GUYS
like
HIM

AIMEE NICOLE WALKER

GUYS
like
HIM

chapter ONE

THE PETITE, FAIR WOMAN WITH CINNAMON-BROWN CURLS AND unsmiling hazel eyes slid a padded yellow envelope through the semicircle opening in the plexiglass window. The tag on her pressed gray shirt identified her as Officer S. Woodley, but the beefy guard escorting Kieran Sullivan out of lockup apparently took the opportunity to make a pun out of her first name.

"Shirley, I can get a smile out of you this morning," he said, laying the cheese on thick.

"Surely not," she deadpanned, and the look in her eyes was enough to melt his cheese. She turned a slightly less hostile gaze to Kieran. "I need you to review the contents and sign a release that states we are returning all your possessions to you."

Kieran dropped his gaze and accepted the envelope, and heat crept up his neck when he noticed how embarrassingly light it was. The contents weren't just the things he'd had on him at the time of his arrest; they, along with the clothes on his back, were everything he owned. His slumlord would've leased his apartment to the first schmuck who'd come along after Kieran missed his rent payment, and there was no way in hell the slimeball had held on to his meager belongings for him. Bouncing the envelope in his hand, Kieran said, "Feels about right."

Woodley's only reaction was a quick double blink. He got the feeling people did her bidding without hesitation. "I'm afraid 'about right' won't cut it, Sullivan. Open the envelope so we can catalog the contents. The sooner you sign the waiver, the faster you're out the door."

He nearly snorted. *Waiver.* As if Arrowhead Correctional Center would mount an investigation if he reported missing items. But Woodley was right about one thing. Kieran was ready to get the hell out of there. Just one more door stood between him and revenge—the thing he wanted even more than his freedom.

"Yes, ma'am," Kieran replied, then picked at the taped seal with his thumbnail.

"What did you think about the Bronco's draft choices, Darren?" Woodley asked Officer Carson, who stood closer to Kieran than he liked.

The freight-sized guard stuck his enormous hand out, palm facing down, and rocked it from side to side. "I won't hold my breath that we'll win the division, let alone make it to the playoffs this year."

Kieran continued working the seal until it loosened enough to pull the tape free, and then he tipped the envelope over to spill the contents onto the stainless-steel counter. "A wallet and a cell phone. Everything is here." There'd been a set of keys to the car he'd allegedly stolen, but those had likely been returned to the owner.

Woodley briefly closed her eyes and shook her head. The officer's deep breath said she had no fucks left to give, so he took pity on her by opening the wallet and rattling off the contents. "An expired driver's license, a reward card for Biggie's Sandwich Shop, and a library card."

"Looks like you've earned a free sub," Carson said.

"They went out of business three months ago," Woodley countered. *Story of my life.* At least the library card was still good, not that he'd have a way to drive there. "No cash?" she asked. Kieran had used every dollar he'd made to pay his rent the day before he'd been arrested. The paycheck prior to that went to an anniversary gift for the guy who'd betrayed him.

"No, ma'am, but I didn't have any when I arrived. Everything is here."

He caught a brief glimpse of pity in her gaze before she slammed the shutters down again. Woodley slid a waiver through the opening and showed where he should initial and sign. "Good luck out there," she said as he scribbled his name.

"Thank you." He slid the form back to her and returned his meager belongings to the envelope.

"He'll be back," Carson said. "Guys like him don't know any other way."

The guard's comment raked his nerves. Carson didn't know jack about him, but Kieran kept his mouth shut. He had one more security door to go through, and he'd be free.

A loud mechanical buzz echoed through the corridor as Officer Woodley assessed him through narrowed eyes. "I don't know. I think this one could be different."

Kieran stepped through the doorway, expecting Carson to remain behind it, but the hulking guard followed him out instead. The door shut behind them, and the automatic lock engaged with a *whir* and a *clank*. Kieran knew he'd hear that sound in his nightmares for years to come.

"I hope you prove me wrong, Sullivan. Maybe you'll find love after lockup," he said, referring to the popular reality show the inmates liked to watch. Even Kieran had gotten sucked into it more often than he wanted to admit, but he wasn't looking for love. Just revenge.

Arching a brow, Kieran studied the guard. Either his bullshit meter had broken, or Carson meant it. Kieran struggled with genuine interactions at the best of times, and his current circumstance definitely didn't fall into that category. His uncertain future was more like staring down the barrel of a gun, not knowing if it was loaded. Emotional Russian roulette. Sarcasm was an old friend—his only friend now—and he hid behind its shield. "Of all the guards, I disliked you the least," Kieran called over his shoulder.

Carson snorted. "Damn straight. Who else would you prefer? Briggs? Dimbly?"

An image of the guards nicknamed Tweedle Dee and Tweedle Dum sprang to mind. "Not in this lifetime."

When Kieran reached the door, he lifted his hands to push it open but froze. His chest tightened with trapped air just like it had when the jury had read its verdict. He took a deep breath to ease the pressure and willed the rising panic away. Kieran was beyond the point of nothing to lose.

"Yo, Sullivan," Carson called out. "You got a ride?"

Grateful for the distraction, Kieran said, "My chauffeur will be waiting." He pushed the door open and stepped out into an overcast March day, wearing the clothes he'd had on when he'd gotten arrested nearly two years prior. It had been a hot summer evening then, and he'd worn cargo shorts, a faded tee, and a pair of flip-flops. Since he didn't have a single person in his corner, he'd remained incarcerated after the arrest and throughout the trial. He'd transitioned from the striped scrubs at the local jail to the bright orange ones at Arrowhead. Wearing his own clothes felt damn good, even if they were too big and provided little protection against the damp, chilly air.

Thick gray clouds hovered overhead, rolling like the anger churning inside him. For the past year, he'd expressed his eagerness to put the past behind him and start fresh. That's what the prison counselors and the people with power over him wanted to hear, so that was the bullshit he fed them. But privately, Kieran tended to his bitterness like a stew on the stove. He knew when to adjust the heat and which ingredients to add to the pot to keep his resentment sharp. And the fucking drab sky and clouds only antagonized him more.

For twenty months, his entire existence had been gray—the floors and walls, the food, and the pallor of the inmates' skin. The only break in the monotony were the prison scrubs. He would happily go the rest of his life without seeing the color orange again. Kieran had foolishly allowed himself to daydream about the vibrancy he'd see on release day, but he'd just gotten more of the same. Everything around him was wet and shiny from the rain, but it was more of a piss on his parade than a refreshing, clean slate. Kieran's olfactory senses zeroed in on the motor oil brought to the asphalt's surface by the shower. It was a scent he knew all too well, and it became a match to his pilot light. Rainwater splashed up on his feet and shins as he walked, but his wrath made him impervious to the chill. Kieran reached inside the padded envelope, removed the wallet, and stuffed it into his back pocket. Then he tossed the envelope with the cell phone into the trash bin. The device was dead, the contract canceled, and there was no one on the contact list he wanted to speak to anymore.

A slight breeze stirred the air, and Kieran closed his eyes and tipped his head back. Yeah, he'd enjoyed fresh air during breaks in the yard, but they never lasted long enough and were controlled by someone else. He'd lived long enough like a marionette, and there was no better time to embrace free will. The weather wasn't what he'd hoped for, but he got to enjoy it outside the fences, and that was a victory he'd stop and embrace.

A rumbling engine caught his attention, and he opened his eyes in time to see a black king cab truck with a silver Redemption Ridge logo stop in front of the facility. The guy behind the wheel wasn't a chauffeur, but he was there for Kieran just the same. A year ago, he set a plan into motion, and Cash Sweeney's presence proved it had worked.

Kieran's good behavior had gained him access to the K9 programs at Arrowhead, where he'd met Cash and his dogs from Redemption Ridge. The front passenger window rolled down, and a familiar black-and-white head poked out. Patsy, a border collie, was the first dog he'd met during the program, and it had been love at first sight for them. It turned out Kieran had a sixth sense when working with animals, especially the shyest ones. His talents had captured Cash's notice, and he'd offered Kieran employment and housing on his ranch, where he rehabilitated horses and dogs. Kieran's participation in the program and the subsequent employment opportunity hadn't been divine intervention or luck; it was all part of his carefully orchestrated plan.

Cash Sweeney's rags-to-riches story was the stuff that made journalists cream themselves. A former inmate himself, Cash got hired to work at a ranch near Last Chance Creek, Colorado, after leaving lockup. He seized the opportunity and turned his life around, creating a software company and becoming a self-made millionaire and a media darling. Information about Cash wasn't hard to find, but how much of it was true? Kieran had seen more dogged investigations performed by Taylor Swift fans when analyzing her videos for Easter eggs than from the so-called journalists reporting on Cash's altruistic endeavors. Kieran knew the leopard hadn't changed his spots, and he was going to prove it.

Patsy let out three excited barks, urging Kieran to hurry. He picked up the pace as the wind kicked up and the clouds threatened to erupt again, but he paused outside the passenger door instead of reaching for the handle. Patsy wiggled farther out the window to lick his face. Pushing his fingers into her silky fur, Kieran said, "I've missed you, pretty girl."

Cash had recently rotated the dogs in the program, and Kieran hadn't seen Patsy in a few months except in photos and videos of her visiting sick kids at the hospital or horsing around at the ranch. Kieran knew the smug ranch owner was watching their interaction because he felt the intensity of Cash's stare. Raising his head, Kieran's gaze collided with intelligent blue eyes.

"She's missed you too," Cash said, his voice deep and gruff.

Kieran held his gaze for a moment before releasing Patsy and sliding over to the rear passenger door. The truck's interior smelled like leather, cinnamon, and something subtle and woodsy like aftershave. It was a welcome reprieve from the misery that clung to every surface in the prison or the motor oil on the asphalt. The door shut with an audible click, and Kieran reminded himself that he was there of his own free will. Patsy let out a triumphant bark, and Cash chuckled as he rolled up her window.

"You didn't have to sit back there. She would've moved with a simple command." Kieran knew firsthand how obedient and well trained Patsy was, but he preferred to sit in the back with his thoughts as company. Introspection had been his existence for the past twenty months. What else was a wrongfully convicted man to do but try to figure out what went wrong, who was responsible, and how he could make them pay? Kieran had a brain full of suspicions and questions, but what he needed was answers. Redemption Ridge was a good place to start.

Cash put the truck in drive and pulled forward, and Kieran was grateful he didn't fill the ride with endless chatter. He played music on the radio with the volume turned low. Kieran kept his gaze on what he could see of the Rocky Mountains through the thick cloud cover. He was just as mesmerized by their splendor as he'd been when he'd stepped off the Greyhound bus when he was twenty-one. Kieran had been California bound with no goal other than to get as far away from Ohio as possible. He'd only meant to hang out in Colorado Springs for a brief layover before catching the next bus, but those craggy mountains and the cerulean sky had held him spellbound. They awakened the artistic side of him he'd locked in the basement of his soul because pretty art was for other people to make and enjoy.

For the first time in Kieran's life, he'd felt like anything was possible. Even now, when all he had found was more hurt and disappointment, he still couldn't imagine a view that didn't include Pike's Peak. The whoosh of the tires on the rain-slicked roads nearly lulled him to sleep as the truck navigated the winding roads, but Kieran forced himself to sit up straighter. He couldn't afford to let his guard down, not for a minute. No distractions. No attachments. While it wasn't fair to blame the entirety of his situation on the man behind the wheel, Kieran's life had taken a sudden downturn the night he learned of his existence. *Cash Sweeney. Mackenzie's Chophouse at 7.* One hastily scribbled note in his boyfriend's handwriting and a clandestine meeting had changed the trajectory of Kieran's life. He'd relived that moment and everything that transpired afterward for nearly two years. The time for introspection had passed; now was the moment for action. And that started with uncovering the role Cash Sweeney had played in ruining his life.

chapter
TWO

ELLS JINGLED OVER THE DOOR WHEN FINLEY ASHE WALKED
into the New Hope Yoga and Wellness Studio. A mishmash
of essential oils and flute music assailed his senses, and the
combination fueled his frustration instead of soothing it. Finley hadn't
come to the shop to be well or get happy. He sure as hell wasn't in the
mood to bend his body like a pretzel, even if he needed a good stretching
session. No, Finley was there to see a woman about a horse.

His mother, Hope Newton, glanced up from refilling a basket with
lotions and potions to offer her visitor a welcoming smile. Her mouth
turned down when she spotted Finley's expression, and the ever-pres-
ent impish twinkle in her dark green eyes dimmed as he approached the
counter. Hope reached for the glasses she wore on a chain around her
neck and placed them on her nose, inspecting him even closer.

"My, my, my," she said. Her honeyed Southern drawl usually
soothed Finley when he'd worked himself into a snit, but it just ruffled his frayed nerves. "Someone's hurting. I'm not sure I've ever seen
such a thunderous expression on your handsome face. You must not

have received the care package I sent back to the ranch with your sister yesterday."

"I didn't get it, but I'm not physically hurt, Mama. Just frustrated."

Hope tsked and shook her head before sweeping her bangs to the side. She'd been letting them grow out for the past few months, and they were in the awkward phase of being too short to tuck behind her ear but too long to rest on her forehead without getting in her eyes. She solved the problem by pushing her eyeglasses onto her head like a headband. Gray-and-white waves framed her face and drew the eye to her impeccable bone structure. Hope continued her perusal and chuckled. "Someone needs to get laid."

"Mom," Finley groaned. Truer words had never been spoken, but they didn't need to come from his mother, and not when a different frustration was riding him hard.

"There are healthier ways to deal with your bad-boy addiction than waging an all-out moratorium on sex." She released an exaggerated shudder at the mere thought of abstinence. And his addiction wasn't bad boys per se. Finley was a sucker for broken souls and sad eyes—both the four-legged and two-legged varieties. That bad boys were often a little broken was a mere coincidence. "You could try dating nice guys for once," Hope continued. "You might even like it. They're not all boring in bed."

"Mom." This time, his voice came out in a low growl.

"Masturbation," she suggested. "Because celibacy doesn't look good on you."

Finley opened his mouth to reply, but no words came out. He ended up choking on his saliva instead. *Christ.* Why was he so crazy about this lunatic who'd brought him into the world?

Nonplussed, Hope reached for her reusable water bottle under the counter and handed it to him. Finley uncapped it and took a drink. The water was chilly and infused with real strawberries and kiwi.

"I started a new line of oils that are so much better than the lubricants you can buy at the drugstore," his mother said. "They're wonderful for your skin, especially in the most sensitive areas, they provide a much better glide, and they don't leave a sticky residue. I even customize the fragrance to enhance the experience."

Finley sprayed a mouthful of water all over her counter and stared at her with a slack-jawed expression. He should've been used to her casual attitude toward sex and, well, everything, but she still surprised him. Heat infused his cheeks, and he looked around the store and the attached yoga studio. Luckily, no one else was around to overhear their conversation or to see his reaction, but Finley should've known better. Hope never hesitated to say outlandish things but never in a manner that would embarrass him in front of others. She had a filter, but she used it selectively. Today was an unlucky day all around.

Hope gasped in outrage, then reached under the counter and removed a hand towel. She tossed it at Finley, hitting him square in the chest. He caught it before it could fall to the floor. His mom retrieved a spray bottle and blasted the counter with a mixture of water and white vinegar, which according to her was also nature's cure-all.

"Sorry about the mess," Finley said as he wiped the counter. The bitterness of the vinegar slashed through the cloying scents in the air, helping him regain his equilibrium and to remember why he came. "I'm not here for sex advice."

"What sex?" she asked. "You quit cold turkey…" Her voice drifted off as she tried to calculate how long he'd gone without sex.

Finley opened his mouth to tell her it was none of her business but, "Six months," exited his lips instead. It had been six long, miserable months since his last breakup when he'd initiated his detox from broken men. Finley wasn't wholly celibate, though. He jerked off in the shower every morning, but it wasn't the same as sharing sex with another person. Finley loved everything about intimacy, especially the sounds a partner made, the press of eager lips, the slide of seeking hands, and the thrill of penetration—his or theirs. He craved the messiness, the tangled limbs, and a climax turning his muscles to rubber and rendering his bones limp noodles. Damn, he missed fucking.

He tossed the towel onto the counter and placed his hands on his hips. "I'm here to see a woman about a horse."

Hope arched a perfectly shaped brow. "Have you finally met a beast you can't tame?"

According to his mother and older sister, Finley's affinity for horses began before he could walk. His memories didn't stretch back that far, but what he could remember usually centered on horses. He'd seen hundreds of pictures of him on the majestic animals as a toddler with his maternal grandfather, a world-class horse trainer in Tennessee, where Finley had grown up. Wealthy clients had sought Finnigan Donovan to ensure their thoroughbreds were in superlative condition to win races and crowns. Occasionally, his grandfather would take on the toughest cases because he believed there wasn't a horse he couldn't train. Then Pops had met Brutus, a chestnut stallion hell-bent on throwing anyone who dared to ride him, including the invincible trainer.

Pops wouldn't give up and sought advice from the best equine veterinarians worldwide. During one such phone conference inside his barn office, Pops heard Brutus neighing from his stall, followed by childish giggles. Finnigan had dropped the phone, run toward the sounds, and discovered his five-year-old grandson had scaled the door to get inside the cantankerous horse's stall. He watched in frozen horror as Finley reached his tiny hand up and stroked Brutus's front leg. Instead of nipping at the boy as he did with the adults who tried to touch him, Brutus rubbed his muzzle against Finley's cheek.

And that's when Finnigan knew his grandson had a special gift. Going forward, Finley was present anytime Pops worked with the horse. After months of patient nurturing and trust-building exercises, Brutus cooperated with his training. The gorgeous stallion wasn't destined for the racetracks, though. Pops bought the horse from his client as a birthday present for Finley, and the two had been inseparable until the cherished horse died of old age. Nellie, a blue roan Appaloosa, reminded Finley of Brutus. And just like that, his frustration with his newest foster horse deflated like a balloon.

"I've met a beast who doesn't want to be tamed," Finley corrected. "I haven't convinced her I'm a friend, not a foe."

"Not everyone wants to be tamed." Hope's voice was gentle, but her gaze was pointed. She wasn't just talking about Nellie or any horse. She meant the broken guys Finley kept trying to fix and turn into boyfriend material. How many times could a person get bitten before they learned? His mother hadn't asked the question out loud, but he could see it shimmering in her empathetic gaze.

He wore the scars on his skin like a badge of honor. They represented the horses he'd rehabilitated through their trauma to flourish. The wounds on his heart caused by men were a different story. They cut much deeper and hadn't healed. Those were a source of embarrassment for him and the catalyst behind his self-imposed relationship detoxification. The thing was, Finley could give up on men much easier than he could on the horses. His battered heart recognized Nellie was exceptional, and he couldn't walk away from her. That didn't mean he wouldn't get pissed when she tried to rip out a chunk of his ass again. It had been a daily occurrence since Nellie had arrived. When she got close enough to rip his back pocket off his jeans, Finley knew he needed to get creative.

"Message received and appreciated," Finley said softly. "I'm not trying to break her spirit."

His mom's mouth quirked up to one side. "But you're digging in your heels."

"Yes, ma'am, and I think you could help me."

"Me? The horse whisperer gene skipped me, my love. What advice could I possibly give you?"

Finley gestured to the row of essential oils on display. "Which one produces calm vibes?"

Both brows went up this time. "Didn't you once refer to my oils as hokum?"

Finley chuckled. "I was young and stupid." And he'd heard the word on *The Big Bang Theory* and wanted to use it. Riling up his mama had just been a bonus.

"It was two years ago," she said, "and you were twenty-three years old."

Finley nodded. "Young and stupid. What would be the harm in using a lotion or body wash that could soothe Nellie's anxiety?"

"None that I can think of," Hope replied. "Lavender is the first one that comes to mind, but—"

Finley shook his head to cut her off. "Reminds me of the little soaps Grandma wouldn't let us use unless it was to wash our mouths out after we repeated the words Pops used." He tilted his head. "Why didn't she wash his mouth out with soap?"

"It would've been a lost cause, and she knew it," Hope replied. "I could go light with the lavender and stronger on vetiver." She picked up a second bottle, unscrewed the lid, and tilted it toward him. It smelled like earth, grass, and lemon.

"I like it," Finley said. "It's worth a shot."

They discussed the different application options for him to consider, and Finley chose hand lotion. He could apply it before a training session and easily wash it off afterward. While he perused the books on her shelves, his mother went into the back to whip up a bottle. Hope was big on mindfulness and meditation, so there were the usual books on those subjects. She'd added a few new yoga instructional books and one that looked like an old leather spell book. Intrigued, Finley picked it up and thumbed through it, realizing it was a guide on how to use essential oils in everyday life.

The front door flew open and the bells above it sounded more like a warning than a gentle announcement that someone had entered the store. Finley turned around and watched as three men entered his mother's store. Their pinched expressions said they were looking for trouble, and Finley was ready to supply it after the morning he'd had. The men's simply constructed brown pants and white button-up shirts identified them as members of Salvation Anew, a cult masquerading as a nondenominational church. The organization had sprung up out of nowhere last year when the casino opened, and they had made life a living hell for the residents of Last Chance Creek. They preyed on the vulnerable and misguided. They picketed, protested, and raised hell about anything and everything. Most of their energy seemed aimed at the sins of gambling, but they'd recently targeted the small businesses lining Main Street. His mother hadn't mentioned the group had bothered her, but three representatives stood in her store, wearing matching expressions of consternation. Then again, it could be constipation, and they could be seeking a holistic remedy.

"I hear castor oil works wonders," Finley said. "Greases up the gears and loosens things up."

Three heads swiveled in his direction, and their calculating gazes swept over him. Besides matching outfits and dour expressions, the men had similar thick beards and closely shorn hair. The man in the middle was the tallest and oldest. He had white hair and piercing blue eyes that gave the impression he could look into your soul or possibly snatch it. The fella to his right was blond with hazel eyes and was significantly younger and shorter. The guy on the left was in the middle, both in age and height, with dark hair and muddy brown eyes.

The youngest man sucked in a sharp breath and pointed to the book Finley held. "It's true, Samuel. There is a witchcraft book in this store."

Witchcraft? What? The tome might've looked like an old leather spell book, but it was nothing more than recipes to ease headaches, soften callused feet, and remove pesky odors from stubborn fabrics. Finley opened his mouth to dispute the claim, but the white-haired man he presumed was Samuel stepped forward and extended his hand.

"Give the evil book to me, son. It's not too late to save your soul."

Save his soul? From using rosemary oil to stimulate hair growth? Finley pulled the book to his chest and tightened his arms around it. They'd have to come through him if they wanted to take anything away from his mama.

The younger man with hazel eyes also stepped forward. His hardened gaze softened to one of pity, and that infuriated Finley even more. Who was this asshole to look at him and judge him lacking? "There's a better way," he said. "Salvation Anew can show you."

Was that the message they'd fed to Keegan, the last guy who'd broken Finley's heart? Keegan's mother had attended the church after losing her husband to another woman, her job to downsizing, and her only son to Finley's evil clutches. He'd known Keegan wasn't completely comfortable with his sexuality, and Finley had backed off when the guy had asked for room to breathe. What he hadn't counted on was Salvation Anew sweeping in and claiming another member for their *flock*. Finley had fluctuated between guilt, shame, and anger when Keegan had broken things off in a coldly written text message. Maybe he'd backed off too far or should've fought harder. Perhaps—

"And I can show you to the door just like I did last week," Hope said as she stepped from the back room. She had one hand on her hip, and the other held a small brown bottle sporting a simple label. He recognized her writing but couldn't distinguish the words from where he stood. "I asked you not to come back, yet here you are."

"We'll defeat you, witch," the dark-haired man snarled.

"Not today, you won't." Hope set the lotion bottle on the counter and lifted her hands to her head. She pressed two fingers to each temple and squinted in their direction. The three spun around and scurried out the door like rats. Hope laughed so hard that she had to lean against the counter for support. Her unhinged cackle nearly sounded like a witch's. "Did you see how fast they ran? Such simpletons."

Finley returned the leather book to the shelf before heading to the counter. He crossed his arms over his chest and stared down at his mother. "You pulled a Sheldon Cooper," he said.

She grinned at him like a lunatic. God, he adored this woman. "Unlike Leonard, those idiots actually think I can make their brains explode."

Finley resisted the urge to laugh with her because he feared the situation was more dire than she realized. "I'm not sure antagonizing them is the right thing to do. Playing into their beliefs that you're a witch could be very dangerous, Mama."

She batted away the notion like a pesky fly. "Those morons don't know what to do with a woman who refuses to cower to their demands. The white-haired guy is supposed to be their fearless leader, Samuel Jeremiah, but he was the first one out the door. Sure, they'll regroup and return, but I'll be ready when they do." She reached down and lifted a massive Super Soaker water gun from behind the counter. "I've added lots of lemongrass oil in here. It keeps the mosquitos away, so why not try it on the human soul suckers too?"

Finley groaned and shook his head. "Does Gary know they're harassing you?" Surely his stepfather would've implored her to use caution when dealing with any type of fanatic.

Hope smiled at hearing her husband's name. "Who do you think went to the superstore down the highway to buy this water gun?" Finley groaned, and she reached over the counter to cover his hand. "And he installed a security system with interior and exterior cameras." She pointed to a device mounted near the ceiling in the room's corner. "Picks up the entire shop. I have one in the back and at each entrance. I'm not taking their threats lightly, but I'm not backing down either."

Finley leaned across the counter and kissed her cheek. "I love you."

"I love you more." She handed him the bottle of lotion, and he read the label. Beast Tamer.

"I'd hate to know what you'd call the lube you wanted to whip up for me." She started to reply, but Finley held up his hand. "No, I would really hate to know."

Hope waggled her eyebrows. "Since you brought it up…"

"No," Finley replied, shaking his head furiously. "It was an accident. My bad." He picked up the lotion and turned to leave, but she placed a hand on his forearm to stop him.

"Fin, I've met someone special."

"Does Gary know?"

"Ha, ha, ha," she said dryly. "Gary picked him out."

Finley shoved the forefinger of his free hand into his ear. "Lalalalalala. I don't want to know what you guys get up to," he said. "You're consenting adults."

Hope pinched Finley's arm through his flannel shirt until he unplugged his ear. "Don't be an idiot. The guy isn't for us, silly. He's for you."

"Huh-uh," Fin said, pulling free of her embrace. "I'm on hiatus, remember?"

"Your pissy, uptight attitude makes it hard to forget. I'd like to remind you that you're on a break from bad boys who break your heart." *Not bad. Just broken.* "You said nothing about good guys. They need nurturing too."

"I don't know, Mama."

She smiled sympathetically. "I hate to see you so unhappy, sweetheart. Just think about it, okay?"

Fuck, he was lonely. Would it be so bad to go on a date with a man?

16

Even if he didn't feel a romantic spark, he always had room for another friend. "Okay. I'll think about it."

Hope's smile was immediate and huge. Finley playfully lifted his hand to shield his eyes from its blinding light, but seeing her happy lifted his spirit. He gave her another kiss before heading toward the door.

"Monkey Grease," she called out before he could reach for the handle. "You know, to spank the—"

"Got it," Finley said. "I knew exactly what you meant. No explanation needed."

She laughed at his discomfort. "It's already on track to become my best seller."

Finley groaned and fled through the door almost as fast as the cult members had.

chapter
THREE

THE TRUCK SLOWED AND TURNED INTO A DRIVEWAY. GRAVEL crunched beneath the tires as Cash drove toward an ornate gate that opened when he pushed a button on his visor. Beyond the black iron, a lane disappeared into a forest of ponderosa pines and blue spruces. The rich greens and silvery blues formed a tapestry of vibrant color that stirred something deep in Kieran's soul.

He'd grown up near a farming community in Ohio, but the land was flat and underwhelming. Kieran's bus ride west had revealed similar topography, so he'd never really associated mountains and forestry with agriculture. "There's a ranch back here somewhere?" Kieran asked, hoping his accelerated pulse didn't reflect in his voice.

"Redemption Ridge comprises forty-five hundred acres," Cash replied proudly. "We only farm a third of the land. Hay and hops are our only field crops, but we also have impressive grapevines and beehives."

"Hay, hooch, and honey. Got it."

Cash laughed again. "We keep the hay for the horses we rehabilitate, and I sell the hops to commercial beer producers, though I plan to change that in the near future. I have my eye on establishing a winery and a craft brewery. Hooch and Honey would make a catchy name."

Kieran studied him through narrowed eyes. "I'd want payment for coming up with the name."

Cash briefly met his gaze in the mirror. "Of course. Do you know anything about making beer or wine?"

Kieran shrugged. "I only know how to drink and serve it."

"Well, that's a start."

Cresting a slight hill, Kieran got his first glimpse at the sprawling ranch below. He didn't bother to squelch his gasp as he took in the scenery. Kieran's gaze skimmed over the buildings and homed in on the vast patchwork of green grass, brown fields, and meadows of purple, blue, and yellow wildflowers. A silvery stream snaked a path through the land and disappeared into a thick forest of trees at the base of the mountains.

"Wow." The breathless reaction escaped unbidden, but he was too spellbound by the magnificence before him to care. The landscape belonged on a canvas. If he closed his eyes, he could smell the paint, feel the weight of the brush in his hand, and hear the strokes it made against the woven fabric. Kieran kept his eyes open and forced his thoughts to his task at hand.

"Incredible, isn't it?" Cash said. "I first stepped onto this ranch twenty-seven years ago." Kieran knew from the articles he'd read that Durrell Padgett, the previous ranch owner, had taken a chance on Cash when he'd answered an ad looking for ranch hands. That was the same year Kieran was born, and their trajectories couldn't have been more different, yet there they were at the same ranch.

The drive to the homestead seemed to stretch on for endless minutes. Kieran shifted his attention to the buildings he'd ignored earlier and noted a mixture of old and new. The original log cabin sat proudly in front while a larger, more modern wood and glass structure stood in the background. Several buildings and barns dotted the landscape, and Kieran assumed they housed equipment and animals. He spotted small cabins grouped in a cluster. Their placement was close enough to give a sense of community but far enough away to offer some semblance of privacy. Was that where the ranch hands lived? He assumed they'd bunk together in one of the outbuildings.

Cash drove past the original homestead and parked in front of the towering structure of wood, stone, and glass. "Let's start with a bite to eat," he said. "I missed lunch, and even if you've eaten, Harry's cooking will far surpass anything they fed you at Arrowhead."

Cash killed the engine and got out of the truck without waiting for a response, whistling for Patsy to follow. Instead, the dog turned in the seat and watched Kieran intently as he decided how to proceed. He hadn't expected Cash to welcome him into his private residence and feed him. He wasn't there to make nice with the man, and he didn't want to accept anything he didn't earn. But Patsy wouldn't budge until he made his move, so Kieran reluctantly opened the door, stepped out, and whistled for her. The dog obeyed immediately, leaping into the back seat and exiting through the open door. And if he proved Cash Sweeney was the rotten son of a bitch he suspected, Kieran would send that asshole back to prison and keep his gorgeous dog.

Kieran turned to walk up the wide porch steps and froze. The two-story structure was even bigger than it first seemed. Shiny windows and soft gray stone broke up the monotony of dark wood. Black iron porch railing, light fixtures, and door hardware perfectly complemented the rustic design. A massive window above the front door stretched to the roofline, showcasing a huge iron chandelier hanging over the foyer. This was by far the most beautiful home Kieran had ever seen, and he knew the vista in the back would be even more impressive with the view of Pike's Peak.

Patsy barked and interrupted his gawking, and Kieran jerked his gaze back to the front door, where Cash waited patiently with an indulgent smile.

"Ready?" he asked.

No, but Kieran nodded and jogged up the steps to follow the rancher into the house with Patsy at his side. "She allowed in?"

Cash laughed. "This is her house. I'm just lucky to live here."

Patsy barked her agreement, and Kieran couldn't resist smiling as he took in the gorgeous home around him. A staircase to the right led to the second story, and a long hallway stretched out in front of them, leading to a massive room with a wall of windows at the back of the house. Gleaming wood stretched as far as the eye could see broken up by colorful furniture settings, artwork, area rugs, and accent pieces. Several doors opened on either side of the main hallway, and Kieran wanted to explore each one to see what Cash Sweeney hid in his closets.

"Cash, is that you?" a woman called out from deep within the house. Her voice was soft, and her accent was more Southeast than Western. Tennessee, maybe.

"None other," the rancher replied.

A red-haired lady poked her head around a corner. Her eyes widened when she saw Kieran, and he recalled his state of dress. Ratty clothes and flip-flops hardly made a good impression, not that he should care. The woman stepped fully into the hallway and stopped with her hands on her slender, denim-clad hips. She was petite, not much over five feet if that, and looked to be in her midthirties. She'd pulled her hair back into a ponytail, but a few wisps of tousled waves framed her delicate face. Who was she? Cash's wife? None of his research had revealed a spouse or significant other, so Kieran had assumed a guy with his looks and money was another playboy.

"Hello, Harry," Cash said.

Harry? He'd imagined a beefy cook who prepared meals for the ranch hands, not this stick of dynamite masquerading as a woman. She shifted her gaze to Kieran. Her eyes were a pale, unusual shade of green as if her maker had made a second pass with a sea-green colored pencil, pressing harder to get a deeper pigment. Harry's expression softened, and she extended a kind smile and a tiny hand. "I'm Harriet Bledsoe, but everyone calls me Harry."

He hesitated a moment before shaking her hand. "Kieran."

"That's such a lovely name."

Shelly Sullivan had named her newborn son after his paternal grandfather because her husband hated the man. She wanted to get even with Kieran's daddy dearest for screwing around while she was in labor as if Kellan needed another reason to resent his son's existence. Shelly's choice of bedtime stories when she wasn't too stoned or drunk to forget about him had always led to a shouting match between his parents. Kellan would swear up and down that Kieran wasn't his kid, and his mother would just laugh because there was no denying his paternity. Everyone had told Kieran he looked just like his dad. Pitying looks and remarks like "Kids like him don't stand a chance" would often follow. Maybe that's why Carson's dig at the jail had rankled him. He'd heard a variation of it his entire life and was ready to change the narrative. He just had one little mystery to solve first, and Kieran thought Cash had the answers.

"Thank you, ma'am."

"Harry, please," she said. "Are you hungry?" Patsy barked and turned in a circle. Harry laughed and ruffled the dog's ears. "Always a given with you, young lady. I was talking to your friend." Kieran's growling stomach answered before he could, and Harry grinned. "Follow me to the kitchen. I made chicken and dumplings for lunch."

Harry spun on her heels and headed back the way she'd come. Patsy nudged him with her nose until he followed while Cash laughed at the dog's antics.

"I'm going," Kieran told Patsy and stepped forward. Since the initial shock of seeing the home had passed, his other senses came alive, and his mouth watered at the smells emanating from the kitchen.

"Do you like dumplings?" Cash asked.

"I don't even know what one is." But Kieran's reticence from before was gone, and he was eager to try them.

Cash explained that chicken and dumplings were like chicken and noodles, but the base was thicker, similar to a stew, and with balls of dough instead of noodles. "Some people don't care for the dumpling texture, so please don't feel obligated to eat something you don't like. I make it clear to the crew that Harry isn't a short-order cook, but there are always sandwich fixings on hand if you'd prefer something else."

"This is where everyone eats?" Kieran asked, finding it hard to believe Cash invited his employees into his home for mealtimes.

"Of course." He stopped beside an open doorway and gestured to a large dining room with a massive table that could seat a dozen people or more. "We'll eat in the kitchen nook today, though."

The rear of the house was one huge open space, combining the kitchen and family room. As Kieran suspected, the entire back of the house was a wall of windows, offering a stunning vista of Pike's Peak. The view alone had to be worth two million dollars. Kieran stopped to gawk until Patsy nudged him with her nose to get him going again.

Harry slid a chair away from the table and patted the back. "Have a seat while I reheat lunch. Don't get used to me waiting on you, though. I lay out the meals buffet style, and you'll serve yourself."

Cash followed Harry into the kitchen while Patsy sat on the floor beside Kieran, rested her chin on his thigh, and peered at him with big brown eyes.

"We have water, iced tea, and a variety of soft drinks. What sounds good to you?" Cash asked.

"Water is fine," he replied.

Cash retrieved two bottles from the refrigerator and walked over to the table, taking the seat directly across from Kieran's before handing the drink to him. "What are some goals you set for yourself before your release?"

Kieran twisted the lid off his bottle and raised it to his mouth, taking a long drink to buy some time. Arrowhead provided classes and training programs to help inmates acclimate to life after their release and avoid recidivism. He'd taken the courses and written up a plan just like everyone else, and he knew Cash had read it before offering him a position at Redemption Ridge. Why pretend he hadn't? Was this a test?

"Maybe let him eat first," Harry called out from the kitchen. Her back was toward them as she stirred the contents in a large pot on the stove.

"Excuse me," Cash said wryly. "I forgot who's in charge here." He looked at me and smiled. "Harry is the COO of domestic operations."

She snorted and rolled her eyes. "I'm the housekeeper."

They continued to banter back and forth, but Kieran shifted his attention to the massive wall of windows. Purple mountain majesty indeed. He lost track of time and the conversation and didn't tune back in until Harry set a bowl in front of him and a cloth-lined breadbasket in the center of the table. It overflowed with golden biscuits, and his mouth watered just from looking at them.

Kieran tried not to be too obvious as he inspected the contents of the soup. He noted shredded chicken, carrots, and celery. As Cash had said, it looked like a richer, creamier chicken soup. He wasn't sure what to think about the dough balls, but the stew smelled incredible. He dipped his spoon in and scooped out a generous serving. A savory symphony of chicken, vegetables, and herbs made his mouth sing. The dumpling texture would take a minute to adjust to, but it tasted incredible. He looked up and caught Harry watching him nervously.

"This is delicious," Kieran said, dipping his spoon in for another bite.

Harry beamed with pride. "I brought my great-grandmother's recipe from Sevierville with me. I'm so glad you like it."

"Sevierville. Is that in Tennessee?"

"Yes, it's near Gatlinburg and Pigeon Forge." She gestured to the mountains and added, "I traded the Smokies for the Rockies."

Cash hummed as he swallowed a bite of food. "Thank goodness you did."

Harry walked back into the kitchen and returned with small plates, butter, a honey pot, and a selection of jellies. Cash broke a biscuit in half and drizzled honey over it.

Kieran had to admit the golden liquid looked delicious. "Did the honey come from your beehives?"

"Sure did," he replied. "Afraid I don't have any hooch to offer you."

"Hooch?" Harry asked.

"Kieran unintentionally gave me an idea for a future endeavor. I might name my brewery and winery Hooch and Honey."

Harry smiled. "Very catchy. I like it." She left them alone to busy herself in the kitchen. As Kieran neared the bottom of the bowl, she reappeared with the pot and ladle to replenish his soup. "Makes me so happy when people appreciate my cooking."

"Would you like a tour of the ranch, or would you like some time to get settled in first?" Cash asked.

"A tour sounds good."

"After you rinse your dishes and put them in the dishwasher," Harry said on her way out of the kitchen, a caddy full of cleaning supplies in her hand.

They carried their dishes to the kitchen once they finished. Kieran rinsed, and Cash stacked them in the dishwasher. They returned the butter, jellies, and soup to the refrigerator, and Cash tucked the honey away in the cabinet.

"Would you like a change of clothes before we start the tour? It's chilly for shorts and flip-flops. I provide your work clothes to you. We keep an excellent selection of styles and sizes available in the general store."

"General store?" Kieran asked.

"It's basically a storage building where we keep clothing and boots for the employees. Ivan, my foreman, once referred to it as shopping at the general store, and the moniker stuck. There's no charge for the items there, and I will give you an advance on your first check so you can buy any personal hygiene supplies you want from a store in town. Would you prefer to start the tour at the general store and get a change of clothes?"

Kieran glanced down at his sole possessions. "I'm fine in this."

Cash shrugged. "Suit yourself."

The ranch was a hive of activity. Cash greeted every person by name, and they responded with a nod or hat tip. Kieran easily recognized the ones who'd served time, though they looked less weary and feral than he felt. He didn't bother committing the names of the buildings or people to memory. No distractions. No attachments.

"There are quite a few entry-level jobs on the ranch. Try them all to see which is the best fit, but I think you'd make a great fit in our horse barn," Cash said as they neared the biggest structure on the property. Once inside, Kieran could see why it was so large. It had dozens of stalls toward the front and a vast arena in the back. Each stall door was open, and a wagon piled high with manure and dirty bedding sat in the middle of the aisle. Several unopened bags of shavings and soft wood pellets dotted the stretch of concrete.

"You want me to work with horses?" Kieran asked. "Why?"

"Animals are drawn to you," Cash replied, gesturing to Patsy, who'd never been more than two feet away from Kieran since he'd arrived. "We have rescue horses who are skittish after being abused, much like the dogs you worked with in the program."

"Why not work with the dogs?" Kieran asked.

"The kennel is fully staffed right now, and Finley could use the help here."

Kieran opened his mouth to respond just as someone inside the barn sang off-key, tentatively at first but gaining fervor with each verse. He didn't recognize the lyrics and wasn't sure he'd identify the voice as human.

Cash chuckled and shook his head as a rake sailed out of the stall and landed on the concrete aisle. "That's Finley Ashe," Cash said, raising his voice to be heard over the ruckus. "He'd be your boss. He can't sing for shit, but he's pure magic with the horses."

A blond guy wearing painted-on jeans and a snug black Henley to show off his athletic build stepped out of the stall and jerked to a halt when he saw Cash, the tune dying on his stunning lips. Kieran had seen chiseled cheeks and a square jaw like Finley's on models in magazines but never in real life. He'd chalked it up to Photoshopping, but that kind of bone structure really existed. Pale green eyes shifted to him and widened. Finley's mouth parted, drawing Kieran's attention to a chin dimple just as a soft gasp escaped his lips. Holy shit. The sweet sound unfurled something deep inside Kieran, a pleasure he'd denied himself for nearly two years to focus his full attention on getting retribution. An alarm bell went off in Kieran's head, warning that this man would threaten his willpower.

"Fin," Cash said, "come meet Kieran."

Finley swallowed hard and said, "Hello, Kieran." His voice had a soft Southern drawl like Harry's. He stepped forward, and his foot landed on the rake tines. Kieran watched in horror as the handle arced upward and smacked Finley on the forehead with a sickening *thud*.

chapter
FOUR

WHAT THE HELL? FINLEY BLINKED A FEW TIMES TO CLEAR his vision, but it still took him a few seconds to realize he was lying flat on his back and staring at the barn rafters. He'd never paid attention to the building's construction before because his only concern was its four-legged inhabitants and the people who cared for them. Those were some big-ass beams supporting the roof and protecting the precious horses under his care. *Why am I on my back? Am I hurt?* His head had landed on a bag of shavings he planned to spread in the cleaned stalls. The world around Finley stopped swimming, and he noticed a high-pitched alarm ringing through the barn. *Was it a fire?*

Panic spiked his blood, making it race through his veins. Finley had to get the horses to safety. But wait… They were already out. He'd been working alone to burn through frustration. His trip to see his mother had only added more stress, and he'd picked up a stupid earworm on the ride back to the ranch. He'd been shoveling shit and singing along with the song playing on an endless loop in his head, and *bam!* Something had knocked him on his ass, but what? Lightning? That didn't feel right. Something had rung his bell, not fried his circuits.

Two faces came into view—one Finley knew well, the other he'd like to know better. Both men looked at him with grave concern. Their lips moved, but he couldn't hear them over the alarm. A fire? He didn't smell smoke. The ringing seemed closer and not as loud as it had been. Finley realized the ringing was in his ears. He locked his gaze on Cash because the other man stole his breath. Finley already had enough problems to contend with and didn't want to add a lack of oxygen to the mix. Was he breathing? Finley inhaled deeply, testing to see if his lungs worked adequately. The ringing got quieter, but he still couldn't make out the words Cash said. His boss looked at the stranger, and Finley couldn't help shifting his gaze too. Christ, he was gorgeous. Black hair swept over a broad forehead. Dark brows slashed down to form a vee over eyes so dark they looked black. The man stared down at him with naked concern and something else in his gaze. The sexy stranger blinked and erected a shield of indifference, but it was too late. Finley recognized the emotion, and it called to something deep inside him like a lone coyote howling for its pack. Butterflies fluttered in Finley's stomach, and his blood heated with excitement. But how had he ended up on his back in the barn staring at this beautiful lost boy?

A flash of memory detonated, clearing out his brain fog and reducing the ringing in his ears to a subdued hum. Lightning hadn't struck, at least not literally. Finley had locked eyes with the sexiest man he'd ever seen, and something inside him had detonated with a *whoosh*. The smoldering stranger had used a flamethrower to light Finley's dormant pilot light after a six-month relationship detox. He'd always been a little boy crazy with a habit of falling too hard and too fast and always for the wrong guy. But this was… Finley scrunched up his face as he tried to find the right word to describe his reaction, and that's when he noticed a dull ache in the center of his forehead.

The entire encounter came flooding back in high definition. Gobsmacked by the newcomer's beauty, Finley had stepped directly on the muck rake. The handle had flown up and cracked him a good one on the forehead, causing him to stagger back and fall onto the bags of bedding. Humiliation heated his cheeks, and he groaned.

"Finley, are you okay?" Cash's concerned tone and worried blue eyes

28

signaled his boss had mistaken the sound as a sign of physical distress, not mental anguish. Finley tried to sit up and clear the air, but Cash placed a gentle hand on his shoulder to keep him still. "Kieran, I need you to find Rueben Sanchez for me. He has emergency medical training and can assess Finley for a concussion."

Finley had rattled his cage pretty well, but he was not concussed. "Not—"

Cash silenced his protest with a gentle squeeze. Finley shifted his gaze to the gorgeous man, who seemed to look right through him with those obsidian eyes. This stunning stranger might just be the most broken boy he'd encountered yet. This guy's pain hovered over him like a rain cloud, stirring Finley's protective and baser instincts. *Oh, baby, come stand under my umbrella.*

"Kieran," Cash said gently.

Kieran. A beautiful name for a beautiful man. He seemed to shake himself out of a trance at the sound of his name. "Um, yeah. Where would Rueben be?" Cash gave directions to the farrier barn. "Farrier?" Kieran asked.

"He's a blacksmith who makes and fits the horses with shoes," Cash explained.

Kieran glanced at Finley once more before nodding at Cash. "I'll be right back."

Finley watched Kieran jog out of the barn with Patsy at his side before knocking Cash's hand aside and sitting up. He paused to ensure the barn didn't spin before meeting his boss's worried blue eyes. "I'm fine."

"You should still lie down until Rueben gets here."

He waved Cash's suggestion away. "I've tumbled off horses plenty of times, and I'm no stranger to head trauma. The rake temporarily stunned me. I'm afraid I made a horrible first impression on Kieran." Finley tilted his head and narrowed his eyes. "Who is he, by the way?"

"He's the newest member of our staff, and I'd just started giving him a tour."

"Recently released from jail?"

"Today," Cash replied. "I just came from picking him up."

"Ah." That explained the rain cloud and broken spirit. Finley put his palm down on the concrete to push off, but Cash extended his hand and helped him to his feet. "Where do you plan to place Kieran?"

Cash rubbed the back of his neck as if carefully choosing his words. The gesture was so uncharacteristic that Finley knew what he planned to say, so he rescued his boss like Cash had done for many others.

"Does he have any experience with horses?"

Cash's lips twisted into a slight grimace. "I haven't asked yet, but I'm going to guess he doesn't."

"Why the stable, then?" But what he really wanted to ask was, "Why me?"

"He had incredible instincts with the dogs in the K9 program, and my gut tells me he'd make a wonderful addition to your crew. There's just something about him that puts animals at ease," Cash explained.

"Horses aren't oversized dogs, though." Thinking of Nellie and her determination to bite the hell out of anyone near her, Finley added, "One false step could have disastrous consequences."

"There's no one better to train Kieran than you."

Finley worried his bottom lip between his teeth. He trusted Cash's instincts implicitly. If he said Kieran was a good fit for his team, he would be. His hesitation had more to do with his reaction to the new guy. Finley hadn't met anyone to tempt him out of his self-imposed detox until locking eyes on Kieran, making him want to answer the lonely howl. *I'll be your pack.* It was instinctual to want to fix Kieran and make all his hurts disappear, but he'd learned the hard way that guys like him only knew how to take. They were vampires, draining energy, souls, and sometimes Finley's bank account, leaving nothing but a broke-ass husk of a man in their wake. He'd worked too hard to heal from Keegan's rejection and couldn't risk a relapse. Before Finley could say anything to dissuade Cash from placing Kieran on his team, the man in question returned to the barn with Rueben and Patsy.

"Hey, Rue," Finley said jovially. "Sorry they pulled you away from your work. I'm fine. The bags of bedding cushioned the blow when I fell."

The lanky Hispanic man removed his thick leather gloves and tucked them into the pocket of a matching apron. "Let me be the judge of that."

He led Finley over to a bench and used the flashlight on Cash's phone to check his pupils. There was a lot of bitching and moaning about Rue blinding him, but he cooperated with his commands to look here and there. Rueben ran through a series of questions that could identify symptoms that could indicate a concussion. Was he nauseated? Did his head hurt? Finley answered no to those questions and the others that followed. Then Rue tested his cognitive abilities. He knew who and where he was and could provide the year and president's name. Rueben asked Finley to stand up and put him through a series of evaluations to check his balance.

"I'm good, Rue," Finley said. "I've had concussions before, and this isn't one."

"I have to agree," Rueben told Cash. "His eyes look good, his equilibrium checks out, and he's coherent."

Cash furrowed his steely gray brows. "But he moaned and sounded like he was in a lot of pain."

"From humiliation," Finley replied. "I only hurt my pride. Trust me."

His boss held his gaze for a long time, and they exchanged an unspoken message. Cash would trust Finley to know if he was hurt if Finley showed Cash the same courtesy with Kieran's placement. Cash could insist he take on the brooding, sexy man, but his boss didn't run roughshod over his employees. Yes, Cash was in charge, but he always gave them a say, which was just one reason they loved and revered him.

Rueben slid his gloves back on and pinned Finley with a somber glance. "Seek medical attention right away if your condition changes. It doesn't take a hard hit to the noggin to cause damage."

Smiling at the soft-hearted man, Finley gave him a Boy Scout salute. "I promise."

Rue replied with the Vulcan live long and prosper before exiting the barn, leaving Finley alone with Cash, Kieran, and Patsy.

"Let me make proper introductions," Cash said. "Kieran, this is Finley Ashe."

Finley buried his reluctance for the moment and extended his hand to the newcomer. If Kieran wasn't a good fit for the equine stable, Cash would hear him out and make the necessary changes. Finley needed to give the guy a chance and maybe trust himself too. Kieran stared at his hand for several moments before pressing his palm against Finley's. Awareness, dark and delicious, unfurled in Finley's gut and spread lower to settle in his groin. He released Kieran's hand and hoped his reaction to him didn't show. The newcomer didn't let on if he'd felt it too, but his gaze dropped to Finley's mouth before meeting his eyes again. Finley had easily adhered to a personal policy of not getting involved with anyone on the ranch, but this lonely coyote with sad eyes would be a dangerous temptation.

Cash's phone rang, and he stepped away to answer it, leaving Kieran and Finley staring at one another. Neither of them spoke or even blinked during Cash's brief conversation. "That's an important call I need to finish back at the house," he said when he rejoined them.

Finley forced himself to look at his boss, whose calm expression didn't match the terse tone he'd used during his phone chat. He offered him an easy smile. "I can take it from here."

Cash slapped his shoulder and turned his attention to Kieran, who watched the rancher intently. "I'm leaving you in competent hands, but please come find me if you need anything."

Kieran responded with a nod and shifted his full attention to Finley, dismissing Cash before he'd even walked away.

"Okay," Finley said. "First, we need to get you out of those clothes."

A dark brow shot up. "Excuse me?" Kieran's voice was soft but menacing.

Just when Finley thought his day couldn't get worse. *Jesus, Finley. Pull it together.* "And into proper work attire," he replied. "Didn't Cash offer you a change of clothes?"

"Yes, but I declined."

Finley attempted a friendly smile but feared it looked more like a grimace. "I'm afraid I'll need to insist." The dark-haired man narrowed his eyes, and Finley could see he would be a stubborn one. He lifted a hand to stave off any protest. "The last thing you want is for a horse to step on your feet while you're wearing flip-flops. It's a liability issue I can't allow. I'm not looking to take away your individualism, but the rules are in place to protect everyone."

Kieran exhaled a long sigh. "Lead the way."

The general store was larger than a shed but smaller than a barn. Rows of jeans, flannels, thermal underwear and undershirts in every color and size were stacked neatly on the shelves along the rear wall. Racks of underwear and socks for every season were on the left of the room, and a shoe store's worth of boots was to the right. Head protection, ranging from cowboy hats to knitted beanies and ball caps, was also available for the ranch hands.

Kieran's gaze swept the room before landing on Finley again. "I can choose anything I want?" Kieran's expression was locked down tight, but he couldn't keep the surprise from his voice. And the coyote howled louder.

Finley nodded and fought off the urge to cover his ears, though it wouldn't do him any good since the soul-piercing sounds were internal, not external. He'd just have to learn to tune them out. "We mark the sizes on the shelves or packaging. Pick out whatever you like and jot it down on the clipboard here," he said, walking over to where it hung on the wall. "Makes inventory for tax purposes easier."

Kieran glanced around the room again. "I'm not sure what size I wear now. I'm leaner in some places and bulkier in others." His comment invited Finley to peruse his body, but he ignored the urge.

"Maybe start with a size or two up or down from what you're wearing now," Finley suggested.

Kieran grabbed the hem of his shirt, lifted it over his head, and dropped it to the floor. Finley's cheeks went up in flames as he tried his best not to ogle Kieran's ripped torso. Finley would bet his pecs, cut abs, and bulging biceps fell into the larger category. God, what he wouldn't give to nuzzle his face against Kieran's chest hair. It was the perfect amount—just enough for him to pet and create the perfect friction against his sensitive nipples. When Kieran reached for his waistband, Finley emitted a strangled sound.

The dark-haired god stopped and jerked his head in Finley's direction. "Problem?"

"No," Finley replied, but his squeaky voice said otherwise. He cleared his throat and pointed to a door in the corner. "There's a dressing room if you—"

Kieran unbuttoned and unzipped his cargo shorts and let them fall to the ground. "I don't have issues with modesty."

"Clearly," Finley said, unable to keep the sarcasm from his voice or his gaze from roaming over Kieran's body. The man had thick, hairy thighs and lean hips. His underwear were no longer whitey, but they were definitely tighty. And thin. Kieran's black pubic hair was visible through the fabric, and Finley wanted to nuzzle his nose in the thatch.

"You don't have a moment of privacy in jail," Kieran explained, "so you get used to dressing, undressing, and, well, doing everything in front of someone else."

Everything? Finley couldn't seem to stop his thoughts from becoming lurid. He swallowed hard and forced his gaze up to meet Kieran's eyes. "That sounds awful." Why did he have to sound as breathy as a Hollywood starlet?

Kieran's expression hardened, and he shrugged. "All part of doing time for the crime." Though his words were flippant, his voice was thick with bitterness. Kieran kicked his flip-flops free and walked toward the shelf with the jeans. Finley could have bounced a quarter off his ass. Now that was a drinking game he could get behind.

"I'll just step outside and leave you to get dressed. You might not be used to having privacy, but you deserve it."

Kieran turned and looked at him over his shoulder. "I didn't mean to make you uncomfortable."

"You didn't."

"Maybe you could jot down what I take off the shelves while I get dressed so we finish quicker."

"Someone is sure eager to get to work," Finley teased.

"I don't like accepting things I didn't earn."

"Fair enough." Finley crossed the room and picked up the clipboard. "You should probably choose extra clothes while you're here. Most of the guys alternate between three or four outfits. There's a laundry room on the backside of this building, and you have access to it twenty-four seven. Or you could come back later to pick out more clothes. We don't lock the store, so you can help yourself whenever."

Kieran slowly panned the room again with a scowl on his face.

"Something wrong?" Finley asked.

"If something seems too good to be true, it's usually because it is."

Kieran's somber gaze tugged at Finley's heartstrings. He could understand why Kieran felt that way, but it was not his responsibility to change the man's outlook. Cash had tasked him with teaching Kieran a skill. Finley would repeat the mantra as often as needed to avoid falling into familiar traps. "Where do you want to start? Jeans, shirts, or boots?"

Kieran held his gaze a heartbeat longer before turning his attention to the shelves in front of him. He grabbed a pair of jeans and stepped into them, pulling the denim up his long legs. The fabric clung to his thick thighs and muscular ass, and Finley forced his gaze away from the alluring sight to fill in Kieran's name on the inventory form.

"These jeans will do," Kieran announced.

Finley glanced over just as Kieran bent forward to choose a long-sleeved tee off the shelf. Denim clung to the most perfect, bitable ass he'd ever seen. Do? Those jeans did a lot. His gaze strayed over with each new item Kieran put on. The man looked better in a flannel shirt and jeans than anyone had a right to, and Finley was both amused and annoyed. He completed his ensemble with thick socks, pull-on boots, and a Redemption Ridge ball cap.

"Would you like a jacket?" Finley asked. "Late March in Colorado means we might see all four seasons on the same day."

"My body temp runs hot, so I'll be fine once I get moving."

Finley just bet it did. He would not think about his hot, naked flesh. Nope. Too late. Finley finished filling out the form and returned the clipboard to its nail.

"I'll keep you plenty warm," Finley said. He wished the ground would open and swallow him whole when Kieran arched a brow. "With all the physical activity we're going to do." The brow crept higher. "*Work!* All the work we're going to do."

Kieran's mouth quirked a little on the right side. Not a smirk and definitely not a smile, but it was a spark of personality. "Ah. Good to know. I'll just pick out the rest of my work clothes later."

"No problem. Would you like to check out your cabin?" Finley asked. "To stow your clothes and stuff."

Kieran removed a wallet from his cargo shorts and stuffed it into the back pocket of his jeans. "I just need a trash can."

Finley gestured to the bathroom slash dressing room in the corner. Kieran nodded and disappeared into the room, returning a few seconds later with nothing in his hands.

"Put me to work, boss," Kieran said, though there wasn't an ounce of enthusiasm in his voice.

Finley led the way out of the store and pondered if he should call his mom later to find out more about the nice guy she mentioned. Detox wasn't working as evidenced by the mockery he'd made of himself. Maybe it was time to try a different approach to love and romance. Then he felt Kieran's gaze on his ass and forgot all about his intentions.

chapter
FIVE

INLEY STRODE TOWARD THE HORSE BARN LIKE HIS ASS WAS ON fire. Then again, based on the heat Kieran had seen in the blond man's eyes, his delectable backside might've been smoldering. If Kieran hadn't kept his back turned in the general store, his new boss would've seen the semierection pressing against his underwear. It had been a dumb move to strip down in front of Finley, but Kieran couldn't resist pushing him. He'd seen sympathy shimmering in the younger guy's pale green eyes and wanted to discourage his interest with crude behavior. It was a tactic that had served him well in jail, and Kieran didn't want to make friends and form bonds on the ranch either.

But his rash decision backfired when his boss's empathy had turned to hunger. Finley's fiery gaze felt like a caress, and Kieran's body reacted. He'd wanted Finley on his knees with those pillowy lips wrapped around his cock. Kieran had stymied his natural urges and resisted any form of physical pleasure for nearly two years. Everything a person did or said in lockup was weaponized against them, especially sexual gratification. Kieran had refused to let anyone see him at his most vulnerable and use it as leverage against him. He figured if monks and priests could abstain for their lifetimes, he could hold out during his sentence. Ignoring the physical and mental ache had been difficult, but he'd learned ironclad control over his mind and body. He wouldn't have been successful if he'd served time with Finley Ashe.

The awareness was enough to light a fire under his ass and cool his ardor. Kieran would've outpaced Finley to the barn if not for the fit and feel of his new boots and his work clothes. Though the items were all excellent quality, they were much heavier and tighter than what he was used to wearing. Lagging behind gave Kieran an excellent view of Finley's ass and long, toned legs. His upper body was lean, but his dark shirt hugged him snuggly, showcasing tight muscles. Ranch work had been good to Finley's physique, and Kieran wasn't the only one who noticed. Several heads swiveled in the blond's direction as he walked by, but Finley seemed unaware of the attention. It stirred uncharacteristic feelings, making him want to mark and claim a man he didn't even know. Where the hell had the urge even come from? Kieran forced his focus, visually and mentally, away from his boss's physical assets and increased his pace. If they were going to work together, he wanted to get past this weird tension between them.

"You never asked why I was in jail," he said. Reminding Finley that he was a felon should throw some ice water on his attraction. "Aren't you curious?"

"Not really," Finley replied. "I trust Cash's instincts."

"Are you two fucking?" *Holy shit, Sullivan. What the actual fuck?* Now that the question was out there, he was dying for an answer. If they were a couple, Kieran felt sorry for Cash because Finley had looked ravenous when they'd locked eyes in the store. Finley stopped suddenly and whirled around to face Kieran. His green eyes blazed hot enough to scorch the entire ranch. *That's right, sexy. Get mad. You don't want a guy like me.*

"Don't do that," Finley bit out.

"Do what?" Feigning innocence had never been Kieran's strong suit.

"Do not disrespect Cash or me." Finley inhaled a deep breath, then released it slowly. His anger seemed to dissipate with his exhale, and his gaze softened. *No, no, no.* Kieran started to panic. He wanted this guy mad enough to keep his distance. "Look," Finley said. "I get it. You're going through a stressful time right now, and it's hard to let your guard down and trust people. I know you don't believe it now, but you will realize you're safe here, and more importantly, you're wanted and valued."

Kieran searched Finley's gaze, looking for any signs of manipulation, but he only saw sincerity. Instead of calming him as Finley had intended, it made him madder.

Kieran caught movement in the corner of his eyes and adjusted his angle to assess the person approaching him. The guy was four to five inches taller than Kieran and carried an extra hundred pounds or more on his frame. The auburn hair peeking from beneath his cap was several shades lighter than his full beard. Kieran recognized the aggressive look in the man's amber eyes. He'd seen it in the yard more times than he wanted to remember, though he'd avoided any major incidents by keeping a cool head. Something about Finley short-circuited his wiring, and Kieran turned to face the threat fully, pulling his shoulders back and pushing his chest out. He might not be built like a ginger version of The Rock, as his opponent was, but Kieran was fast and built for endurance.

"Just great," Finley grumbled. "Another banty rooster in the barnyard."

Ginger Rock reached them in a few strides. "Is there a problem, Finley?" he asked without taking his eyes off Kieran. The man's soft voice was jarring. Kieran had expected something deep and rumbling, but he had to strain to hear him.

"Not at all, Ivan," Finley said, moving into Kieran's periphery. "Everything is fine."

The big man's expression didn't falter, and his gaze remained locked on Kieran. "Why don't I believe you, Fin?"

Kieran had several replies ready to unleash, but Finley beat him to the punch.

"Because you're a suspicious bastard." Finley's voice was light and laced with humor, undercutting the sting of his words.

Big Red's lips twitched, and he finally broke eye contact with Kieran to smile at Finley. "This coming from someone who is way too trusting."

"Touché." There was a wistfulness in Finley's voice that intrigued Kieran, and he wanted to see if his expression matched the tone, but Red's calculating amber eyes were back on him. Finley snorted. "Ivan, this is Kieran Sullivan. Cash assigned him to work in the equine program." When neither man acknowledged the introduction, Finley huffed out a sigh. "I'm just going to let you two pound your chests like alpha gorillas and get it out of your systems. Make it quick, Kieran. We have a lot of work to do." He pivoted on his heels and headed back toward the barn, leaving Kieran to square off against the bear-sized man.

"Ivan Gallagher," Ginger Rock said after a few awkward moments. "I'm the foreman around here. I answer to Cash, but everyone else answers to me."

"Explains the swagger," Kieran replied.

Ivan blinked twice but didn't react otherwise. "If you do one thing to upset Finley, I'll bounce you off this ranch so fast and hard your ass will leave potholes in the gravel. And I won't care who protests or tries to intervene. Keep your nose clean and your hands to yourself."

Heat rushed to Kieran's face as he bristled with anger. This asshole didn't know the first thing about him but had already pegged him as a threat to Finley. Kieran wanted to push back, to get in his face and insult him, but he couldn't blow the opportunity. He gave Big Red a curt nod and followed Finley, but the foreman held out his arm like a crossing gate. Kieran jerked to a stop and glared at the man.

"I need to hear the words, Sullivan."

Kieran counted to five and tried to throw a fire blanket on the flames of his rising fury, then calmly said, "Heard and understood."

Ivan studied him through narrowed eyes. Had he wanted a pinky promise instead? After another intense stare-down, the burly man relaxed a little and said, "Get back to work."

Kieran fought off the urge to salute him as he turned to follow Finley. He was surprised the blond man hadn't made it too far, considering his earlier gait. Maybe he wasn't as indifferent to the standoff as he'd pretended to be. Kieran quickened his steps and caught up to him in a few strides.

"Who won?" Finley asked.

Kieran glanced over and saw a smile flirting at the corner of his mouth. "Excuse me?"

"The pissing contest," Finley clarified.

Kieran snorted. "It was a tie."

Finley sighed heavily. "Guess I can expect more chest-thumping in the future."

"The foreman seems mighty concerned about you. Warned me off and everything." Kieran wanted to take the words back because they implied he cared about their relationship. He didn't. It was just an odd conversation to have right out of the gate.

Finley stopped and whirled on him again. *Fucking great.* Ginger Rock was probably storming toward them. He was surprised the earth wasn't shaking with the man's fury. "Are you going to accuse me of screwing Ivan too?" Kieran tried to respond, but Finley hadn't finished his tirade. "Because we're not. And just to be clear, I'm not fucking my way through the staff."

Son of a bitch. Why did the hurt shimmering in Finley Ashe's eyes bother Kieran so damn much? Shit. He'd have to triple his efforts to keep an emotional distance from this guy, but he wanted to do it in a way that wasn't cruel to someone who'd only shown him kindness.

"What I said about you and Cash was crude and rude. I was out of line."

Finley arched a brow as his mouth ticked up at one corner. "That's a lazy apology."

Kieran fought off the urge to smile. "It's more a statement of fact."

"Apology accepted," Finley said before turning back toward the barn. Once inside the structure, he turned and looked at Kieran again. "Aren't you going to ask what I did to get locked up?" Kieran snorted and shook his head. "What? I could be dangerous."

Of that, Kieran had no doubt. "I know when a guy has done time. I can tell by the expression in his eyes and in his demeanor. Rueben has done time. Ivan has done time. Several of the other guys I've met have also been locked up. You? No way in hell. The spitfire who manages the house? Not a chance."

Finley's lips curved into a smile, and Kieran felt a tug low in his belly. "Never underestimate Harry. She'll make you pay." Kieran didn't doubt that either. He noticed their eye color and accents were similar, making him think they were related. Siblings? Cousins? He was curious but wouldn't ask.

Finley's conduct turned to all business when he gave Kieran a barn tour. The enormous structure housed an impressive tack room, a veterinary examination area, a breakroom, and ample storage for their equipment and tools. Their last stop was Finley's office. The space was small but tidy with wood-paneled walls and standard furniture—a desk, lamp, computer, and chair. A red loveseat tucked along one corner added a pop of color, but the gallery of framed horse paintings, wildlife photography, and family snapshots hanging on the wall behind the desk was the real showstopper. The largest image was of a little blond boy sitting astride a black horse, wearing a cowboy hat that was bigger than he was. Kieran wasn't sure how old the kid was, but it was unmistakably a younger version of the man who stood beside him.

"This is where you'll check in each morning at six," Finley said. He walked over to a clipboard where he posted daily tasks and assignments. He flipped through a few of the daily sheets, summarizing each chore and when they performed it.

"I'll train you on each task the first week, supervise the second week, and turn you loose the third week if you've got it down. I will assign the tasks each morning, and you'll initial once you're done."

"Sounds fair," Kieran said.

Finley grabbed a second set of tools and gestured to the stall area. "We'll pick up where I left off with everyone's least favorite task—shoveling shit." Kieran nodded and followed him back to where they'd first met. He could still hear the sickening thud of the rake connecting with Finley's head, and his stomach tightened as he thought about it. Kieran listened as his boss discussed the importance of clean bedding for horses. "Filthy living conditions can lead to life-threatening illnesses." They removed manure daily with a muck rake and used a pitchfork to remove the bedding every few weeks. "We use a combination of wood pellets and shavings, or we'd have to change the bedding every four or five days. New shavings get added between deep cleans as needed. You'll have the hang of it in no time."

They moved on to the next stall, and Finley demonstrated the best techniques for removing the filthy bedding. Kieran did his best to keep his eyes trained on the action inside the tight space, but occasionally, his attention and gaze strayed to Finley's ass. After a few scoops, Finley straightened up and extended the pitchfork to him. "Your turn."

It had looked simple enough, but the manure and urine-soaked bedding weighed more than Kieran had expected and smelled awful. There were undoubtedly worse situations he could find himself in. He pushed the shovel in, scooped out an enormous amount, pivoted, and flung it into the wagon. Kieran felt a slight twinge in his lower back but ignored it.

"Can I give you some advice?" Finley asked after he repeated the process three more times.

Kieran stilled and straightened up. "Sure."

Finley walked into the stall, which seemed to shrink the surrounding walls, and took the pitchfork from his hand. He demonstrated again but slower, giving tips to prevent injuries to his shoulders, neck, and lower back. "There's no doubt you're in great shape, but you'll use different muscle groups than with bodybuilding." Kieran bit back a scoff. He used every single muscle when he worked out. Maybe not all at the same time, but he gave them equal attention in the gym. "I'm not leaning and twisting with my waist as much, so I'm putting more weight on my legs and less pressure on my back."

"Yeah, okay," Kieran said. He tried it Finley's way a few times, but he couldn't leverage his strength as much. Therefore, his shovelfuls were smaller, which meant more twisting and shit-throwing. Kieran's way would be kinder to his body, so he returned to the method that worked best for him.

Finley said nothing, so he continued working until the dirty bedding was gone. He paid close attention to the volume of wood pellets and shavings to use. They moved to the next stall, and Kieran took the lead, digging his fork right in. Finley grabbed his tools and moved to the next pen so they could work side by side. Kieran's brain was full of questions, and since none were personal, he let them fly.

"Why are you shoveling shit if it's the most dreaded job?" he asked. "Why not delegate it?"

"I'll never ask my team to do a task I'm not willing to do myself," Finley replied. "A horse's environment is critical to its health, and everyone needs a break from the tedious tasks to prevent burnout and harmful shortcuts." Finley heaved a girthy sigh. "And I needed the physical work to burn off frustration."

There was the wistfulness Kieran had heard in Finley's voice earlier. He paused and looked at the wall separating their stalls. It had to be eight feet tall, so not even the jolly red giant could peer over the sides. More questions arose, and it was on his tongue to ask about the source of Finley's melancholy, but he didn't. Kieran reshuffled his questions like a deck of cards until he found one he could voice. He heaved a shovel of shit into the wagon and said, "How many horses do you have here?"

"Twelve right now, but the number always fluctuates. Some of our guests are here to train for various equine skills; others we foster until they've completed rehabilitation. We eventually find forever homes for the fostered horses. Some require more therapy than others." There was a hint of frustration in Finley's voice, but it was gone when he added, "We can house twenty horses right now, though Cash will build another barn if our program continues to grow."

"That's cool," Kieran said, and he meant it. He'd never been around horses, but he thought they were beautiful and graceful. He couldn't believe anyone would want to harm them, but people had no trouble hurting innocent kids and other animals.

"You okay?" Finley's voice came from the front of his stall, not beside it.

He snapped his head around, alarmed he hadn't noticed the movement. Hell, Kieran hadn't been aware he'd even stopped working. He'd stood there staring off into space with a shovel full of manure in his hands. "Yeah. I was just thinking how much I don't like people who abuse animals."

Finley sighed, and his eyes shimmered with an emotion more

unwelcome than pity. The last thing Kieran wanted was for Finley to admire or even like him.

"Might want to move," he said gruffly, hoisting the shovel. "You've already had the shit knocked out of you. No need to be covered in it too."

Finley laughed and shook his head. "You make an excellent point." He whistled as he headed back to his stall. Kieran was just grateful Finley wasn't singing and returned to his work. They worked well together and finished the remaining stalls before pivoting to food and water. Finley emphasized the importance of ensuring the horses had plenty of clean water.

"They will drink anywhere from five to ten gallons of water per day."

"Each horse drinks that much?" Kieran asked.

Finley smiled. "Yes. Wait until you see how much they eat."

Kieran continued asking questions as they marked one task off the list after another.

They were about to clean tack when a loud neighing sound came from the paddock, followed by several frenzied shouts.

"Damn it," Finley bit out. "What has Nellie done now?" He took off running from the barn, and Kieran followed when curiosity got the best of him.

The outdoor arena was pure chaos as people moved horses to the opposite end from where a magnificent beast bucked and kicked. Nellie, he assumed, had a blueish-gray coat with black spots all over like someone had splattered paint from one end to the other. Her black mane and tail were on full display as she alternated between tossing her tail and kicking her hind legs.

"Never stand directly behind a horse," Kieran said somberly. As if to emphasize his point, Nellie's back hoof connected with the fence's top rail and nearly splintered the wood. "Ever. You can argue form when shoveling manure, but never question this rule."

"No, sir," Kieran said automatically. He was too caught up in the sight before him to realize what he had said until the sexy blond chuckled.

"Finley or Fin will do," he said.

"Yes, sir."

Finley expelled another weighty sigh as if he couldn't decide who was more infuriating—the horse or the new guy. He stuck a few fingers in his mouth and let out a shrill whistle. Nellie stopped bucking and jerked her head in Finley's direction. The whites of her eyes were showing, and Kieran thought that was a bad sign. He didn't have any experience with the animals, but even he recognized she was terrified. She immediately started pawing the ground with her front hooves and panting heavily.

"What caused this flare-up, Tyler?" Finley asked.

"I just tried to brush her," the dark-haired guy said. He pulled a brush from behind his back, and the horse started kicking again.

"Someone hurt her with a brush before," Kieran said. Nellie looked in his direction when he spoke. She stopped trying to kick her way out of the paddock and pranced a few feet away from Tyler. "Lose the brush," Kieran called out, and the trainer tossed the item over the fence. Nellie volleyed her attention between the handler and Kieran before settling on the newcomer. "No one's going to hurt you here," Kieran told her. His voice was softer and gentler than he dreamed he was capable of, and Nellie seemed slightly appeased. Her eyes weren't as big, and her pawing decreased. "That's a good girl," Kieran said as Tyler slowly approached with a carrot. Nellie accepted the peace offering, and the handler moved around her with more confidence.

"Atta girl, Nellie," Tyler cooed as he gently petted her neck.

"Amazing," Finley said softly beside him. Kieran felt his stare and turned to meet his gaze. "I'll be damned if Cash wasn't spot on about you."

Kieran clamped his jaw tight and swallowed his response. He guaranteed Cash hadn't pegged him right or he wouldn't be there. Once Nellie settled down, they returned to the barn to continue working. By the time they finished, Kieran ached in places he never knew existed.

"I think you've had enough for one day," Finley said as he handed Kieran an ice-cold bottle of water from the refrigerator in the break room. "You did great work."

"Don't take pity on me," Kieran replied. "I will pull my weight around here."

Finley gestured to the completed tasks on the clipboard. "You have, and you've earned a shower and a fresh change of clothes. I'll show you to your cabin and let you retrieve a few more outfits from the store. There will be basic supplies like soap, shampoo, and deodorant in your cabin to get you started, but Cash will advance part of your check so you can go into town and buy the supplies you want."

Kieran didn't mention his expired license. He was stretched too tight, overstimulated, and needed some quiet time to process. He'd worry about getting a ride to town with someone at a different time. "Thank you."

Finley stopped outside a cabin and gestured to the door. "Cash has a set of keys so you can lock the place up for privacy. You have your own bathroom and access to satellite television. It's a pretty sweet setup. Harry, or someone on her crew, cleaned the cabin and stocked it with the essentials. You'll keep it clean going forward, okay?"

"Yeah, of course," Kieran replied, then winced when a muscle spasmed in his lower back.

"I have a special salve my mom made for aching muscles. I'll make sure you get some too. You're strong and fit, but you'll need it for the first few weeks." A protest danced at the tip of his tongue until Finley added, "We all need it from time to time. Dinner is at six sharp. Don't be late."

"Or Harry will make me pay?" Kieran asked.

Finley laughed and shook his head. "Not about that, but the rest of the hands will devour your share. They're like animals."

Recalling the lunch he'd had, Kieran couldn't blame them. "I won't be late."

"See you at dinner."

Kieran watched him walk away before heading to the general store. He chose two more outfits and a few packs of socks and underwear. Kieran might double up on his socks to cushion against the leather boots. He already had blisters forming and thought the extra padding might help. Kieran filled out the form on the clipboard, marveling again at the honor system Cash trusted the ex-cons to use before heading back to his cabin.

He pushed the door open and stepped inside. The space was barely big enough for the full-size bed, loveseat, and television, but it was a thousand times nicer than his previous accommodations. The décor was a standard Western theme of bears, moose, trees, and mountains on a red-and-black plaid background. No orange in sight, thank fuck. He had a microwave and coffee pot on the counter and a small refrigerator nestled below it. The bathroom was barely big enough to turn around in, but Kieran liked how the shower curtain and small rug matched the rest of the cabin. He looked at the mirror and studied his reflection. He looked tired and weary, but he couldn't deny the shimmer of pride in his eyes after a day of hard work.

Kieran's gaze shifted to the shower. He hadn't washed by himself for too long and couldn't resist the lure any longer. He turned on the faucet, expecting it to take a long time to heat, but steam filled the room before he stripped down. Kieran stepped beneath the spray and moaned when hot water pelted his skin. The water pressure would probably feel average to most people, but it felt like a massaging caress to him. Kieran's body came alive in ways it hadn't during lockup, nerve endings sparking as his blood traveled south, plumping his dick and making his balls tingle.

There was no need for him to abstain any longer. Kieran could touch himself now without everyone on his cell block listening and knowing. He could moan and cry out as much as he wanted. Kieran tried to resist the pull, to maintain the mastery of his body, but the need was too great. His brain made a last-ditch effort to correct course, reminding him that just his hand wouldn't be enough for long, and he'd seek pleasure with another person, opening himself up to rejection and betrayal. Kieran's need to come, to feel alive, overrode the voice of reason that helped him during lockup. He tried to blame his weakness on his exhaustion or the water's enticing sensation against his flesh, but he knew the source.

Kieran conjured up his image now, those green eyes and plush lips. He imagined Finley on his knees, begging for more with his gaze as Kieran fed his dick into Finley's greedy mouth. The urge to fist his cock and get himself off fast pressed against his brain, but Kieran ignored it. He grazed his callused fingertips over his rigid flesh, relishing the tremors in his body and the need clawing at his gut. His balls tightened from the simple caress, and Kieran tilted his head back as he lifted his free hand to pinch his nipple and twist it.

The pleasure was so acute he cried out, nearly choking on a mouthful of water. His need to come overtook his desire to draw out the pleasure. The drag of his callused palm over sensitive flesh created the most delicious friction. Kieran would've preferred a slicker glide, but he didn't want to stop and reach for the conditioner. His mind returned to mesmerizing eyes and a wicked tongue dancing around his cockhead, sucking it into a hot, welcoming mouth. Kieran shot his load after a few strokes. The intensity of his orgasm sent him to his knees, where tears of joy and shame racked his body.

Kieran remained there, panting through his anguish until his legs felt strong enough to support him. His body already craved the next orgasm before the tides of pleasure from the last one faded. He tipped his head under the stream and reminded himself he'd done nothing to warrant his guilt. Finley's image formed behind his closed eyes, and he jerked them open and reached for the soap.

He made a deal with himself. He could jerk off as much as he wanted to, but he wouldn't think of Finley Ashe while doing it. Should be easy enough now that the man was out of Kieran's system.

chapter
SIX

THE TANTALIZING AROMA OF TOMATOES, FRESH HERBS, AND
Italian sausage greeted Finley when he entered Cash's house. He
wanted to arrive before everyone else to have a private conversation
with his sister and perhaps grab a little snack while he was there. Harry
was at the stove with her earbuds in place, humming and swaying side
to side. Knowing her, she had the volume turned up so high an elephant
could sneak up on her. He could've been a dick and scared her, something
he'd done more times than he could remember, but Finley wanted to
stay on her good side. Harry wouldn't divulge coveted information if
he scared her.

He helped himself to a few grapes from the fruit dish and leaned
against the island, knowing she'd eventually turn around and spot him.
A bowl of ricotta cheese sat on the counter along with dozens of cooked
lasagna noodles resting on foil-lined cookie sheets. Kieran was in for
a treat because Harry's lasagna was the best. She made her meat sauce
from scratch using tomatoes and herbs she grew on the ranch. Finley
had mowed through the first handful of grapes and reached for a second when Harry turned around and squealed.

His sister covered her heart with both hands and aimed a mutinous glare at him. Then she briefly closed her eyes and cycled through a few deep breaths before meeting his gaze again. Harry removed her earbuds and dropped them into her apron pocket. "You're an asshole, Fin."

Usually, he'd feign innocence, but this time, his wide-eyed expression was legit. "What did I do? I was only standing here."

She put both hands on her slim hips and narrowed her eyes. "Don't play dumb with me. You knew damn well I didn't hear you come in. You should've let me know you were here."

"Like I did the last time?" he asked. "You nearly punched your hand through my chest." He rubbed the spot as if the bruise was still there. "I'm damned if I do and damned if I don't."

Harry studied him for a few heartbeats before she grinned and shook her head. "Okay, you might have a point."

Finley's mouth fell open in genuine surprise. "What? You're admitting you're wrong?" he teased.

"Don't push it, brat."

"I can't seem to help myself." Finley reached back toward the fruit bowl, but she swatted his hand away.

"You'll ruin your appetite."

Finley laughed and retracted his hand. "Yes, ma'am."

Harry was older by thirteen years and often felt more like a bonus mom than his sister, especially when she bossed him around so much. He'd hated it when they were younger but had grown fond of her overprotectiveness. Their mom had had Harriet with her first husband, who hadn't stuck around to help raise the fiery redhead. Finley's sperm donor, who was Hope's third attempt at a happily ever after, wasn't much better at parenting. Hope, Harry, and Finley formed a tight bond, adopting an "us against the world" mentality until Hope met Gary, ending her streak of toxic relationships and expanding their family. For her, the fourth time was the charm. Finley's stepfather was the reason his mother could speak about rehabilitating the heart and finding true love with conviction. She hadn't given up and didn't want her only son to either. It seemed she was trying to prod his healing process along, and

Finley was positive she wouldn't have brought it up to him without discussing it with Harry first.

"I know how you can get your mind off your stomach," Harry said.

Finley tossed up his hands in surrender. "Fine. Put me to work."

"Do you want to assemble the lasagna or make the salad?" she asked.

"I'll do assembly." Finley stepped over to the sink. He pumped the soap dispenser twice, lathering his hands thoroughly before rinsing them. "Who's the guy Mom wants me to meet?"

Harry moved to the refrigerator and retrieved a freezer bag full of mixed greens and several containers of vegetables and salad fixings. "He's someone Gary knows. His name is Michael, and he recently moved to Last Chance Creek. That's all I know."

Finley pinned her with a disbelieving stare. "How's that possible?"

Harry shrugged. "I didn't ask questions. I'm trying to stay out of your business. And before I forget, Mom sent a jar of her special salve for muscle aches with me yesterday, but I forgot to give it to you last night. It's in that small purple bag by the refrigerator."

The salve's arrival was perfect timing since he wanted to give some to Kieran, and he was down to his last jar. "Thank you," Finley said, "and since when do you stay out of my business?"

Harry slapped him lightly on the arm. "Since you've become a grown-ass man who can care for himself."

Finley quirked a brow as he dried his hands. "So this morning?"

His sister aimed a cheeky grin at him. "Yep. I told Mom to stay out of your business, but it sounds like she didn't listen to me." Harry set her bounty on the island counter and pulled an enormous bowl from the cabinet beneath it. "I gotta admit she has good taste." Then she removed three large rectangular casserole dishes for the lasagnas.

Finley retrieved the pot of meat sauce from the stove and set it on the workstation. "You've met Michael?"

Harry shook her head. "She showed me a picture. You could search Gary's social media profiles for friends or followers named Michael." Their stepfather was a very successful real estate agent with tons of connections, so Harry's suggestion sounded like finding a needle in a haystack. "He has dark hair and eyes like the hunk Cash brought home today," Harry continued, fanning her face with both hands. "The solemn expression in that guy's eyes really punched me in the chest. He reminded me of a stray puppy." Harry sucked in a sharp breath as she realized what she said. Finley could feel her stare but didn't turn to meet her gaze. "Where did Cash place the new guy? His name started with a *K*. Keith. Kevin."

She damn well knew his name, but he'd take the bait. "Kieran."

"That's it," she said, snapping her fingers. "Do you know where Kieran is going to work?" When Finley started assembling the first dish without answering, Harry groaned. "Oh no."

Finley finished the first layer of noodles in the casserole dish nearest to him. "It will be fine, sis."

Harry placed her small hand on his forearm, and Finley looked at her. "Kieran is the ultimate fixer-upper. I get the attraction, but I'm worried about you working with him so closely."

Finley was worried too, but he put on a brave front for his sister. "Kieran isn't dangerous."

"He is to your heart," Harry countered. "You are the best person in the world, Fin. You deserve so much better than you allow."

Two of those remarks were one hundred percent accurate, but he wasn't so sure about the other. Finley tried to be a good person, but he was sure there was someone more deserving of the best-person title. "Which is why I'm giving serious consideration to Mom's suggestion. Who better to guide me through picking a good partner than Hope? I can benefit from all her knowledge without the messy divorces."

Harry removed her hand from his forearm and placed it on her chest. "You don't want to become a spinster like me?"

Finley snorted. "You would've been considered a spinster two hundred years ago. Now you're just smart because you refuse to settle." Hope would say Harry refused to take chances, but Finley wasn't as brave as their mother. He wished his sister would open her eyes and heart to the possibility of love. It might be closer than she realized.

Toenails clicking on the hardwood alerted them to company moments before Patsy and Cash appeared. The rancher pulled out a stool and dropped onto it while the black-and-white beauty rounded the island so she could get closer to the action. Cash tilted his head back and sniffed the air. "Lasagna. My favorite." His mouth curved into a smile, drawing attention to his full lips and neatly trimmed mustache and beard. The salt-and-pepper bristles contrasted with his unlined, almost youthful-looking complexion. Cash's gray hair was several shades darker than his facial hair.

He'd come from his office and still wore his black glasses. He'd rolled up his sleeves, revealing muscular forearms, a particular weakness for Finley. He nearly laughed out loud when he recalled Kieran's presumption that Finley and Cash were lovers. He'd have to tell Harry about it when they were alone again. Cash came across as an open book, a gorgeous one, but Finley didn't know anyone who kept it locked down tighter than his boss. Was he curious about Cash? Hell yes, but Finley respected him more, and there wasn't a single spark of chemistry between them.

Pale blue eyes focused on Finley, signaling he had Cash's full attention. "How'd Kieran do today? I meant to circle back but got tied up with one call after another."

"He did great," Finley said, and it was true. "He didn't shy away from any task, took direction well, and asked a lot of great questions. I'm pretty sure Nellie has a crush on him." If he kept Kieran close enough, he might not need the lavender and vetiver lotion his mom had made for him. His brain tried to suggest how close Kieran could get, but Finley tamped it down. He needed to get through dinner with the guy before he could allow that thought to run free, preferably while his hand shuttled up and down his erection.

A slow smile spread across Cash's face, softening his angles. Finley hadn't realized his boss was tense until his shoulders eased. "I had an inescapable feeling Kieran belonged here with us."

"I've learned not to question your judgment," Fin said as he resumed lasagna assembly.

The three of them chatted about the latest true crime documentary and their favorite podcasts while Cash handed them the ingredients they needed to complete dinner. The topic reminded Finley of his encounter with the cult.

"A trio from Salvation Anew visited Mom's store today," Finley said. Harry snapped her head up and searched his face. "No, Keegan wasn't one of them, but the encounter was just as disturbing. They think our mother is a witch." He recounted the entire interaction for Cash and Harry. "I want to dismiss the incident as no big deal, but I'm worried about Hope."

"I don't like it either," Harry replied, "but Mom can handle herself. Gary will take all necessary steps to keep her safe."

"I received a lengthy email from that Samuel guy this week," Cash said. "Most of it was arcane gibberish, but the gist is that he doesn't approve of my hiring practices. I'd like to dismiss him as a harmless buffoon, but true crime aficionados like us know better. I just don't know the best way to counter his influence."

Voices and laughter echoed down the hallway from the dining room, signaling the crew had arrived for dinner. Finley caught himself listening for a particular voice as he removed plates from the cabinet. Either Kieran hadn't arrived, or he wasn't joining in with the others. Then again, his voice was soft and would easily get drowned out by the more boisterous tones.

"I got this," Harry said, placing a hand on Finley's arm when he opened the silverware drawer. "You go hang with the guys."

Finley stepped away from the open drawer so Harry could resume the task. He looked at Cash, who was scowling down at his phone. "Are you coming, boss?"

Cash met his gaze and shook his head. "I won't be joining you for dinner. An unexpected opportunity has come up, and I don't want to miss it." Cash slid off the stool, reached into his back pocket, and withdrew a white envelope with Kieran's name scrawled on it. "Would you mind handing this to Kieran? It's his payroll advance."

Finley accepted the envelope. "Of course."

"See you tomorrow," Cash called over his shoulder as he exited the kitchen.

Another burst of laughter erupted from the dining room, pulling Finley's head in that direction.

Harry put her hands on his shoulders and steered him a few feet forward. "Go." She must've had second thoughts because she tightened her grip. "Just guard your heart."

Finley chuckled and shook his head. He placed Kieran's envelope next to the bag from his mom's store and kissed Harry's cheek. "It's fine."

"Not worried about *it*. I'm worried about my baby brother."

"Whom you called a grown-ass man moments ago," Finley reminded her on his way out of the kitchen.

He stepped inside the dining room and locked eyes with Kieran Sullivan, who looked better than any man should in double denim. A faint blush stole across Kieran's cheeks before he dropped his gaze to stare at the floor. *What the hell was that all about?* Finley's inquisitive mind wanted to know, but the information wouldn't lead him to any place good. It sure as hell wouldn't guide Finley toward the mystery man his mom wanted him to meet.

Rueben took the seat next to Kieran and started talking. Finley couldn't hear what they said, but he enjoyed seeing the two men interact. Talk about night-and-day differences in personalities. One man didn't know a stranger, and the other's tense posture screamed "stranger danger." Before Kieran arrived, Rue was the newest crew member. Finley thought he was the quickest to settle in and the most improved out of all the guys. Rue had seized his opportunity and run with it. He was the poster child for what Cash wanted to accomplish for the men. Meeting Kieran's gaze once more, Finley suspected Cash had found another diamond in the rough. Something alluring shimmered in Kieran's dark eyes, and it took Finley a few seconds to realize it was a silent plea for help, which was like the bat signal to the broken-boy magnet. Rueben's friendliness probably seemed cloying to someone like him, so Finley took the empty seat across from Rue and engaged him in a conversation about blacksmithing. A glance in Kieran's direction revealed another slight blush and an inscrutable expression Finley couldn't decipher. But damn, he wanted to decode the enigmatic man. No, no. He wanted to meet a nice guy who wasn't carrying a ton of baggage. Like the guy his mom wanted to introduce to him? What was his name again? It started with an *M*. If Finley continued staring into Kieran's eyes, he'd probably forget his own name too. He'd sure as hell forget his no-more-broken-boys rule.

Finley forced his attention to Rue, who was all too eager to tell him everything new he'd learned that week, but he pivoted the conversation around to Finley's health.

"How are you feeling?" Rue asked. He'd kept his voice down, but the question seemed to pull everyone's attention toward Finley.

"What happened?" Tyler asked.

"I'm fine," Finley replied. He wasn't aware he'd lifted his hand to touch the sore spot on his forehead until Kieran's gaze followed the movement. Fin hadn't been aware his eyes had shifted back to his newest employee either. He tried to recall the mystery guy's name. *Mitchell? Marcus? Matthew?*

"Tyler didn't ask if you were fine," Ivan said. "He wanted to know how you got hurt?"

Finley forced himself to look at the burly foreman, who was staring holes through Kieran, instead of meeting his gaze. "Well, I made a rookie mistake," he replied, then embellished the story to make everyone laugh and pull Ivan's attention back to him. Rue added his two cents, and the entire table was laughing and teasing Finley when Harry brought in the first casserole dish. She set it down on the buffet and recruited volunteers to help her transfer the rest of the food. Finley pushed back his chair, eager to get a break from Kieran, but Kieran stood up as he rounded the table, and Finley nearly plowed into him. Kieran gestured for him to go first, so Finley stepped around him and headed toward the kitchen.

They put the food and beverage pitchers on the buffet, then formed a line at the far end, where the plates, silverware, and napkins sat. Finley fell in behind Kieran and tried not to stand too close. He found it curious how the same soap could smell so different on everyone. The familiar components of Irish Spring were present, but it somehow smelled deeper and lusher on Kieran's skin. Finley allowed his gaze to roam over Kieran, noting his wet hair and taut ass before a throat cleared behind him. Finley looked over his shoulder at Rue, who smiled impishly and gestured to the sizable gap between him and the temptation in front of him.

Finley had gaped at Kieran long enough for the line to advance, and the hungry crew behind him was getting restless. He couldn't afford a mutiny, so he tossed a sheepish apology over his shoulder and stepped to the buffet to pick up his plate and utensils. As much as Finley loved Harry's lasagna, it didn't always love him back. He took a small corner piece, loaded a heaping portion of salad onto his plate, and snagged a hunk of garlic bread.

By the time Finley returned to his chair, Kieran had already tucked into his food. Rueben resumed his seat and whispered to their newest recruit, but Finley picked out enough words to realize he was cautioning Kieran to eat slowly and be mindful that the food was richer. Finley hadn't thought about it much, but the abrupt switch from bland jail food to Harry's indulgent dishes could wreak havoc on a person's digestive system.

Kieran absorbed what Rueben said, then looked over at him. "Thanks," he said. "I appreciate it."

Never one who liked to be excluded, Finley leaned forward and whispered, "He just wants more for himself."

Kieran's lips twitched at the corners, but he didn't smile. Not yet. One day, Finley would earn one. Damn it. This was how it started. A quest to make them smile would lead to other challenges. Finley would work to earn a laugh and a gentle touch, then a kiss. He'd obsess about kissing until it was no longer enough. His gut clenched as he realized he might be the problem. The guys who'd broken his heart hadn't set out to do so. Finley had gotten greedy, wanting more than they could give. His fork fell to the plate with a clang, and the surrounding conversations halted. All eyes were on him while he stared at his hands as if they'd failed him.

"I'd hoped this phase was gone for good," Harry said from the opposite side of the table. "Between the ages of six and ten, my brother dropped everything."

Finley leaned forward and turned his head so he could look at her. He'd never gone through a clumsy phase, which she knew all too well.

His big sister was doing what she'd always done—bail him out of trouble. Finley shot her a wink and said, "A kid breaks one thing, and his sister never lets him live it down." He looked back at his plate, retrieved his fork, and scooped up another bite of tomato-y, cheesy goodness. "Makes it hard to hold a grudge when she cooks this good."

A smattering of chuckles bounced around the table, then the eating and chatting resumed.

"I can't believe Cash missed this," Tyler said, forking a bite into his mouth.

"He's been gone a lot lately," Owen said. He and Tyler had been inseparable since arriving on the ranch two years ago. Owen was Tyler's opposite in every way. Where Ty was fair-skinned and dark-haired, Owen was sun-kissed and golden-haired. Tyler was more laid-back to Owen's assertiveness, yin and yang. "Maybe he's met someone."

"Something's up, and it's gotta be big," Tyler replied. "He never misses lasagna night."

Kieran's brow furrowed, and Finley recalled his remark about the ranch and its owner being too good to be true. He leaned forward, catching Kieran's eye, and quietly said, "They're only teasing. Nothing nefarious is going on."

Tyler pursed his lips for a few seconds. "Or maybe—" His words died when he saw the glower Ivan aimed at him.

"Or maybe you should shut the hell up and mind your own business," their foreman said.

Tyler's face flushed red, but instead of defending himself or making excuses, he nodded and tucked back into his food. Everyone else did too, and the conversation stopped until they pushed back from the table with full bellies. They heaped praise on Harry's cooking as they gathered their dirty dishes. Harry waved off the compliments with one hand and urged them on with the other. She stood and gave a mock bow before declaring her work done.

"We're each responsible for carrying our dirty dishes to the kitchen," Rue told Kieran as they stood up. "We rinse and put them inside the dishwashers. Teams of two or three alternate the daily kitchen duties, starting the dishwasher, cleaning the counters, and storing leftover food. That kind of thing. Ivan will let you know when it's your turn."

"I'll put Kieran on your team and bump Dylan over with Tyler and Owen," the foreman said.

"Great," Rue said. "We're up tomorrow."

Kieran nodded and followed Rue out of the dining room. The crew continued their usual banter as they took turns cleaning off their plates and rinsing their cups and utensils before stacking them inside the commercial-grade dishwashers. Finley hung back and watched them interact like they'd known each other all their lives. The crew felt like a mishmash of people Cash had pulled into his orbit. *Found family.* Finley had heard of it but hadn't realized he'd been experiencing it since accepting a job from Cash four years earlier. He'd tried his hand at real estate for a few months after moving to Colorado, but it didn't feed his soul the way working with horses did.

Finley's gaze landed on the small purple bag from his mother's store, and he grabbed it along with Kieran's payroll advance. Kieran was already outside, walking toward the cabins with Rueben, who continued to talk a mile a minute. Finley noticed Kieran's posture wasn't nearly as tense or rigid. He might not be doing much of the conversing, but he didn't look put off by it.

"Kieran," he called out. The two guys stopped and turned to face him. Finley extended the bag to him, but the taller man stared down at the offering like it might contain a deadly snake. "It's the salve I told you about," he explained. "Harry picked it up from our mom yesterday. And Cash asked me to pass along your pay advance."

"You'll want to use the salve," Rueben said. "If you think you're stiff now, just wait until morning." *Stiff?* He wasn't walking or carrying himself funny. Had Kieran mentioned he was hurting or had Rue known from personal experience? Kieran scowled at the shorter man until Rueben laughed. "I was new here once, and it wasn't so long ago I can't remember. I refused Finley's kind offer and regretted it deeply."

Kieran took the bag from Finley's hand and met his gaze. "Thanks."

"My pleasure." Had his voice sounded husky, or was it his imagination? Neither Kieran nor Rueben reacted, so it was just his inner tramp wanting to come out and play. A montage of images featuring how Finley could please Kieran rolled through his brain, and he needed to get away before making a fool of himself.

"I'm heading into Last Chance Creek tomorrow," Rueben said. "Want to tag along?"

"Yeah," Kieran said. "That'd be great. Thank you."

Finley bit back his disappointment. He'd planned to offer Kieran a ride to town, but Rueben taking him was probably for the best, considering the way his body and brain reacted to Kieran. "See you fellas at breakfast."

Rueben said goodbye while Kieran turned around and walked away but not before Finley saw his cheeks flush again. Where else would he turn that pretty pink color? He tamped down the thought until he was alone in his room at the original homestead where he lived with the other two supervisors. Dylan was in charge of the dog kennels, Finley supervised the horses, and Ivan was the ranch daddy, though no one was brave enough to call him that to his face.

The images Finley had repressed came flooding back the second he locked his bedroom door. Heat rolled over him like a hot flash, making his clothes feel too tight and itchy. He pulled them off as he stumbled toward the bed, an oasis where he could get a much-needed reprieve from the sensation overload. Once bare, his skin felt wrong—tingly and pulsing as if a million ants marched beneath the surface. He smoothed a hand over his chest and sucked in a sharp breath when his fingertips brushed over his nipple. Finley's core tightened and thrummed with need. His cock was rock hard and aching for relief.

Instead of fighting the urge, he reached inside his nightstand for the two things that would restore his balance. He affixed his dildo to the headboard with the suction cup, then squeezed lube along the shaft. Finley picked up the throw pillows and shoved them between the wall separating his room from Ivan's and the headboard. He didn't need to broadcast just how hot and hard the new guy made him. Finley yanked his covers down and tossed his pillows to the end of the bed. He climbed onto the mattress and positioned himself on his hands and knees in front of the dildo.

He reached for the lube and worked his asshole open a little because it had been a long time since he'd ridden a dick or anything shaped like one. Just the friction of his fingers over his pucker and stretching his nerve-laden hole was enough to make him hump the air, his balls swaying angrily between his legs. Finley pulled his fingers free and backed up until the wide dildo pressed against his greedy hole. Finley kept one hand braced against the mattress, gripped his cock with the other, and pushed back until the large cockhead penetrated the first ring of muscle.

"Oh god," he whispered. The burn hurt so good, and he pushed back a few more inches. Black dots danced in front of Finley's eyes, and he realized he was holding his breath. He released it with a lusty sigh and pushed back until the silicone balls were flush against his ass. His channel tightened around the intrusion, and his dick throbbed in his hand. Though he hadn't entirely abstained from sex, jerking off didn't give him the same thrill. Finley knew he'd come fast, so he stayed there, stretched wide and filled with a fake dick. Anticipation zinged through him, tightening his balls until he couldn't hold back.

Finley eased forward until the fat head of the dildo was the only thing inside him, then slowly rocked back, feeling every inch of the silicone cock scraping against his nerve endings. He repeated the motion but slid his hand along his shaft. The images that had teased him earlier gained intensity, morphing from random clips to a pornographic movie. Kieran had one hand on Finley's hip and the other gripping his hair as their flesh slapped together. Finley bit his bottom lip to keep from crying out as he increased the tempo to keep up with fantasy Kieran.

The black dots from earlier reappeared, and his vision dimmed around the edges. Finley didn't care about breathing or any other bodily function except the one gaining strength in his core. Fantasy Kieran bent over his body, pressed his lips to Finley's ear, and growled, "Come on my cock. Right fucking now." Then he sank his teeth into Finley's neck, marking and claiming him. *Lone coyote no longer.*

Finley released his dick, dug both palms into the mattress, and shoved back against the dildo once more. His release exploded from him, spurting all over the bedding. He quickly grabbed a pillow and bit down on it to dampen the sobs of pleasure as he rocked and rocked, riding the wave until the current pulled him under. He barely had the strength to ease off the dildo and collapse onto the bed. The orgasm continued to roll through him like an aftershock, and he shivered against his comforter, both hot and cold at the same time.

Eventually, his breathing calmed, and his body settled. He pushed to a sitting position and winced at the tenderness in his ass. *I'll feel that in the saddle tomorrow.* He'd also be lucky to be able to look Kieran in the eye without his face going up in flames. Fantasizing about his employee was a big mistake, but he couldn't work up the energy to regret it. This brief episode was just a moment of weakness to release some steam. He'd regroup in the morning, and no one would be the wiser. Not his know-it-all sister and definitely not the star of his fantasy. He'd get back on track, call his mom, and...

He couldn't remember why he wanted to call her. Finley closed his eyes and searched his memory. The answer was right there. He reached out a hand to grab it and fell into oblivion.

chapter
SEVEN

"**S**O WHAT DO YOU THINK ABOUT THE RANCH?" RUEBEN asked not five minutes after they'd climbed into the truck.

Kieran had known when he accepted the invitation that they wouldn't spend the trip to Last Chance Creek in contemplative silence. Rueben didn't do quiet, probably not even in his sleep. Normally, Kieran would've avoided spending free time with someone as chatty, but his hands were tied. He wanted to get some basic stuff from town, and the alternative would be to ask Cash for a favor or hitch a ride with Finley since the others were still cautious around him. Kieran didn't trust Cash as far as he could throw him, and Finley tormented him, even in his sleep.

It had horrified him to wake up in a pool of his own jizz in the middle of the night. He'd rolled onto his stomach at some point and humped the mattress while dreaming of going balls deep inside Finley's sweet ass. Kieran couldn't remember the last time he'd had a wet dream. Even worse, the realization had only made him hornier when he should've been humiliated by the loss of control.

He'd found clean sheets in a cupboard and changed the bedding before taking a quick shower. Kieran had ignored his insistent dick for as long as he could, but tossing and turning on the bed only created friction against his overstimulated body. He'd refused to give in and only managed fitful sleep the rest of the night, which left him cranky as hell when the alarm clock went off. Kieran's brain might've been tired, but his supercharged dick tented the bedding. He'd reverted to his teen years with the perpetual hard-ons since walking out of Arrowhead. He couldn't risk an inconvenient boner during chores, so he yanked the nightstand drawer open and removed the small bottle of clear liquid he'd found in the purple bag. The label read Monkey Grease, and Kieran hadn't been sure what the liquid was for until he'd read the directions. His eyes nearly bulged out of his head when he realized it was lube for jacking off. Was this a standard goody bag given to new arrivals? Then Kieran found a handwritten note that made him realize the contents were specifically for Finley, a gift from his mother of all people. He should've put everything back in the purple bag and returned it to Finley, but then Kieran would have to explain how he knew the items weren't meant for him. He'd rather wrestle a grizzly than confess to Finley that he'd read his mother's message.

My son,
Different cures for different aches.
Love,
Mom

Kieran's desperation won out over decency, so he uncapped the Monkey Grease and sniffed the contents. He didn't know what the scent was, but it was pleasant. A hint of vanilla maybe. Then he had to test out the viscosity by squeezing a small dollop on his middle finger and rubbing it against his thumb. It was slick without being thick and sticky. He couldn't stop thinking about what it would feel like against his dick and how it would feel to have someone else use it on him. He'd splayed his legs on the softest mattress he'd ever felt and fingered his hole while jerking off, wishing it was Finley's hands and fingers and coming hard enough to see black dots.

The first person he saw at breakfast was Finley, whose hair was still damp from a shower. He smelled woodsy, citrusy, and delicious, stirring something inside Kieran he didn't understand. Sure, the guy was gorgeous, but he'd met plenty of good-looking men who didn't wage this level of chaos on his libido. Abstaining for nearly two years probably had a lot to do with it, but Kieran didn't pop wood whenever the wind blew, and he didn't fantasize about the other hot guys on the ranch. Only Finley affected him this way.

Kieran had a hard time meeting Finley's gaze and only offered a cursory response when his boss asked how he'd slept. Taking the hint that he wasn't in the mood to chat, Finley made an excuse to go into the kitchen. Kieran's dick move made him feel guilty, and he started to apologize, but then he noticed a slight hitch in the man's usually graceful gait. Was Finley stiff because he'd given the salve to him? He didn't have time to bring it up before the rest of the crew arrived and teased Finley mercilessly about how he'd injured himself. The outlandish remarks and Finley's good-natured responses made him smile and eased his guilt. It was plain to see how much the crew respected and cared for one another. But then some of the remarks turned a bit suggestive, sending Kieran's thoughts down an entirely different path. Finley's face flushed bright pink, and he darted his gaze in Kieran's direction a few times. If he didn't stop looking at him, the crew would think Kieran had put that hitch in his giddy-up. Luckily for them both, Ivan shut the comments down. The guys offered token complaints until Harry diverted their attention with a platter of pancakes.

Kieran ended up in line behind Finley again, and his mind returned to the gutter when he caught a whiff of Finley's soap or aftershave. He wanted to press his nose against Finley's skin and discover where the scent was strongest. Kieran's gut clenched and his lust stirred. *Christ.* If he stayed at the ranch long, he'd need to add masturbation as part of his morning ritual. Wake up, stretch out the stiff muscles, brush his teeth, shower, and jerk off. There were much worse ways to start each day.

"Probably too soon to tell if you like it, huh?" Rueben asked, snapping him back to the present.

"The ranch is gorgeous, and it's honest work." It was basically a nonanswer, but it would have to do.

"Did you use the lotion Finley's mom made? Stuff works wonders."

"Yeah. It helped a lot."

Kieran bit his bottom lip to keep from laughing. Rueben had surely referred to the salve, a true miracle worker, but he couldn't stop thinking about the Monkey Grease. If he were honest, he couldn't wait to get back to the cabin and use it again. He'd spent five hours working closely with Finley, and it didn't take long for sweat to mix with the scent of his soap. The combination had only revved Kieran's motor, which had pissed him off and made him surlier. The madder he got, the harder he wanted to fuck.

Kieran might've been removed from the dating scene for a few years, but he could tell Finley found him attractive too. He wasn't used to having people invade his personal space, but his boss didn't seem to have any qualms about it. Kieran would detect a slight hitch in Finley's breath, witness a nostril flare, or catch that green, green gaze raking over his body whenever they bumped into one another.

Their chemistry was a recipe for disaster or explosive sex. Christ, he had to get out of there before he did something stupid like push Finley up against a stall and kiss his lush mouth. It wouldn't stop there because he knew Finley was right there with him in the insane attraction. He wasn't sure if that made him feel better or worse. A one-sided fascination would be easy to navigate, but he wouldn't stand a snowball's chance in hell if Finley gave him the green light. And if the gorgeous blond made the first move? Spontaneous combustion came to mind.

"Just hang in there," Rueben said. "I promise you'll adjust quicker than you think. The other guys will warm up to you, and the work gets easier."

Kieran thought of Ivan, the beefy foreman, who either watched him like he might steal the silver or gazed at Finley with puppy dog eyes. Why that bothered Kieran was a mystery. While he had no intention of stealing from Cash, he had ulterior motives for being there, and Ivan instinctively knew it. Kieran just had to be careful not to screw up and give Ivan ammunition to use against him. As for Finley, he had no claim on the man's time or body. Ivan obviously had tender feelings for Finley, and Kieran would be wise to encourage the sexy blond in the ginger giant's direction. He tried to picture them together, locked in an embrace, but it just made his blood boil. He forced his attention back to the stilted conversation Rueben was trying to have with him.

"I actually like the work," Kieran said. "It's physical and rough on the body, but you can step back and see the fruits of your labor." There was no waiting for things to click into place or pan out. Working with the foster horses would be a different story, but he figured it would take a while for him to advance to that point, and he planned to be long gone by then. "I'm used to being the one on the outside looking in," Kieran said. "It doesn't bother me." *Anymore.*

"Nah, that's not how it works here, amigo. We're family. Maybe not by blood but how it counts. I know the perfect solution. Come to poker night at the old homestead. Give the guys a chance to get to know you."

The suggestion made Kieran's skin itch. No distractions. No attachments. But he couldn't afford to raise red flags with the crew and draw tighter scrutiny from their foreman. "I don't have much money," Kieran said, hoping that would give him an out.

Rueben snorted. "No money needed. We play for bragging rights only."

Well, fuck. There went that excuse.

"And remember," Rueben said, "Harry has plans, so we're fending for ourselves tonight."

Kieran recalled the way the guys had razzed her over lunchtime about going on a date while Dylan had dropped his gaze to his plate. He didn't need to be on the ranch long to notice the guy's infatuation with the lovely redhead. Harry waved off their ridiculousness and assured them there were plenty of leftovers on hand if no one felt like rustling something up on their own.

"We'll order pizza and scrounge up some snacks. It's a great time. Happens every Saturday at seven at the original homestead."

"Sounds fun," he lied. "Who all plays?" With Harry gone, it might be a good time to search the big ranch house if Cash was distracted with poker. It wasn't like he could come right out and ask Cash what his connection was to his ex-boyfriend, and he didn't expect an honest response if he did. Kieran needed irrefutable evidence tying them together. How many chances would he get to look around the big ranch house unimpeded?

"Ivan, Dylan, Owen, Tyler, and me," Rueben said.

"What about Cash?"

Rueben slowed the truck and signaled for a turn. "Sometimes, but he's gone again this weekend."

Again? Interesting. He embraced his good luck rather than press for more information about Cash. "Not Finley either?" *Damn it.* Why the hell had he asked about him? Rueben chuckled, and Kieran looked over in time to catch his sly grin before it faded. He debated on correcting Rueben's assumptions about his interest, but if he did, he'd only validate the guy's suspicion, not dissuade it.

"Nope. Finley's usually out on the town Saturday nights." Rueben's countenance darkened as if a giant cloud had blocked the sunshine. A quick glance out the windshield showed a perfectly sunny afternoon. "Well, that was the case until about six months ago."

Before Kieran could ask what happened, Rueben shook his head as if he'd heard the unspoken question. Then again, it would've been a natural reaction if someone had spoken out of turn and let something slip they hadn't meant to reveal. Kieran had learned several things about Rueben in the twenty-four hours he'd known him. The man might talk a lot, but it was never mindless chatter, and he wouldn't hurt a fly, let alone someone like Finley, and divulging personal information would definitely fall under that umbrella.

"It's not my story to tell, and I was wrong to say that," Rueben said, bolstering Kieran's opinion of the man.

"And it's none of my business," Kieran replied, though he had to wonder who he was trying to convince. Rueben's obvious distress bothered him on a few levels. Kieran shouldn't care, but he did. He shouldn't want to ease the man's mind, but he did. "No harm, no foul."

Only a day after leaving Arrowhead, his carefully cultivated control was slipping away. He pictured it in his mind, a steady rope to grasp hold of, but it turned into a tendril of smoke as soon as Kieran reached for it. *Poof.* Frustration simmered in his gut, and if he wasn't careful, it would boil over and ruin his carefully laid plans.

"So anyway," Rueben said. "What do you think about poker night? You in?"

Not if he could help it. "Let me think about it," Kieran replied instead of betraying his real thoughts. At least he hadn't lost control of his mouth. "Tell me about Last Chance Creek."

"I don't know much," Rueben replied. "I've only been here a year. I was born in Los Angeles, but my family moved to Denver when I was ten." Kieran was curious about Rueben's past and the crime or crimes that landed him in lockup, but he didn't ask. Rueben deserved the opportunity for people to know the man he'd become, not who he'd been at a low point in his life.

"Last Chance Creek is a pretty little place," Rueben continued. "Used to be a mining town during the big gold rush. Looks like a set for a Western movie. There's not a ton of shopping in town, but there's a general store attached to the feed mill, but I think they're overpriced. My first stop after arriving was a neat thrift shop. The owner always has a good variety of options and sizes. Finley asked me to stop by the feed mill and pick up a small order. You can wait for me in the truck, and we'll head downtown together afterward or you can take off on your own."

"I think I'll head over to the thrift shop and check it out." Kieran didn't want to hurt Rueben's feelings, but he really needed some quiet time. Keeping his guard up around some people was harder, and it drained his battery faster.

"No problem," Ruben said, then told him where to find the secondhand shop.

The feed mill was at the edge of town. Its front was a throwback to a bygone era where people would've rolled into town on wagons or horses instead of pickup trucks. Its rear was modern concrete with multiple bays for easy loading. Rueben backed up to one and killed the engine.

"Want to meet me back here in an hour? I'd like to take a nap before poker tonight so I'm extra sharp."

"Sure," Kieran replied, though he doubted he'd need that much time.

Walking down Main Street in Last Chance Creek felt like traveling back in time because each storefront mimicked the Old West style of the general store. Well, all except the large casino at the end of the block. The color of the building matched the others and fit in well. It looked like a hotel some weary traveler might stay at after a long trek across the country. The neon sign out front, though designed to look old, clashed with the rest of the town. It was more Bugsy Siegel than John Wayne.

The streets were more crowded than Kieran expected for the middle of the week, especially in front of the casino. The thrift shop, This and That, was located between a bookstore that caught Kieran's eye and an old-fashioned soda shop. He wanted to spend cash in all three, but he needed to budget wisely. He'd start with necessities and reevaluate afterward.

A kind-eyed man with more hair on his chin than his head looked up from a paperback and smiled. "New in town?"

"Just passing through," Kieran said. It was close enough to the truth. He'd put Colorado in the rearview mirror once he received the answers he deserved. "I forgot a few items, and I'm looking to replace them."

The clerk shut his paperback with a snap. "You've come to the right place." He grabbed a paper bag off the stack on the counter and extended it to Kieran. "All you can fit for ten dollars."

He would've spent more than that on a graphic tee at a department store. Kieran accepted the bag and opened it. "Challenge accepted."

He'd dreamed of sweatpants for twenty months while wearing scratchy prison scrubs, but he didn't find any in the store. He located a few pairs of super soft flannel lounge pants in his size, though. Kieran grabbed a variety of shirts, a hoodie, and a jacket. He didn't see any other clothing items he needed, but the clerk had said anything that fit inside the bag was ten bucks. He picked out a pair of aviator sunglasses and a Denver Broncos hat. The colors and mascot were drastically different from the modern team logo. His gaze landed on playing cards, an art kit, and a sketchbook. None of those things were necessities, but his soul longed to create art, and they would fit in his bag. Kieran was just about to head to the counter when he noticed a display of books. The selection was small, but the range of options was vast, covering everything from fantasy to historical romance and paranormal to thriller. His gaze landed on a copy of *The Outsiders*, and he reached down to grab it.

The book had been assigned reading in high school. Most of the kids he'd run with had bitched and moaned about the book, but he'd secretly loved every word, even if it wasn't the most uplifting story. He could relate to the greasers and always felt like he was on the outside looking in, never belonging to anyone or anything.

The book's presence felt like serendipity, a reminder that he didn't belong on the ranch. Kieran could admit to himself that he was on the verge of loosening up when it came to Finley and possibly Rueben, and he was already smitten with a horse named Nellie. But he had to maintain his focus or spend the rest of his life drowning in bitterness. Kieran approached the counter with his paper bag, then noticed a display of watches. Without a phone, it was difficult to keep track of time. He found one with a simple brown leather strap and added it to his sack once he confirmed it still worked. The gentlemen didn't inspect his paper bag or look to see what he'd picked. The items fit inside, and that was all that mattered to him.

"Ten bucks," he said.

Kieran removed the bill from his wallet and passed it to the shopkeeper. He still had ninety dollars from his advance but decided to hold on to it rather than explore the bookstore or the soda shop.

"Thank you for your business," the clerk said. "I hope you enjoy your visit and come see us again." With that, he picked up his book and resumed reading.

Kieran stepped outside and donned the sunglasses, watch, and ball cap before continuing down the sidewalk. The crowd in front of the casino had grown considerably during his brief jaunt inside the thrift store. Kieran noticed the outfits the people wore belonged in the same period as the buildings. Modest slacks and shirts for the men and long, shapeless dresses for the women. All were made from drab-colored fabric and lacked any adornment.

A white-haired man stood in the center of the gathering. The platform he'd perched himself on elevated him above everyone else. He lifted a bullhorn to his mouth and said, "Sinners repent. Salvation can be yours if you—"

Kieran slammed a mental door shut, blocking out the rest. He halted and turned to head back toward the truck and smacked into someone on the sidewalk. Thankfully, it was only Rueben.

He gripped Kieran's biceps long enough to steady him, then dropped his hands. Rueben's gaze shifted to the protesters, and his lips curled into a sneer. "Christ, those people need to get a life."

"Who are they?" Kieran asked.

"Some outfit called Salvation Anew. They basically hate anyone who doesn't look or love like them."

Kieran snorted. "Makes us enemy number one."

Rueben shifted his gaze back to Kieran and winked. "Some of us are a double whammy."

"I think I'll head on back to the truck," Kieran said. "These killjoys have put me off shopping or sightseeing."

"I'm with you," Rueben said, pivoting to face the same direction as Kieran. "Find any good bargains?"

"I did. Thanks for telling me about the shop."

"Us sinners need to stick together," Rueben teased. He had little to say during their walk back to the truck, which Kieran found unsettling. Rueben always had something to say, and the quiet felt uncomfortable and solely for his benefit. The guy had made Kieran feel welcome, and he wanted Rueben to be himself.

"So which of you makes the stiffest poker competition?" Kieran asked.

Rueben grinned and glanced over at him as he navigated the road out of town. "Piqued your curiosity, huh?"

"Maybe a little," Kieran said.

"I suck at poker, but I'm not in it to win. I just play for fun."

Kieran found his honesty refreshing. "And the others?"

"Ivan and Dylan are pretty laid-back but more competitive than me," Rueben replied. Kieran tried to picture what laid-back looked like on Ivan, but he couldn't get there. Dylan was so reserved that Kieran wanted to check his pulse to make sure he was still kicking. "Tyler and Owen are cutthroat. They'll either hate you or respect you if you beat them."

Kieran found that curious—two vastly different reactions to the same outcome. "What triggers the Jekyll and Hyde reactions?"

Rueben guffawed at the reference. "It's in the delivery. They respect someone who beats them with skill, but they don't appreciate showboating."

No one liked that. "Good to know."

"Because you plan to join us?" Rueben asked, a hint of pleading in his voice.

Kieran chuckled, "I'm thinking about it." It surprised him to realize it was the truth, then he gave himself a mental shake. He needed to get his priorities straight with Harry and Cash both away from the ranch. "What made you interested in blacksmithing?" Kieran asked, changing the subject.

"I see what you did there, but I'll let it go," Rueben replied before filling the rest of the drive with conversation about his ironworking.

His passion came through on the subject, and Kieran was envious. He'd always felt aimless and uncertain. What must it be like to wake up with a purpose each morning? Even his artwork had been more of a hobby. He didn't get very far in his pondering before they arrived back at the ranch. Once more, the sheer beauty of the property struck Kieran. He spotted Finley in the paddock with a few horses when Rueben parked the car. His blond hair shone like a beacon in the sunshine, and Kieran had never wanted to go to the light more than he did right then. Rueben snickered when he pushed his door open, and Kieran knew he'd caught him ogling Finley.

"See you tonight, Kier," Rueben said as he walked toward his cabin.

Kier? No one had ever shortened his name. It was Kieran or some expletive. When he climbed out of the truck, he felt Finley's eyes on him. The desire to look back and offer a simple wave was strong, so he kept walking. He tossed his clothes from the thrift store into the center of his soiled bedding, then bundled it all up and headed to the laundry room attached to the general store. He brought his paperback, sketchpad, a charcoal pencil from the art kit, and the deck of cards. Kieran wasn't sure how many machines there were, and he couldn't stand idle hands. Luckily, there were several washers and dryers, so he could use two machines at once and finish quickly. Ninety minutes later, he'd read a quarter of the book and played several rounds of solitaire. The notebook and pencil remained untouched. He hadn't sketched in so long and doubted his ability. And worse, despite the amazing scenery everywhere around him, Kieran was only interested in drawing one subject, and he couldn't allow it. Drawing a person felt as intimate to him as sex, and the last thing he could afford to do was obsess over perfectly capturing Finley's incredible bone structure. But damn, the man was made to be sketched and appreciated.

As if Kieran had conjured him out of thin air, Finley walked into the laundry room with an overflowing basket of dirty clothes. He stiffened in the doorway and looked unsure if he should come in or not.

"Want me to come back?"

"No," Kieran replied truthfully. The ranch was Finley's home, and he didn't want him to feel uncomfortable. "There's plenty of room."

Finley carried his burden to the washing machines and set it down with a thud. A light blue jockstrap fell off the top of the pile and landed on the floor. Kieran's fingers itched to pick up his pencil and sketch Finley laid out wearing nothing but the skimpy scrap of fabric. Christ, that bubble butt framed by pale blue strips of fabric… That wasn't all he was itching to do. The urge to pick up the jockstrap and sniff it nearly bowled him over. What the hell was wrong with him? Sure, he'd deprived himself of sexual stimulation and relief, but he was worried about himself.

"Oh god," Finley groaned as he leaned over to pick the jockstrap up off the concrete floor. Kieran imagined him saying those words while beneath him in bed. "I do or say the most embarrassing things when you're around." Finley quickly turned his back on him to load the washer, allowing Kieran to adjust his crotch.

The buzzer on his dryers went off, and Kieran launched out of his seat like a rocket. Christ, he had no chill. Kieran took the clothes from one dryer and added them to the one with the sheets, then wadded everything up again. Would Finley want to know why he was washing his sheets already? Would Kieran answer honestly if he asked?

"Want to borrow my basket?" Finley asked.

Kieran tucked his bundle of clean clothes under one arm and said, "I got it, but thanks. See you later."

"Wait!"

He jerked and spun around, nearly colliding with Finley, who held the stuff he'd left on the table. "Oh, yeah," he said, accepting the neatly stacked bundle. "Thanks."

"Sure." Finley didn't look quite certain what to do with his hands and tucked them into his front pockets. "Did anyone tell you about poker night?"

"Rueben did."

"Well, I hope you join us."

Us? Rueben had said Finley didn't play. What had changed? "Yeah? You any good?" Was this what happened when a person basically quit talking for nearly two years? He'd never been a great communicator, but this was ridiculous. "At poker," he added lamely.

Finley's eyebrows arched toward his hairline, and an impish smile curved his full lips. "Damn good." The heat shimmering in his gaze said he was definitely not referring to poker.

A persistent voice insisted he should stay the course and search Cash's house. It started loud but reduced to a barely audible whisper as Kieran's blood ran south and his mind flirted with the gutter. "Guess you'll have to show me what you got."

"Guess I will."

"See you at seven," Kieran tossed out after he left the laundry room. *Stupid, stupid, stupid.* Then he recalled the heat in Finley's gaze and that skimpy blue jockstrap on the ground. He wouldn't take it back even if he could. He'd search the house another time.

chapter

EIGHT

FINLEY STOOD ROOTED TO THE SAME SPOT FOR SEVERAL MOMENTS after Kieran disappeared from sight. Were they flirting? It sure felt like it. Was six months away from the dating scene long enough to forget the basics? Maybe that was why he'd stumbled all over himself since Kieran had arrived on the ranch…*yesterday.* Finley had to keep reminding himself that he'd only known the guy for twenty-four hours. Their acquaintance wasn't nearly long enough to justify the hold Kieran had on his thoughts and emotions. Finley had always believed one should strike while the iron was hot, but this was ludicrous, even for his standards.

He forced himself to focus on the task at hand and turned back to the row of laundry machines. His gaze landed on the blue fabric on top of the clothes pile. Heat crept up his neck as his brain replayed the jockstrap incident in slow motion. The *thunk* of the plastic basket hitting the concrete, followed by the mound of clothes teetering before settling again. Then that insignificant scrap of blue fabric with a mind of its own toppling to the ground like a bright blue flag in a sea of gray machines and concrete floors. He'd been mortified until he saw the hungry expression on Kieran's face.

Hell yes, they'd been flirting, and wasn't that what he wanted when he'd orchestrated their run-in? The washer and dryer at the old homestead were in use, but he could've waited for them to become free. It wasn't like he had big plans later. But Finley had chosen to drag his overflowing basket of clothes to the crew's laundry room because he'd seen Kieran go in there earlier. He tried to convince himself that it was just curiosity and not him giving in to the magnetic pull he felt toward Kieran. But he'd never grow and change bad habits if he continued lying to himself, so he acknowledged the hard truths. He'd purposely sought out Kieran because he wanted to be near him, even though Kieran was giving him lukewarm signals, aloof ones at best. Yet there were moments when Finley witnessed something delicious sparking in his dark gaze, and he felt a resounding howl in his soul. A persistent voice whispered that Kieran needed him, that they needed each other. The question was: what was Finley prepared to do about it? He closed his eyes and inhaled a deep cleansing breath. He felt calmer and more focused when he reopened his eyes. The answer arrived swiftly and resolutely. *Nothing.*

Kieran's arrival changed zilch. Finley's love life was still on hiatus. He was determined to turn over a new leaf and only engage in healthy romantic relationships, but only after he sorted himself out. The pull he felt toward Kieran was nothing more than horniness. Finley snorted when he realized that the howling he'd heard was probably coming from his mournful libido. He was just horny, which explained the dildo incident that had left him sore enough to attract notice. It was also the reason he lied to Kieran about being good at poker just to have an excuse to be near him. He'd never played poker a day in his life. Though he knew enough about the game to know his fib was called a bluff, which Kieran would call during their first hand.

Finley could always claim his boast was about something else entirely, but that would lead him into dangerous territory. He should make an excuse to back out of playing and busy himself doing anything else. But would spending another Saturday night in solitude be the best way to combat his loneliness? Or should he start working on strengthening his resistance to Kieran by placing himself around him more often? Didn't his mother have a meditation lesson on exposing oneself to temptations to build resistance? Avoidance hadn't worked out for him, so Finley decided to try exposure in a controlled environment. He and Kieran would be surrounded by people at the poker game. What could be the harm? Other than humiliating himself when it became obvious he wasn't a card shark.

The solution was simple. He'd overheard the guys use terms like "five-card stud," "jacks or better to open," and "progressive" enough to know they were significant. He typed the words into YouTube and found a host of tutorial videos on how to play the game and spot other players' tells. Two hours later, Finley was confident he could bullshit his way through one evening. If he tanked, he could just blame it on luck, which wasn't exactly going his way lately. As game time approached, his confidence faltered, and he redirected his energy into something useful. He located Ivan in their kitchen. The big guy had a cell phone in one hand and a takeout menu in the other.

"Mind if I take over food duties for the night?" Finley asked. "I thought we might expand the menu a little."

Ivan arched a brow but handed Finley the menu. "*You're* coming to poker night?"

"Yep."

The big guy narrowed his eyes. "Why tonight?"

Finley tried for a casual shrug, but it felt more like a nervous twitch. "First you bust my balls for never playing, and now you're going to give me the third degree when I relent?"

"*Third degree?* It was a single question." Realization dawned slowly on Ivan's face before his handsome features morphed into a scowl. "The new guy is going to be there, and you want to make a good impression."

"Do not," Finley scoffed. He shifted his gaze to the menu in his hand and mentally prepared an order.

"Mmmhmm." Ivan's tone said it all. "It's fine with me if you want to fancy up poker night for the hot guy, but don't forget to order the stuff the rest of us like too."

Finley snapped his head up to meet Ivan's gaze. "Pepperoni,

pineapple, and anchovies." Ivan's lips curled into a sneer, and it was impossible to tell which annoyed him more—the pineapple or the anchovies. "I wouldn't dream of forgetting the standard meat lover's or supreme pizza. I just thought I'd add some wings, garlic knots, and a few other options."

Ivan pursed his lips and rocked his head from right to left. "I wouldn't turn up my nose at either of those options. Kind of annoyed I hadn't thought of it myself."

"Harriet, the hostess with the mostest, isn't your sister, so you're excused."

The big man arched a brow, and Finley prepared to have his first bluff called that evening. Instead, Ivan said, "I want to try the atomic wings."

Finley tapped his temple. "Already on the list."

"Let me know how much I owe you," Ivan said.

Finley was going to protest and insist on paying for the extra food, then thought better of it when he saw Ivan's scowl. "Okay," he said.

The foreman shook his head and walked away. "I'll pick up the order so you can have extra time to primp for Romeo," Ivan called over his shoulder.

Finley tried to come up with an appropriate rebuttal, but he hadn't thought of one by the time Ivan's bedroom door shut with a firm *click*, making his friend's displeasure known. He rolled his eyes and placed the order, texted the amount and pickup time to Ivan, then retreated to his room to find something to wear. Fifteen minutes into the search, Finley realized he was treating poker night like a date and returned the pressed Western-style shirts to his closet. He yanked a faded gray hoodie off the hanger and closed the door—literally and figuratively. No more debating outfits or his motives. In the shower, he spent his time replaying video clips he'd watched on YouTube instead of easing the ache between his legs. Finley caught himself reaching for the cologne on top of his dresser and stopped. *Poker night. Not a date.* But his heart sank when he caught his reflection in the mirror. Finley's eyes shimmered with excitement and anticipation that had nothing to do with playing cards. No wonder Ivan had called his bluff. He didn't have cartoon heart eyes popping out of his head, but he might as well have.

"No. This is not a date, and I'm not romantically interested in Kieran." *I just really want to fuck him until neither of us can see straight.* No, Finley shook his head, half expecting his reflection to have a life of its own like in *Mary Poppins*. No doubt his body double would nod vigorously or laugh at his ridiculous claim.

"Yo, Finley," Tyler called from downstairs. "Food's here. You already look pretty enough, so get down here."

Finley and his reflection scowled at one another. He was not pretty. His jaw was too square and his bone structure too prominent. The only remotely lush or soft feature was his mouth, and he had received plenty of compliments about it from his romantic partners. Finley had even seen Kieran's focus drop to his lips a time or two when he spoke. That he reached for his lip balm had zero to do with impressing Kieran; his lips looked dry. Nothing more. Finley couldn't sit around the table with the guys until he got his emotions in check. He tried to summon a topic that would take his mind in the opposite direction of lust and attraction. He either was too tired to think of something or he just didn't want it badly enough because his mind drew a blank.

"We'll eat without you," Owen yelled up the stairs.

That got Finley moving. Inspiration struck when he spotted a pair of sunglasses on top of his dresser. Several of the poker professionals wore accessories at the table. Some probably wanted to look cool, but others wanted to hide their tells. He snagged his shades and debated footwear. He decided against his boots and padded down the stairs in his socks instead, which meant the rest of the crew didn't hear his approach.

"This is some spread," Dylan said. "Is it someone's birthday?"

Finley pulled up short outside the dining room, where everyone had gathered to eat before the games started.

"Finley picked the menu," Ivan said. "He put together a welcome for the new guy." His voice was as soft as ever and devoid of emotion to anyone but Finley, who felt the unspoken insinuation in his marrow.

A soft thump reached his ear, followed by Rue's exuberant, "Welcome, Kier." He must've slapped Kieran on the back.

Finley had halfway convinced himself that Kieran wouldn't show, but there he was. *Kier*, huh? The aloof man didn't strike him as someone who used nicknames. Had Rue made that up, or was it a name Kieran had shared with him? Finley hadn't asked how his trip to town went, but it appeared the two men had gotten along well.

"Thanks, man," Kieran replied softly.

"Wow," Tyler said. "Finley's coming to poker night? That never happens."

"As surprising as that is, I'm more shocked that he hasn't found his next ex-boyfriend yet," Owen teased.

"Who had Finley still single after six months?" Tyler asked.

Ugh. He'd forgotten all about the crew's stupid bet. Finley knew the guys meant nothing with their comments, and it wasn't anything they hadn't said to his face multiple times. He wasn't hurt or angry, but he wasn't sure how to enter without them knowing he'd listened outside the dining room like a creeper.

"Y'all can be assholes," Rueben told them. "Pretty sure I would shut up and eat the food if I were you. My abuela used to say, 'Rue, if you look a gift horse in the mouth, it might just haul off and bite you.'"

"She's talking about Nellie," Owen teased.

"Nah," Tyler replied. "That she-devil doesn't need a reason to bite."

Bless Rue and his abuela-isms. Finley pulled his hood up and slid his sunglasses on before pushing off the wall. He entered the room right as Owen asked why salad had been added to the menu.

"Colon cleanse," Finley replied, "because some of you are full of shit." Owen's cheeks turned pink, and he looked embarrassed. Finley offered a playful wink to let him know there were no hard feelings but remembered he wore the dark shades. He probably deserved to squirm a little anyway.

"Nah," Tyler replied. "The meat lover's pizza is dripping in fat, and it will grease the gears."

Ivan chuckled and shook his head. "Pretty sure Finley meant you two idiots will shovel shit until the end of time for talking smack about him."

Finley hooked an arm around Owen's neck in a one-armed hug. "They know better. I don't have a vindictive bone in my body."

"Damn good thing," Tyler said as he loaded his paper plate with everything but salad. "You could really make things difficult for the last boyfriend if you outed him." Tyler looked up and smiled. "But you'd never do anything so cruel."

"No, I wouldn't."

"I saw him today in town," Rueben said. "He was protesting near the casino with a group of Salvation Anew members."

Finley felt Kieran's intense focus and turned to face him. *Yes, that's right. I chased my last lover straight into the arms of religious fanatics.* Kieran's expression was curious and pensive, but Finley didn't expect him to voice his thoughts, especially about anything as personal as Finley's relationships.

"What the hell are you wearing?" Kieran asked, his lips quirking at the corner.

Finley was grateful for the subject change and played dumb. He looked down at his body, though it was more difficult to do with his dark sunglasses on. "A ratty old hoodie and a pair of jeans."

Kieran snorted. "I can see that. I'm talking about your hood up and the dark aviators, Eight Mile."

Owen leaned closer to Ivan and said, "I was thinking more Unabomber."

The Eminem reference made Finley want to smile, but he crossed his arms over his chest instead. "This might come as a surprise to you since you're new, but I wear my heart on my sleeve, which means I'll tip my hand with my expressions."

Kieran arched a brow so high it nearly disappeared. "But you said you were pretty good at playing poker."

This felt like a continuation of their flirty conversation in the laundry room. Finley wasn't sure what surprised him most—that they'd picked up where they'd left off or that they were doing it in front of everyone else. God, that sounded dirty. "No, I told you I was damn good. And that's because I take extra measures."

Kieran narrowed his eyes as if he could smell the bullshit Finley was peddling across the room. After a moment, he shrugged and said, "Guess we'll see."

"Guess we will."

"What's happening?" Tyler whispered to Owen.

"If he has to tell you, then you don't need to know," Ivan informed him.

A round of snickers met the foreman's reply, and Kieran tore his gaze away to glance around the room. Finley couldn't tell by his expression if he'd picked up on the subtext of the exchange. The last thing he wanted was for Kieran to feel uncomfortable around him. Finley felt like he should say something to divert attention when Dylan took care of that with a perfectly timed remark about the food offerings.

"Mmmm. Is that chicken bacon ranch pizza? And what's the kind with white circles and leaves on it? Looks like abstract art or something."

Finley shook his head and walked over to the guy who had a mad crush on his sister. "It's called Margherita pizza. The white circles are melted slices of mozzarella cheese, which is usually higher quality than the shredded stuff. The green leaves are fresh basil. It just so happens to be Harry's favorite pizza," he said.

Dylan looked at him with a hopeful puppy expression. "Will she be here tonight?"

"She has a date," Tyler replied. "Don't worry about it, Dylan. She's as unlucky in love as her brother."

Dylan's cheeks flushed with heat, and Finley felt sorry for the guy. "Why would you say that? It's nothing to me." Yet he added two pieces of Margherita pizza to his plate and a heaping serving of salad.

Finley pushed his sunglasses down his nose and pinned Tyler with a dark look. "Harry is having a girls' night with some friends in town. She's not on a date." He didn't want to give Dylan false hope, but he'd seen the furtive glances Harry sent Dylan's way when he wasn't looking. "I don't see anyone beating a path to your door, Ty. Maybe we cut the chitchat about our dating lives and eat so we can get down to business."

"Sounds good to me," Rueben said.

It didn't take them long to get their fill of food, though Ivan stopped Finley before he could stow the leftovers in the refrigerator. He leaned closer and said, "I'll give you a hint. Tyler is an emotional eater. When the cards aren't looking good, he'll grab a slice of pizza and munch on it."

"Thanks," Finley said. "Any other tips you care to share?"

"A card shark like you shouldn't need them." Ivan chuckled as he walked away because he knew Finley was full of shit. The foreman resumed his seat and picked up his cards. "Five-card stud. Jacks or better to open. Progressive."

"Anything wild?" Kieran asked.

"Deuces," Ivan replied.

The foreman's laughter at Finley's expense didn't last, and he tipped an imaginary hat to Finley after he won the first three hands. It was mostly the luck of the draw, but it didn't take him long to discover the other players' tells. Tyler ate when he had a shitty hand but didn't want to fold. Owen stroked a finger over his brow when he had good cards but still needed one or two to make them great. Ivan shifted in his chair when he got the card he wanted. Dylan didn't bother to hide his reactions. He snickered when something good happened and groaned when his luck took a downward turn. Rue drummed his fingers on the table when he was bluffing. Kieran was the only opponent who didn't give his thoughts away, and he didn't need to hide behind a disguise. Each of the first three hands came down to the two of them, and he knew it was only a matter of time before Kieran started winning some chips back. Turned out he was right because Kieran won the next three.

"Too rich for my blood," Owen said, tossing his few remaining chips onto Tyler's pile. He saluted Finley with a piece of cold pizza. "Want to join us again next week?"

Finley smiled. "I'm going to the art festival in Last Chance Creek on Saturday." Since he was studying Kieran closely, he noticed a slight tick near his mouth. Was that in response to his answer? Did Kieran like art? Did he wonder who Finley was going with?

"That lasts all weekend, right?" Tyler asked. "Can't you go on Friday and do poker on Saturday?"

"Are you that eager for me to wipe the floor with you again?" Finley asked.

Owen swallowed another bite and said, "We're in it for the food."

Finley promised to think about it, then returned his full attention to his hand. Interest waned when the food ran out and the same two players battled for the win each time. One by one, the guys shuffled out of the room in search of better entertainment or bed. Ivan held out the longest, probably acting as chaperone, but even he waved them a good-night and lumbered down the hall to his bedroom around midnight. And they played on. The stack of chips between Kieran and Finley was even. Neither of them seemed brave enough to risk going all in. Was it because they preferred to play it safe or because their night would end if one of them won it all? Tension built in the room with each hand. Their fingers brushed when dealing cards, their feet bumped under the table, and they stared at one another when not studying their cards. Finley had lost the glasses and hood halfway through the night because he couldn't see worth a shit and Kieran amped up his body temperature, making his head itchy and sweaty.

Kieran chewed the corner of his mouth while looking at his hand. Finley had thought it was a tell at first, but the assumption had cost him a ton of chips. He focused on his hand and didn't worry about anything else. Neither had a pair of jacks to open the first round, a pair of queens to open the second, nor a pair of kings to open up the third deal. The next hand required a pair of aces to open the betting, and Finley only had one—the ace of hearts. He also had the ten and queen of hearts, which was a good start toward a royal flush, but it wouldn't do him a damn bit of good if Kieran couldn't open the bet. He could technically open with a bluff, but it was pretty damn risky.

He looked up and found dark eyes locked on him. Finley didn't have a clue if he planned to open or not. Saying nothing, Kieran scooted a tall stack of chips to the center of the table. It was the boldest move he'd made all evening. Maybe he was ready to call it a night. Finley could either place an equal bet or fold. He looked at his cards again. The chances of landing a royal flush were slim, but he reminded himself they weren't playing for real money. Finley pushed the same size stack of chips to the center and followed it with another.

Kieran pursed his lips and studied his cards. Their eyes met again as Kieran matched his bet.

Finley picked up the deck of cards and said, "How many?" Kieran removed one card from his hand and slid it facedown across the table. Finley swallowed hard, realizing his chances didn't look good. He dealt the card to Kieran before removing the two off-suit cards from his hand. "The dealer takes two," he announced. He snapped the top two cards off the pile in front of him and held his breath when he lifted the corners up for a peek. *Holy shit.* He had the jack and king of hearts to make a royal flush. It became nearly impossible for him to squelch his excitement.

He glanced up and caught Kieran watching him intently. The man didn't reveal a single thought in his expression or body language. How was that possible? The longer they stared at each other, the harder it became for Finley to remain still and quiet.

"You look so damn smug right now, Eight Mile," Kieran said. "I should fold."

Finley placed his elbow on the table and leaned forward. "Why don't you?"

Kieran pushed the rest of his chips into the center of the table, leaving Finley with only one choice. He added his remaining stash to the kitty and smiled at Kieran and said, "That's that."

"Or is it?" Kieran asked.

Finley cocked his head to the side. "Are you suggesting an additional bet?"

Kieran bit his bottom lip and nodded. Finley nearly broke out in a sweat, and his mind raced with the dirtiest wagers he could think of. Win or lose, he wanted to be on his knees for Kieran. "I'm game for anything." He sounded breathy and bratty.

Kieran swallowed hard and shifted slightly in his chair. "Loser takes the winner's kitchen duties for a week." Finley huffed out a sigh of disappointment, earning a smirk. "Too risky?" Kieran asked.

"Too tame," Finley countered. "But I'll take it."

Kieran kept his cool as he laid his cards down to reveal a full house.

"Not bad," Finley said, then showed his royal flush.

Kieran's lips parted in surprise. "I don't believe it."

"Doesn't make it less real," Finley said as he leaned forward and raked in his fake loot. "'Cause I'm damn good."

"Yeah, you are." Kieran's voice was husky and raw, and Finley swore he heard that coyote howling again.

"Tuesday," he whispered.

Kieran blinked. "Huh?"

"That's my next day of kitchen duties."

"Oh, yeah," he replied, pushing back from the table. Finley stood up when Kieran did, though he didn't know why, and when Kieran exited the dining room, Finley followed. Kieran turned and faced him at the front door. "I should stay and help you clean up."

"No way," Finley replied. He could see the protest forming on Kieran's lips and needed to thwart him. He suspected Kieran had made the offer because he was reluctant to part ways too. Finley was teetering on the precipice like his stupid blue jockstrap on the mountain of laundry. One false move and he and all his effort would topple onto the concrete. "That wasn't part of the wager."

They simultaneously reached for the door handle and their hands collided and lingered. Finley snapped up his gaze to meet Kieran's and saw the awareness flickering there too. They both took a half step closer, and Finley felt Kieran's body heat radiating off him. The battle of needs and wants waged inside him until he couldn't tell which category Kieran fell into. Did he want to kiss him or did he need it? Kieran took a deep breath, then stepped back and dropped his hand from on top of Finley's.

"I had a great time, Eight Mile," he whispered.

"I did too, Kier."

"You're as good as advertised," Kieran replied with a teasing lift at the corner of his mouth.

"Not bad for my first time."

Kieran narrowed his eyes. "You've got to be fucking with me."

Finley quirked a brow and released the wickedest smile in his arsenal as he opened the front door. "You'd know it if I were. Sleep well."

Kieran's nostrils flared with his sharp inhale. "Sleep well," he replied hoarsely.

Finley stood in the open doorway and watched him walk across the porch. When he reached the top step, he said, "Would you like to go to the art festival with me next weekend?"

Kieran stiffened but didn't turn around. Finley hadn't planned to say it, but he couldn't exactly take it back. He could clarify that he meant the trip as a friendly excursion only.

"Yes," Kieran said, then continued down the steps. "Goodnight."

"'Night."

Finley shut the door and leaned against the cool wood. What the hell just happened? And not just the parting bit. He'd cleaned house at poker, gotten out of kitchen duties for the week, and made plans with Kieran the following weekend. "What the hell just happened?" This time he voiced his thoughts out loud.

"Sounds to me like you ended your dry spell and have a date for next weekend," Dylan replied.

Finley flinched and jerked his head toward the staircase where Dylan stood in a pair of boxers and a tank top.

"Not a date," Finley told him.

Just two guys going to town to enjoy an art festival. Now he just needed to convince his heart.

chapter
NINE

KIERAN'S GAZE KEPT DRIFTING FROM THE HOOF FINLEY CRADLED in his left hand to the perfect ass cradled by his too-tight denim. How the hell did he move as fluidly as he did without painful ramifications? Why couldn't he quit staring at the man's ass or stop fantasizing about him? Kieran had been there a week, and the only thing he'd accomplished was plowing his way through the bottle of Monkey Grease. To his defense, Cash had returned Sunday evening and hadn't left since, eliminating the opportunity to search the big ranch house. The lack of circumstance should've made Kieran mad at himself for choosing poker with the crew over looking for his answers, but he'd had such a good time matching wits, a.k.a. flirting, with Finley that he couldn't work up an ounce of regret. Instead, Kieran promised that he'd renege on the art festival trip if Cash left again the following weekend, but the ranch owner remarked at breakfast that he was looking forward to a quiet Saturday at home. Kieran wanted to be disappointed, but he was looking forward to the trip to Last Chance Creek with Finley.

"She needs her hooves trimmed," Finley said, drawing Kieran's attention back to the task at hand. Finley still held the horse's foot in his hand, but he'd tipped his head back to peer up at Kieran, reminding him of the numerous fantasies he'd had of the man on his knees in front of him. His scalp prickled as his body started to heat. His expression must've tipped Finley off that his mind was elsewhere because he smirked and said, "Did you catch that?"

"Yes," Kieran replied, though how he'd retained the knowledge was beyond him. He'd learned an overwhelming amount of information about horses over the past week. Harry had boasted that her oatmeal was excellent brain food and would stick to his ribs, providing vital energy for a physical workday. Kieran needed both things to keep up with his boss and his new responsibilities. Buttercup, the tawny horse, let out a noise that sounded like a snicker. *Snitch.* The horse whinnied and tossed her lustrous mane.

Finley looked up and volleyed his gaze between horse and man. "Why do I feel like I'm missing out on a private conversation?"

Kieran shrugged and stroked a hand over Buttercup's muzzle. Finley sighed and shook his head before returning his attention to the horse's hoof. "Do you remember how you can easily tell if it's time for a trim?"

"You couldn't draw a straight line from the coronet to her elbow," Kieran replied.

"Technically, I couldn't draw a straight line with a ruler, but you are correct. We need to let Rueben know so he can give her a pedicure." Finley released Buttercup's foot, then stood up to move to her other front leg. A soft hiss escaped his lips, and a wince flashed across his handsome features.

Kieran narrowed his eyes and caught a slight hitch in Finley's step as he moved to Buttercup's flank. It was similar to the one he'd witnessed the previous Saturday. Maybe wearing those tight jeans was cutting off the circulation to his nether regions or perhaps he needed the salve more than Kieran had. He saw the same wince when Finley squatted to inspect the next hoof.

"Are you hurt?" Kieran asked before he could think better of it.

Finley stiffened and kept his gaze on his task, but Kieran witnessed the blush creeping up his boss's neck. The temptation to rub his nose against Finley's flesh to see if it was warm to the touch caught Kieran off guard and nearly sent him running. *No attachment. No bonding.* Canoodling with his boss would break both those rules.

"Just a little stiff," Finley said.

"You didn't give me all your salve, did you?"

"No," Finley said, "I just didn't use it."

He rose to his feet and finished the health check they performed regularly on the horses to catch injuries before they turned into something more threatening. Once Buttercup received a clean bill of health, Finley showed Kieran how to groom the horses. He sent Buttercup off with her handler once they finished and retrieved Skipper, a gorgeous young horse with a gait that exuded confidence.

"He's a little full of himself," Finley said, "but he's an excellent horse for you to train on."

Like the day before, Finley stayed close while Kieran ran point. He offered suggestions and gentle reminders as Kieran made his way around the horse, checking hooves and searching for injuries. He'd nearly made the mistake of walking behind the horse, but Finley grabbed his arm and pulled him back in time. Kieran's face heated from the rookie mistake, but Finley wouldn't let him stew about it. He distracted Kieran by asking what he should do next. He let go of his irritation and continued the inspection, pointing to a shallow scratch on Skipper's hip.

"Good eye," Finley said. "He's rubbed up against something. Based on the location, I'm thinking a splintered piece of wood at the paddock or in his stall. We'll check both places."

After they groomed Skipper, Finley showed Kieran how to apply healing ointment and explained what the signs of early infection would look like. He used a gentle touch and an even gentler voice as he treated the animal. Kieran glanced up at one point and caught Finley staring at him with an expression that looked too much like adoration for Kieran's comfort, but Finley blinked, and approval replaced his heart eyes.

They continued the wellness checks and grooming for three more horses before taking a water break. Kieran averted his gaze from Finley's mouth wrapped around the bottle and his throat as it worked up and down to swallow the cold liquid. Both things reminded him of the fantasies he'd had about his boss.

Finley tossed his empty bottle into the recycling bin. "Ready?"

Kieran held up his finger and downed the rest of his bottle. Finley didn't have any qualms about watching him, or maybe he wasn't aware of the laserlike focus he aimed at Kieran's mouth. A little devil whispered in his ear or shoved his pitchfork into Kieran's brain, urging him to test his boss. Kieran pulled the empty bottle from his mouth and licked his bottom lip, catching the lingering droplets and Finley's full attention. The man continued staring until a bark of laughter echoed through the barn. Finley jumped and jerked his gaze up to meet Kieran's just as Owen and Tyler stepped into the supply room. Shock and shame shimmered in his pale irises, and Kieran regretted giving in to his impulse.

Tyler and Owen stopped inside the door when they spotted Kieran and Finley. Their conversation faded as they looked between their boss and the newcomer.

"We just stopped for a drink and were heading out," Finley said.

Owen's lips tilted into a smirk as he assessed the situation, and a new tension filled the air. It was clear he suspected something was going on between Finley and Kieran. "Of course, boss."

"We're getting a drink too," Tyler said. "We should make it champagne after surviving Nellie's shenanigans this morning. That crazy horse nearly tore a chunk out of my ass."

Kieran stood taller, feeling the need to advocate for her. What had they done to rile her up? Someone had obviously abused her with a brush. What other items had been used against her?

The comment about Nellie coerced a huge smile from Owen's lips. "She barely grazed you."

Tyler turned around, thrust his ass toward his friend, and pointed to a back pocket. The fabric was loose at three corners and dangled by a fourth. "I just got these jeans."

"Ivan can fix them," Finley said. It wasn't the first time someone referenced the big guy having nimble fingers and a gentle touch. Kieran had also learned that he was the head beekeeper, a skill he'd learned in Arrowhead. "Better yet," Finley said, "he could teach you how to fix them."

"It's better to teach a man to fish than to feed him one," Owen agreed. "Keep your wits about you today, though. Nellie girl is in a mood."

"Thanks for the warning," Finley replied. "I have a trick up my sleeve that might calm her down a little." He glanced at Kieran. "Maybe two tricks."

"We should start a friendly wager," Tyler said.

Kieran didn't like that bet any more than the stupid stakes they'd placed on Finley's love life. "Maybe we should bet on the horse instead of against her."

Owen's shoulders went back, and he puffed out his chest. Finley halted the bigger man before a rebuttal could form on his lips.

"We all love Nellie," he said, patting Owen's shoulder as he passed. "Let's get back to it, Kieran."

Owen held his gaze, a challenge shimmering in his eyes. Kieran didn't start fights, but he never backed down from one either. Technically, they weren't fighting, but the tension sparking between them could easily flare into an altercation.

"Kieran!" Finley called out from the hallway. And, damn, he really liked the way his name rolled off his tongue, especially when it held a hint of command. Kieran didn't think he had a power dynamic kink, but he was already trying to figure out ways to entice the bossier side out of Finley.

Kieran forcibly shifted his brain back into work mode to concentrate on doing a good job. He picked a rock from Biscuit's hoof and identified another wound for Sarge. He and Finley worked through the rest of the stable, saving the feistiest beauty for last. Before they retrieved Nellie from her stall, Finley reached into his pocket and pulled out a small bottle.

"I hope this works," he said, squirting a small amount into the palm of his hand.

A hot flush crept up Kieran's neck when he recognized the New Hope Wellness logo, but Finley was too busy striding purposefully to notice. His boss stopped a few feet away from the stall door. Nellie approached slowly, snorting and tossing her mane. Kieran stopped beside Finley and took a deep sniff, picking up earthy tones and a hint of something floral.

"What's that?" he asked.

"Hopefully my secret weapon." Finley kept his attention on the horse, gauging her reaction to the scent. As for Nellie, she only had eyes for Kieran once he arrived. "It's lavender and vetiver. My mom said it might put out a soothing scent to help calm Nellie as I figure out just how deep her trauma goes."

Kieran wondered what would happen if Finley reached a verdict that the beautiful horse couldn't be rehabilitated. Surely, they wouldn't destroy such a magnificent creature. Tears burned the back of his eyes and nose, reminding him that living like a caged animal for twenty months hadn't turned him into one. He nearly resented the truth more than the thought that had provoked it. He squared his shoulders, determined that Nellie would never face such a horrible fate, and crossed to her stall door.

"Hold on a minute," Finley said. "I know she likes you—"

Kieran ignored him, opened the door, and reached for her reins. She snorted and tossed her head, her nostrils flaring.

"Careful now," Finley urged. "Those are signs of high stress."

"It's okay, pretty baby," Kieran cooed. "You're safe. No one will harm you." Nellie stopped tossing her head and snorting to stare at him. "That's right. We've got this. Now come out of there so we can check you over." He gently tugged the leather rein in his hand, and she eased out of the stall and walked beside him.

"There's a good girl," Kieran said as they walked to the examination room. "No need for potions and hysteria, is there? You just need someone who understands you." He talked to the horse, telling her everything they were going to do and why. Kieran knew she didn't really understand him, but she seemed to like his voice. He hadn't done a lot of talking since going into lockup, but he'd make an exception for this beauty. They encountered Owen and Tyler, who gaped at the pair with open mouths. "Never bet against me, fellas."

Nellie whinnied as if to add, "Me too."

Tyler and Owen tipped their hats, and Owen held up his hand for Kieran to fist bump.

Kieran led the horse into the examination area and secured her lead to the post. "Remember what I said," he cooed. "This is for your own good. We gotta make sure your shoes still fit right and that you don't have any wounds." Finley had explained that he preferred for the horses to go barefoot whenever possible, but Nellie's hooves had been in bad shape when she'd arrived at the ranch, and she needed the added stability that horseshoes provided. He stepped back and petted her velvety crest. "And we need to do something about the state of your mane. I've seen dudes in jail look more polished than you do right now." Nellie neighed and butted against him. Her spunky nature thawed his frozen heart a little. "Don't get sassy," he cajoled. "You're still the prettiest girl in the world, and we saved the best horse for last."

Kieran turned to get his tools and to make sure no brushes were in Nellie's line of sight. Did she hate all grooming implements or just brushes? He pulled up short when he caught Finley watching him from the doorway with an awed expression on his face. It was very similar to the one earlier yet different. His green eyes glittered with intensity as he shifted his gaze from the horse to Kieran. Finley blinked, but the expression didn't disappear like last time. If anything, it took on a dreamier quality like maybe his mind transported him someplace else.

"Incredible," Finley said, his voice a guttural whisper.

"I know she is," Kieran said, deflecting the praise and pretending it didn't feel like a caress down his spine. He couldn't allow anything to develop here. Finley had relationship written all over him, which was the opposite of what Kieran needed. He wasn't sticking around and had no desire to leave a trail of tears and heartbreak in his wake.

Finley blinked several times, and his eyes focused once more. His full lips curved into a lush smile, drawing Kieran's gaze to the bitable dimple in his chin. "Let's get started so we can get cleaned up and head to town for the festival. I figured we would grab dinner at my favorite diner." Finley's brow furrowed slightly as he continued to look at him. "That's if you still want to come with me."

With him, on him, in him. Kieran would settle for near him. He swallowed the earnest response and went with a safer choice. "Yes, if it's still okay with you." Finley had given him an out, but he hadn't taken it.

"Of course," Finley said. He stepped closer to supervise but didn't crowd them, and he didn't offer input unless asked a question.

Kieran moved from one task to the other, talking sweetly to Nellie as he went. She bunched her muscles at times or shifted to the left or right. When that happened, Kieran stopped and soothed her with gentle strokes until she calmed down.

"I've been thinking about her aversion to grooming brushes," Finley said once Kieran finished his exam. "Let's try putting blinders on her so she won't see the brush."

"Blinders?"

"Ever heard the adage about putting blinders on?" Finley asked him.

"I have but didn't realize it referred to horses."

"Blinders ensure they won't see objects or other horses in their periphery. They can only see what's in front of them. The devices are used a lot in horse racing and driving, but they come in handy in other situations. Let's see how she does with them on. Limiting her vision could cause her more distress than seeing the brush, but it's worth a shot."

Kieran stood in front of Nellie and smoothed a hand over her muzzle while Finley attached the leather disks to her bridle's cheekpiece. She stayed calm until he stepped away to retrieve the grooming tools. Kieran moved back in front of her and looked at Finley for guidance.

"For today, let's keep you where Nellie can see you. I'll take care of grooming while you sweet talk her."

Kieran shifted his gaze back to the horse, whose eyes were widening in fear. "Don't be afraid, pretty girl. No one here will ever hurt you. No brushes to break your spirit."

They worked together—Kieran cooing softly while Finley went to work with the grooming tools. Nellie got a little animated when he started working tangles from her mane, so Kieran sang "Brown Eyed Girl" to her. The song seemed to come from a place he hadn't known existed. Was it a memory of his mom before their lives went to hell? The words rolled off Kieran's tongue without any provocation from him. He felt Finley's attention but kept his eyes on Nellie, who looked at him as if he were her lifeline. Kieran started the next verse of the song. It was a strange feeling to pull lyrics from his subconscious mind without knowing how they'd gotten there. Finley stepped back when he finished, and Kieran let his voice trail off.

"We can take her blinders off now," Finley said, moving closer to remove the devices.

Kieran got a whiff of the lotion he'd put on to help calm the horse. He couldn't say it worked, but the stuff sure smelled good, and he appreciated the lengths Finley would go to for Nellie. The horse neighed and shook her head from side to side, allowing Kieran to see the pretty braid Finley had woven into her mane. He reached up and ran his finger over his boss's handiwork and let out a soft whistle.

"Prettiest damn horse ever," Kieran said.

Nellie must've felt it because she practically pranced back to her stall. Once she was secure, Finley called Tyler over and told him which horses had abrasions and asked him to scrutinize their stalls and check the fence for large splinters.

"Yes, sir," he said. "Sure you don't want to play poker with us again tonight?"

"I'm sure," Finley replied. "Maybe next weekend."

After washing up in the sink, they grabbed more water and headed out.

"Be ready in an hour?" Finley asked him when they stopped outside Kieran's cabin.

"I can be ready in twenty minutes." *Fuck.* Did that sound too eager?

Finley laughed and continued toward the old homestead. "See you in thirty minutes."

Kieran didn't dare linger long in the shower, though rubbing one out before getting in a cramped space would've been smart. He didn't have many shirts to choose from and went with a deep-red button-up that was nice enough to wear to the festival without looking like he'd spent fifteen of his thirty minutes trying to decide what to wear. He found Finley waiting for him at a silver truck with a black logo on the sides—the opposite of Cash's truck. And speak of the devil, Cash stood with his elbow propped on the edge of the truck bed and smiled at whatever Finley was saying.

He felt foolish for surmising they could be lovers. It hadn't taken him long to realize the only thing between the two men was a friendship and mutual respect, though the pair couldn't be more different. Finley was warm and open where Cash was aloof and enigmatic, but they shared a work ethic that was unparalleled. Since the time he arrived, he'd witnessed Cash working in the trenches with everyone else, including shoveling shit in the horse barn. He didn't complain or make excuses for someone else to do the dirty work. Cash greeted each of the horses with affection and snuck them treats when Finley wasn't looking. Even Nellie seemed to tolerate him well. She hadn't tried to bite his ass even once.

Cash had laughed and said, "We understand each other. I pay for the food Nellie likes to eat."

Kieran had thought about that for a few days while observing everything happening around them. The farm operation and payroll had to cost a small fortune. Was he supposed to believe Cash paid that out of his personal wealth? He understood the ranch generated income from selling hops and honey but enough to float the operation? Did Cash have a partner or silent investors? Every time Kieran turned around, he had more questions about Cash Sweeney, and many were ones he could ask the rancher himself without raising suspicion. He should be hanging around the ranch and trying to get answers instead of going to the art festival. Then Finley glanced over at him and smiled. Kieran's heart skipped a beat, and he decided he could chat Cash up at breakfast the next morning.

"No way, Fin," Cash said when Kieran reached them. "Thank goodness Kieran is here to settle the debate."

Kieran arched a brow. "I'll try."

"If you only got to choose one dessert to eat for the rest of your life, would it be cherry crisp or coconut cream pie?"

"Cherry crisp."

"Yes!" Finley said, punching the air. His smug smile only made his lips look more kissable.

Cash sighed and shook his head. "I'm so disappointed."

Finley patted him on the shoulder. "Luckily, you aren't forced to settle for cherry crisp, and I will bring you back a piece of coconut cream from the diner."

"And that's why you're my favorite," Cash said, causing Finley to snort and roll his eyes. "You guys have a great time."

Favorite? Kieran looked between them, trying to figure out the private joke.

Finley must've read the confusion in his gaze because he said, "Which one of us is Cash's favorite is a running joke on the ranch."

"Is there a point system?" Kieran asked. "A cash prize for the winner?"

Cash tilted his head back and laughed. "Bragging rights. Don't give these guys any more incentive to become menaces." He pushed off the truck and stepped forward. "Don't let me keep you guys. Drive safe."

"Always," Finley said as he rounded the vehicle.

Cash whistled a jaunty tune as he headed toward the house. If Kieran stood there watching him too long, Finley might get the impression that he had the hots for the rancher. He pulled the passenger door open and climbed inside the cab, which was spotless and smelled like a forest. Kieran glanced at the rearview mirror and saw a cardboard tree with the New Hope logo swinging from it.

"Your mom makes air fresheners too?" Kieran asked as Finley started the engine.

His boss shifted the truck into drive and pressed the accelerator. "She dabbles in a bit of everything."

Kieran thought about the little bottle of lube and shifted in his seat when his pants felt too tight. "What do you like to use besides the salve?" Why the hell had he asked that? It was too personal, and he'd only imagine the man using each product. Too bad he couldn't take it back.

Unaware of his discomfort, Finley rattled off his favorites. "She customizes shampoos and conditioners to meet individual needs and lets you choose your own scents. They look like bars of soap, so there's no plastic waste. I like her goat's milk soaps, deodorants, and lip balms.

She also makes a thick hand lotion that helps prevent cracking during the winter months."

As he feared, Kieran pictured Finley running through his morning routine and had to shift in his seat again.

"Her products are affordable if you want to stop in while we're in town and check them out. Just don't divulge too much about your romantic woes, or she'll try to fix you up with somebody."

Kieran glanced over at Finley and caught him smirking. He wanted to ask about his woes but wouldn't. "Is that what she does to you?"

"Sometimes."

"You ever take her up on her offer?" Kieran pressed, then silently cursed himself.

"I haven't yet."

Yet. The paltry word implied there was a possibility Finley could or would let his mom set him up with someone. "Sounds like you're thinking about it."

Finley briefly met his gaze before returning his attention to the road. "I am."

"Because of the guy who joined the cult?" So much for not pressing for more information. Kieran wished he could take the words back as soon as he'd said them. "Never mind. It's none of my business."

A ghost of a smile formed on Finley's lips. "It's okay. I have a history of dating the wrong guys, and Keegan was just the nail in the coffin. Since I no longer trust myself, I figured why not let my mom take a swing at it."

"I'm sorry."

Finley glanced at him again. "Don't be. And it's okay to ask me anything. If I don't want to answer, I won't."

A slew of things came to mind, but the one that escaped Kieran's lips was, "What's the deal with the jockstrap?"

Finley applied the brake a little too hard at the stop sign, and Kieran's seat belt tightened across his chest and abdomen. He grunted and loosened the belt when Finley eased up on the brake. "Sorry about that," he said sheepishly.

"Not sorrier than I am about my question. What the fuck?"

Finley burst out laughing, which eased the tension gripping Kieran's heart. He checked both ways, then accelerated forward. "I wear a cup when I work with the friskier horses that might buck or rear back. I've had my balls racked enough to know better."

"Oh," Kieran said, his voice too flat for his liking. "Makes sense." Even though it was damn disappointing. What did he expect? That Finley would confess he had an OnlyFans channel where he sprawled on a bed wearing nothing but a jockstrap and did delectable things to his tight body?

"They've come in handy at other times too," Finley offered. Kieran jerked his head in Finley's direction and caught him smirking like the devil. "Football," he said. "Get your mind out of the gutter."

"I... It wasn't in the—"

"Liar," Finley said. "All you boys go gaga eyes over those things, so why the hell wouldn't I use it to show off my best asset when I want to impress a guy?"

Kieran's shirt suddenly seemed too tight around the neck. He hated that his desire for Finley was so naked. He released the top button, even though he knew it wasn't the problem. He deeply regretted not rubbing one out before they'd left when his dick started to harden.

"I'm sorry," Finley said, his voice heavy with genuine regret. "That was really inappropriate of me to say to an employee. I don't suppose we can pretend I never said it?"

Kieran looked over and met his solemn green gaze. There was a fat chance in hell he'd forget, but he said, "What were we talking about again?" The tension in Finley's jaw eased, and he knew it was the right thing to say.

Last Chance Creek had turned the fields at the edge of town into an event parking space, and it was already packed with cars when Finley found a spot big enough for the ranch truck. Main Street was closed to traffic so booths and vendors could set up on both sides of the road. There were more people in Last Chance Creek than he'd seen in a long time, and for a moment, the crowd seemed to close in on him. Kieran took a few deep breaths, and the panic receded a little.

"Too soon?" Finley asked softly.

Kieran made Finley's green eyes his center of focus until the rest of his tension eased. "I want to be here."

Finley held his gaze for a few moments, then nodded. "We can leave anytime and without question. Just let me know."

Kieran's next breath flowed in and out without a hitch, and he knew he was ready. He tilted his head toward the festivities and merged into the crowd. Finley fell into step with him, and Kieran had the sudden urge to reach for his hand. Every medium of art and craft seemed to be on display as they wandered between the booths. He feasted his eyes on vibrant oil paintings depicting life in the Rockies, admired charcoal sketches of wildlife, and ran his fingers over an intricately woven tapestry. Finley posed for a caricature drawing, and the artist turned him into a cowboy superhero.

"With a jawline like yours, I couldn't help myself," she told him.

"Thank you," Finley told her. "I've never seen myself that way."

"Your horses do," Kieran said.

Finley turned his jewellike eyes on Kieran and smiled. God, how easy it would be to palm his neck and pull him in for a kiss. Finley's gorgeous lips parted like he could read his mind. Someone bumped into Kieran, jostling the idea out of his head before he could do something stupid. They continued down the row of booths without making a colossal mistake. He glanced over at the storefronts and found the bookstore he'd seen during his first visit.

"Mind if we go in there?" Kieran said, gesturing to the shop.

"Not at all. It's my favorite store in town." He leaned closer and said, "But please don't tell my mom."

Kieran chuckled. "I won't."

The bookstore was completely empty, allowing them the freedom to roam without fear of bumping into anyone. Kieran took a deep breath, enjoying the smell of paperback books. "Almost as good as a library," he said.

He'd gone to his local library after school nearly every day before his parents died. No one argued or did drugs there. He could read until his heart was content without someone making fun of him. One of the few regrets Kieran had of his childhood was sacrificing his love of books and reading to peer pressure as a surly teen. Cool kids hung out, got drunk, and banged girls or boys. By that point, everyone had given up on him and his future, so he had too.

"Oh," Finley said softly. "That's so sad."

Kieran blinked him back into focus. "What?"

Finley's cheeks turned pink, and Kieran realized he'd spoken some or all of his thoughts out loud. *Well, fuck.* How did he do damage control when he didn't know exactly what he'd said? "Cash has an amazing library, and it's available to the crew. And a gym," Finley added hastily. "But he probably already told you that." Finley had tossed him a lifesaver, and he grabbed it with both hands.

"No, he didn't. We didn't get very far into the ranch tour before he was interrupted. Thanks for telling me." Kieran couldn't explain to Finley that he'd rather eat a bowl of razors than accept anything else from Cash. Then why wasn't he trying harder to find answers instead of having fun with Finley? Kieran turned in case his frustration was as obvious as his attraction to Finley. He started roaming the shelves for bargain books to put some distance between them. Luckily, most of them were used and marked way down, so he stacked a few in his hands.

"Here," Finley said, handing him a basket.

Their fingers brushed when he accepted it, and Kieran felt like someone had hooked jumper cables to his heart. Damn, this attraction was getting out of hand. "Thanks."

Finley headed to the opposite side of the store, allowing Kieran's heartbeat to return to normal. He'd nearly filled the basket when his eyes landed on the book that had gotten him through his jail term and given him a purpose. He picked up the copy of *The Count of Monte Cristo* as reverently as he could muster. Its presence now felt like serendipity, a reminder of his mission. He gently laid it on top of his stack and headed toward the counter. The clerk greeted him with a smile and rang up his purchases while Finley milled around at the opposite end of the store. His entire haul of books cost him under fifteen dollars, and he was quite pleased with his bounty when he walked up to Finley with a bulging reusable tote.

"Ready to eat yet?" Kieran asked.

Finley replaced a book on the shelf and snorted. "Always."

When they stepped back onto the sidewalk, the atmosphere at the festival felt vastly different. An oppressive lull had replaced the carefree vibe, and it didn't take long to figure out why. Several members of the Salvation Anew group had clustered in the middle of the street near the casino. The white-haired guy was back on his soapbox, preaching the evils of sinning. Two men—one tall and brunet and one short and sandy blond—stepped out of the casino and stopped next to the protesters and kissed passionately. The entire group of protesters turned to face them and started shouting. Kieran couldn't hear what they were saying because of the blood rushing through his ears. He recognized the taller brunet who smiled against his lover's mouth as the people raged around them. He seemed fearless and brave, but Kieran knew him to be a deceitful coward.

The rage he'd stoked for months flared to life, making him dizzy and breathless. His brain urged him to duck into a nearby store and seek cover, but he couldn't move. The two men ended their kiss and turned in Kieran's direction. His brain screamed for him to duck into the crowd, yet he remained rooted to the spot. Firm hands gripped his biceps and pushed him into a narrow alley between two businesses. His fight-or-flight instincts had failed him at the worst moment. Finley spun him around and backed him against the wall. His mouth moved, but Kieran couldn't hear him over the ringing in his ears. In his periphery, he saw Ritchie Alvarez and his lover walk into the gap between the two businesses. If they turned their heads to look down the alleyway, they'd see Kieran and Finley.

Fuck! Fuck! Oh fuck!

Something in Kieran's expression must've clued Finley in because the blond pressed his body against Kieran's, gripped the back of his neck, and planted a kiss against his lips. The rest of the world faded away—religious zealots and heartbreaking backstabbers alike. The tote bag fell to the ground, and Kieran would have too if not for the gorgeous man pinning him against the building.

Lust grabbed Finley by the balls and twisted hard enough to make his eyes water, but at least it temporarily took his mind off his aching ass after another night of debauchery on his dildo. Nothing had ever hurt so good, except for maybe the bruising grip Kieran had on his hips in the alleyway. Finley unleashed a soft whimper and melted deeper into him. It would be so natural to part his lips and invite Kieran's tongue into his mouth, but he hadn't completely lost his mind. Or had he?

Finley cracked his lids open, shifted his eyes to the right, and confirmed the men had moved on. He broke the kiss, and his conscience confronted him immediately. Blood and shame rushed to his face, turning his cheeks bright pink.

"I'm sorry," Finley whispered. "I shouldn't have done that."

"Why did you?" Kieran's voice was deeper, richer. After just one kiss? What would he sound like when he was aroused?

"You looked like you'd seen a ghost," Finley said. Kieran swallowed hard but didn't say anything. "Then I glanced over and saw two guys kissing. When they turned in your direction, you went from seeing a ghost to becoming one, so I acted on instinct and provided cover." Kieran inhaled a shaky breath, and Finley knew his instincts had been right. "You know those guys?"

"One of them." His voice sounded as fractured as his spirit. It didn't just tug on Finley's heartstrings; it yanked. Kieran could've wrapped said string around his finger a dozen times or more if his digits weren't currently digging into Finley's hips. Their kiss might've ended, but they'd remained pressed together from chest to toes.

"Want to talk about it?" Finley asked.

"Not really."

Finley blew out a frustrated breath and reached for the next best thing. "Want to get something to eat? You must be hungry after the day we've had."

"Starving." Kieran's voice dropped lower, making Finley think he was referring to a different kind of hunger.

And that's when he noticed a very pressing need—Kieran's, not his. If he didn't remove himself from the vicinity of Kieran's enormous erection, he might drop to his knees in broad daylight and do something about it. Finley's self-preservation woke from its nap and stretched. He released Kieran's neck, because of course he'd still held on to him, and stepped to the side, promptly tripping over the tote bag Kieran had dropped and spilling some of the books.

"Christ, I can be so clumsy," Finley said, squatting down to repack the bag. But truthfully, he was glad for the opportunity to put some distance between himself and—

Holy shit. Dropping down had put him at eye level with Kieran's crotch and gave him an eyeful of the long, thick erection pressing against a pair of Levi's. His mind immediately spun through the delicious things he could do with that beast, but his pucker clenched in protest.

Kieran knelt and started reaching for his spilled items, reminding Finley to do the same. Just how long would he have stared at the man's dick if Kieran hadn't taken charge of the situation? *Mmmm.* Take charge. Jesus, he was acting like a teen boy who'd just discovered the cool thing his dick could do and who lived to do it again as soon as humanly possible. Some things apparently didn't change. Thankfully, he hadn't said the "holy shit" thing out loud. A quick glance at the smirk on Kieran's lips said maybe he had. Oh no. Oh no, no, no, no, no. Finley averted his gaze to the remaining items on the ground and noticed a paperback of *The Count of Monte Cristo.*

Finley picked up the book and dusted it off. *The Count of Monte Cristo* had been required reading in high school. He'd looked at the size of the book and dreaded reading it over the summer, but it hadn't taken long for him to fall into the story of redemption and revenge. Finley held the book out to Kieran, who carefully placed it on top of the items in his bag. With everything now restored, he had no excuse to squat down and avoid meeting Kieran's gaze. Finley pushed up on his legs and barely avoided a moan when his body protested. Kieran hadn't missed his discomfort in the barn, and it didn't slip by him in the alleyway either.

"You sure you're not hurting?"

Finley wanted to strike a quid pro quo bargain. He'd confess to Kieran that he'd ridden a dildo while fantasizing about him as soon as Kieran told Finley why he feared those guys spotting him. But Finley didn't make the suggestion because it would've been just as inappropriate as him kissing a subordinate. "So…dinner?" Finley asked when they were both standing upright in the alley.

Kieran puffed up his cheeks and released his breath in a long exhale. "I'm still going to need a minute."

Finley dropped his gaze as any masochist would and noticed the Beast, as he now inappropriately thought of Kieran's dick, was still primed and ready to fuck. Incarceration had to be hell in so many ways but especially on his sexual health. Finley recalled Kieran's comment about never being alone. It probably wouldn't take much to get the Beast off. Finley could unzip his jeans, slide his hand inside, and—

"You staring at it doesn't help," Kieran said gruffly. "And please don't whisper 'holy shit' like my dick is the first, last, and only one you want to ride."

Finley jerked his head up as heat rushed to his face, and he moaned in mortification. "I said that out loud?"

Kieran pierced Finley with dark, glittering eyes. "Yes, and you moaning like I'm balls deep inside you isn't helping either. I'm on the verge of coming in my pants, Finley." He briefly closed his eyes and swallowed hard. "I don't want to do that. I can't handle the loss of control right now. Can you give me a few minutes to regroup? I'll meet you at the diner. Please." The last word sounded like he'd forcibly ripped it from his soul.

"I'm so sorry," Finley whispered. He could say he'd only been trying to help all he wanted to, but his actions had been selfish. "I'm horrified by my behavior."

Kieran's gaze softened. "I'm not." He lifted his hand toward Finley but stopped and lowered it to his side. "I am horny, though. And hungry."

Finley's guilt eased enough to free his feet. He sidestepped toward the alley, unwilling to take his eyes off Kieran. "I'll go grab us a table." A horrible thought occurred to Finley. What would he tell Cash if Kieran left the ranch? Cash implicitly trusted Finley to look after the horses and recruits, and he'd betrayed his faith.

"I won't run," Kieran said softly. "We're good."

Finley hated that his emotions were so transparent. He had no choice but to believe Kieran and head toward the diner. The sign at the hostess station told guests to seat themselves, so he chose a booth overlooking Main Street to observe the people enjoying the festival, not to watch for Kieran like a lovesick fool. What he felt wasn't love; it might not even be like. Lust was a tumbleweed barreling into Finley, and he didn't mean those puny props they put in movies. He was talking about the authentic kind that could knock an adult to the ground and leave them scraped and bloody. He'd been a heartbeat away from falling back into unhealthy patterns with Kieran. The realization stung as if someone had doused him with lemon juice after the tumbleweed had had its way with him.

Finley's breath hitched when a familiar figure stepped out of the alley and crossed the street with purpose. He wanted to think the man was eager to eat dinner with him, but he knew better. Kieran kept his head down to avoid making eye contact with anyone who might recognize him. With his gaze glued to Kieran, the waitress caught him by surprise when she set down napkin-wrapped silverware. He jumped like someone had shot him, causing the petite brunette to jolt too. Water sloshed over the edge of the pitcher she held in her hand and splattered against his sleeve. Finley didn't recognize her, but her tag identified her as Merri.

"I'm so sorry," Finley said as he heard the bell jingle over the door.

"No, I'm sorry," Merri replied. "Let me go get some extra napkins. You'd think it was my first day."

Finley waved off her gesture. "It's fine. Have you worked here long?"

"Here, no. I recently moved from Santa Fe, but I've been waitressing for six years. So sorry I startled—" Her words died when Kieran stepped around her and slid into the booth opposite Finley. "I...um..." Yeah, Kieran Sullivan was that good-looking. "I'll go grab another set of silverware. Be right back."

Kieran looked from her retreating figure to Finley. "What did I miss?"

"I was daydreaming and not paying attention to my surroundings, and Merri startled me when she set the silverware on the table. My jumping triggered a chain reaction, and she splashed water on me." Finley lifted his arm so Kieran could see the wet spot. He turned over both water glasses and filled them. "Oh, and Merri recently moved here from Santa Fe."

Kieran arched a brow. "You move fast."

Finley, who'd just taken a drink, nearly spat the liquid on the gorgeous man across from him. He managed to swallow it and set the glass down without incident. "Move fast?"

Kieran shrugged. "You haven't been here long, and you already know where she's from."

"Oh, it was a natural progression from our conversation."

The brooding man across from him either didn't buy the explanation, didn't care, or both. He lifted a menu tucked behind the condiment caddy and extended it across the table.

"I already know what I want." Finley's voice sounded husky and low, probably giving Kieran the wrong idea. "I have the menu memorized, but I already worked out what I was going to order the moment I planned the trip into town." Finley hoped that set the record straight.

Merri returned with Kieran's silverware before he could respond. "Do you guys need more time, or do you know what you want?"

Kieran returned the menu to its spot and said, "I'll have what he's having."

Merri smiled at Finley. "Which is?"

"Open face roast beef sandwich with mushroom gravy, mashed potatoes, honey glazed carrots, and rolls instead of biscuits. Sweet tea to drink, please. Oh, I'll also want cherry crisp and vanilla ice cream for dessert. And I'll take a piece of coconut cream to go."

Merri finished writing the order, then looked at Kieran. "Still want what he's having?"

"Yes, except for the coconut cream pie," he replied without looking away from Finley.

"I'll have your orders out in a jiffy," she told them.

Once alone, Kieran shifted his gaze out the big window. Was he people-watching or avoiding him? Finley couldn't be sure, but he was content to observe Kieran watching everyone else. Merri returned with their drinks a few moments later, but Kieran continued gazing out the window. Just when Finley was prepared to be on the receiving end of the silent treatment, Kieran met his gaze.

"Tell me about Last Chance Creek."

"It was a thriving mining town in the mid-eighteen hundreds but abandoned after the Gold Rush ended. In the early nineteen hundreds, Ezekiel Chance and his extended family stumbled onto the empty town on their way to California and planted their roots here instead of moving on."

"Why Last Chance Creek and not just Chance Creek?"

Finley shrugged. "Some historians said he was an odd man, looking to create a utopia and thought this town would be his last chance to realize his dream." Kieran scowled like he didn't buy it. The jury was out for Finley too, but it was a good story. "The businesses you see today aren't the original buildings, but historians preserved the

Chance homestead and turned it into a museum if you ever want to kill some time. Everything on Main Street was built to look like structures from that era, though. Gives it a quaint vibe."

"Except for that tacky-ass casino," Kieran said, tipping his head toward the monstrosity with the neon lights.

Finley agreed, but he couldn't resist leaning across the table. "Keep your voice down or people from Salvation Anew will try to recruit you."

Kieran snorted. "When I first saw them last week, I thought they were period actors running through a scene for the tourists. I thought the guy at the podium was portraying a snake-oil salesman until he started shouting through a bullhorn. And tonight…" Kieran's voice trailed off as he turned his attention back out the window.

"Nothing you say leaves this booth," Finley said. "Or anywhere else you confide in me…if you confide in me."

Kieran met his gaze again, and his battered soul was right there in his beautiful brown eyes. The need to soothe Kieran's hurt caught Finley by surprise. Need, not want. Of course he wanted to help Kieran, but this feeling went much deeper, and Finley didn't understand why. Kieran looked on the verge of saying something but shook his head instead. The intimacy of the moment shattered when Merri arrived with their food.

Kieran looked from his plate to Finley's. "You're actually going to eat all this plus dessert?"

Finley nodded enthusiastically as he unrolled his silverware from the napkin. He draped the cloth over his lap and tucked into his meal. He scooped up a big bite of beef, potatoes, and gravy, then paused with the fork near his mouth. "Hell yeah. I'll eat mine and whatever you don't finish. My mama calls me a human garbage disposal."

Kieran's lips ticked up slightly on the right. It wasn't a smile, not even a smirk, but it was progress. "Where do you put it?"

"Goes straight to my ass," Finley replied before shoving a forkful of food into his mouth.

"Explains the jeans," Kieran mumbled.

Finley pretended not to hear him and said, "What was that?"

Kieran shoved a bite into his mouth and pointed to it with his empty fork. Finley snickered and let it go. He was just grateful he hadn't scared Kieran off, though he was desperate to learn something about the man. He'd offered to talk about his crime the day before, but Finley had waved him off. Had that been a mistake? He broached the subject midway through their meal.

Kieran's posture tensed briefly, but he took a drink of tea and said, "A jury convicted me of stealing a luxury car."

Finley studied him closely as he chewed, wondering about Kieran's phrasing. "But you didn't do it?"

Kieran cocked his head to the side. "That isn't what I said."

"I heard what you didn't say," Finley replied. "You didn't say you stole it. You said they convicted you of stealing it."

"Same difference."

Kieran set his fork down and gave Kieran his full attention. "I've worked with a dozen guys who've served time at either Arrowhead or Four Mile. None of them talk about their convictions, just the crimes they committed. You didn't steal the car." Kieran clenched his jaw tight enough to crack his teeth. "Did you go to jail to protect someone else? Maybe one of those guys playing tonsil hockey on Main Street." That comment earned a sneer. Okay. Not that. He recalled Kieran's reaction to seeing the men, and said, "One of them set you up."

Kieran blinked twice but otherwise didn't react. "What makes you say that?"

Finley tapped his temple with two fingers. "Intuition. You have the look of someone who's been let down by others more than a few times in their life." Kieran's gaze shimmered with moisture, but no tears fell. Finley expected him to break eye contact, but he held on. "Am I right?"

Kieran's nostrils flared as he inhaled. "Everyone I've known has let me down, including my parents and the system that was supposed to protect me. And especially Ritchie Alvarez." Kieran's breath hitched and his cheeks heated. Still, he held on.

"And you saw him just now?"

Kieran nodded. "He was the taller guy with dark hair."

Finley had so many questions but wasn't sure what he should ask. Then he noticed Kieran looked a little more at ease. His back was still ramrod straight, but his shoulders were more relaxed. His color was back to normal, and his breathing had evened out. He decided to press for a little more information. If Kieran didn't want to answer, he wouldn't. "Was Ritchie your friend or a romantic interest?"

"My boyfriend."

"And he betrayed you."

Kieran nodded. "Ritchie cut me deeper than anyone ever has."

Finley saw red but kept his emotions in check. "And what does this asshole do?"

"Owns a body shop and detailing business in Colorado Springs. He's very successful."

"Let me guess," Finley said dryly. "He specializes in high-end luxury cars."

"Yep."

"And boosts them as a side hustle, probably accounting for his real wealth." Kieran said nothing, but he didn't have to. "One of those natural conclusions," Finley said. "Which is why it's odd the police didn't look into Ritchie after your arrest." He tilted his head to the side and ran through the scenario out loud. "You got caught driving a stolen car, and the cops settled for the little fish instead of going after the big one. I bet you have an idea why that is."

"I do."

"But you're not ready to tell me," Finley said. Who could blame him? "Is he here to make trouble for you?"

"Doubtful," Kieran replied. "He's always had a thing for gambling. Blackjack is his poison. I only knew him to play at Black Hawk, though."

"The casino here is newer and closer to Colorado Springs." So his presence could be a coincidence, at least it had better be. Finley dropped his gaze to the tote bag and recalled the book it contained. "I hope I'm around to see you go all Edmond Dantès on his ass." Kieran's eyes widened just enough for Finley to know he'd guessed right. "You don't trust me now, but you will. I'm going to be the one person who doesn't let you down. The Jacopo to your Edmond."

Kieran's mouth formed a real smirk, and Finley fought the urge to fist-pump the air. This was more a cause for alarm than celebration because getting Kieran to let his guard down just the tiniest amount made Finley thirstier for more peeks behind the curtain. He nearly snorted out loud. Yeah, information was what he was after. Not more kisses and definitely not an up close and personal introduction to the Beast. Finley tried to summon the discipline he'd found the past few months, but it eluded him. All he heard and felt was the howling coyote.

chapter
ELEVEN

KIERAN AND FINLEY CLEANED BOTH THEIR DINNER AND DESSERT plates before tapping out. His stomach ached in protest, and he was grateful he'd had a week of Harry's amazing cuisine before attempting the diner stunt. Tension had eased between them while they were shoveling food into their mouths, but it returned tenfold when they were alone in the truck, heading back to the ranch with Cash's pie sitting on the console between them.

"I'm really sorry," Finley said softly. "I feel like I should tell Cash what happened in the alley."

That snapped Kieran out of his food coma. "What the hell for?"

"My behavior was inexcusable, and I betrayed Cash's trust and yours."

Kieran would've sighed heavily, but he worried the air would come out in an embarrassing belch. "Cash has nothing to do with what is happening between you and me." Too late, he realized how that sounded.

"What *is* happening between us?" Finley asked.

"Fuck if I know, but it doesn't have a thing to do with our boss. And I'm not sorry about the kiss. I don't want you to be either."

Their kiss had been brief and chaste, something that should've barely registered on the Richter scale of embraces, yet it had rattled Kieran's bones and left him achingly hard. He hadn't felt violated or threatened, but the memory of Finley's sweet lips pressed against his threatened to upend his focus and possibly his sanity. Finley's determination to be the person who wouldn't let Kieran down was even more arousing than the kiss, putting everything he'd held dear in jeopardy.

Doing time for a crime he hadn't committed had threatened to destroy him in ways his parents' abandonment and the welfare system's neglect had not. Continuing to work with Finley could be the biggest mistake he ever made, but he'd rather find out and fail than miss out on a single second with the alluring man.

"Okay," Finley agreed. "I don't really regret our kiss."

But it couldn't happen again. Anything more would constitute a full disclosure that he wasn't ready to give. Kieran needed to keep his head on straight and start looking for answers. He'd had all the time in the world to reflect on everything he knew about Ritchie. Kieran had talked to the inmates who were serving time for boosting cars. They told him about an auto theft ring that would pop up and disappear like a ghost. No one knew who was behind it. Bits and pieces started clicking into place, and he realized Ritchie had to be involved, but there was no way in hell the dumbass was the one calling the shots. It would take a savvy person who was above reproach and had the right connections. Was Cash Sweeney that someone? Was his ranch a recruiting ground?

They spent the rest of the drive back to the ranch in silence, and he set his tumultuous thoughts aside until he was alone in his small cabin. Then everything he'd suppressed came rushing back to him— seeing Ritchie, kissing Finley, and divulging more than he was comfortable sharing. He'd revealed little, but it was more than he'd planned to tell anyone, another warning sign he'd ignored. Overstimulated in more ways than one, Kieran stripped out of his clothes and took a scalding hot shower. His skin tingled beneath the spray and his dick stood at attention. Fucking his fist wasn't another delay tactic; it was an act of necessity, just as important as breathing when Kieran remembered the way Finley had licked his lips upon seeing his erection.

He came fast and hard but at least stayed upright. Surely, his urges and reactions to the man would settle down with time. Kieran soaped his body and washed his hair as soon as his breathing returned to normal. He felt much calmer once he dried off, dressed, and settled on the loveseat with a throw blanket over his lap and a paperback in his hand. One positive takeaway from serving jail time was finding pleasure in the simplest things. The soft flannel pants, cotton tank, plush blanket, and comfortable furniture were a luxury he refused to take for granted.

Calmness washed over him as he opened his book and read, but it didn't last long. Someone knocked on the door before he finished the first page. Not someone. Finley. Kieran knew the identity of his visitor without looking. He debated not answering for about ten seconds before throwing off the blanket and setting his book on the coffee table. Kieran recalled the determination shimmering in Finley's gaze and couldn't resist his lure.

He opened the door, and sure enough, Finley Ashe stood on his stoop with a DVD in one hand and a package of microwavable popcorn in the other. He'd showered too but was dressed in another pair of jeans, a darker wash than earlier, and a different Henley in a light gray. The hue made Finley's eyes look darker as they took in every inch of his body. His gazed lingered on Kieran's bare feet before snapping back up to lock eyes with him.

Kieran crossed his arms over his chest, and that green gaze fell to his biceps. He didn't need a mirror to know his arms look ripped in the pose. Tension filled Kieran's body, making his biceps bunch even tighter. Finley swallowed hard and met his gaze once more. Damn, he was truly the most beautiful man Kieran had ever seen. "That better not be an apology," he said gruffly.

Finley's cheeks colored a little, and he inhaled shakily. "Just a surprise."

Kieran lifted a brow and leaned against the doorjamb. "You've piqued my curiosity."

Finley lifted the DVD to reveal *The Count of Monte Cristo.* "There's an extensive selection of movies in the library. I thought you might enjoy this one, so I grabbed it when I dropped off Cash's pie." Finley skimmed his gaze over Kieran once more, then extended the movie and popcorn package to him. "I just wanted to drop these off for you to enjoy when it's convenient."

Finley's words said he didn't plan to linger, but his eyes communicated something else entirely. Hope was a dangerous emotion, and Kieran had no right to flirt with it or to lead Finley on.

He accepted the offering with a thanks, then added, "I don't think I have a way to watch the movie here."

Finley scrunched up his brow. "You should have a DVD player."

Shaking his head, Kieran said, "It isn't on or in the entertainment center."

"The closet?" Finley asked.

"No. Just my clothes and bed linens are in there."

"Probably inside the coffee table," Finley said.

Kieran looked over at the rustic wooden trunk in front of his loveseat. It looked like a movie prop. He faced Finley again. "That thing works?"

"Yeah, the top slides open instead of lifting."

"How do you know so much about the cabins?" Kieran hated the little green monster that rose to the surface anytime he imagined Finley with another guy. *Freaking ridiculous.*

As if reading Kieran's mind, Finley rolled his eyes. "I lived in one of them when I first started working here. I moved to the old homestead once Cash promoted me to the equine supervisor position."

Kieran resented the relief flooding his system. He hadn't been a choir boy before they'd met, so why was he holding Finley to a different standard? Because Finley made him want things he had no business coveting. "Mind showing me how the coffee table works?"

"Of course."

Kieran turned away and took the few steps to the loveseat. The door shut softly behind him, and anticipation skimmed down his spine. The place had been small when it was just him, but it felt like all the air had been sucked out of the space when Finley joined him.

Kieran moved to the other end of the trunk and turned in time to see Finley push the top open to reveal more folded blankets, some board games and card games, and a DVD player with all the cables and a remote.

"I'll be damned," Kieran said. "That's pretty badass."

"Well, you're all set unless you need help hooking it up," Finley said.

He wasn't insulted; he knew plenty of people who weren't good with electronics or technology. "Nah, I'm good."

"Then I'll just head out," Finley said. "Enjoy your movie. It's a wonderful adaptation of the book, and that isn't something I say often."

Kieran should've squashed the hope shimmering in Finley's gaze, but he couldn't. "Or you could stay and watch the movie with me." Kieran looked down at the popcorn. He was on the verge of saying he didn't have room for more food, but it would give his hands something to do other than reaching for Finley.

"Are you sure?"

Sure this was a mistake? Yeah, but he wouldn't take back the invite if he could, and severing his own finger would've been easier than rescinding the offer. Kieran really enjoyed having Finley in his space, even if it would be cramped on the couch. Or maybe especially because it would be a tight fit. He'd be in big trouble if he let his dirty mind pick up that thread and run with it. "I'm sure. I'll make the popcorn while you set up the DVD player."

"Deal."

Kieran headed toward the kitchenette. He removed the wrapper, popped the package into the microwave, and pressed the popcorn button. "I don't have anything to drink. Is tap water okay?"

"Sure."

Kieran filled two glasses and poured the buttery kernels into cereal bowls until they nearly overflowed. Sharing the bag wouldn't be a good idea. If Finley's hand grazed against his, there'd be no telling how his body would react. The sexy blond had already made himself comfortable on the love seat with the remote on his lap. He reached up and accepted the bowl and glass Kieran extended to him. Luckily, their fingers didn't touch and put his willpower to the test right out of the gate. He returned to the kitchen to get his own snack and drink. Finley had toed out of his shoes and covered himself with one of the spare blankets from the trunk. He would've teased his guest about making himself right at home but knew Finley would issue a string of apologies, and Kieran would feel obligated to cut them off with a kiss.

Kieran set his popcorn and water on the closed coffee table and settled onto the cushion beside Finley's. He covered his lower body, which would help disguise his reaction to any wayward thoughts, but it turned out the precaution wasn't necessary. The movie sucked Kieran in from the very start, and he was barely aware of Finley's presence—a miracle in itself—or the passing time. All the emotions he'd felt while reading the book the first time resurfaced, taking him on a roller coaster ride that left him feeling motivated when the credits rolled at the end. The story was powerful and stirring on paper but even more spellbinding on the screen, and it put things in perspective for him. Kieran was stunned to discover he hadn't taken a single bite of popcorn or one sip from his water glass. He'd sat there completely mesmerized.

The rest of the room came into focus, namely the beautiful blond watching him with a tender expression. Finley blinked, and a single tear slipped down his cheek. He turned his head and brushed it away, but the damage was done. For the first time in nearly two years, Kieran wanted there to be room for something more in his heart than loathing and vengeance. It turned out his soul was more resilient than he realized. A voice in his head reminded Kieran that he wasn't staying, but this time a softer voice reasoned, "But you could. Just give up on your vendetta." Another first that left him reeling and frozen in place until Finley threw back his blanket and reached for his shoes.

Something had shifted inside Kieran at the diner. He hadn't said a lot, but when he did, an invisible weight lifted off him, making it easier to breathe. What would happen if he opened up to Finley more? Would the thorny vines of bitterness surrounding his heart unravel? Did he even want them to? By the time he'd decided, Finley had both shoes on and was rising.

"Ritchie asked me to drive a client's Jaguar to the warehouse for safekeeping until they returned from a trip." His voice sounded as strangled as his heart at first but gained strength as he spoke. Finley didn't say anything; he simply sat back down and gave Kieran his full attention.

Those shimmering eyes encouraged and soothed him at the same time. "It wasn't an odd request or scenario. Ritchie's clients were super wealthy and would drop off their vehicles for detailing or service on their way out of town. He always had limited space at the shop, so he rented a warehouse when his business grew to help with his overflow problem."

"What a convenient place to hide stolen cars," Finley said.

"Yeah, but I was too dumb to realize it." Kieran blew out a breath. "Instead of driving straight to the warehouse, I took a brief detour because I'd never driven a car as smooth and fast as the Jag. I truly understood what luxury and performance meant. According to the cop who pulled me over, I didn't signal when making a turn. He ran the plates, and the vehicle came back stolen. Next thing I knew, multiple officers with drawn weapons had surrounded me and were screaming at me to get out of the car with my hands up. I complied right away, and two of them rushed forward and knocked me to the ground, bloodying my lip and scraping my face on the asphalt. I was scared out of my freaking mind, but finally found the presence of mind to ask why they were arresting me." Kieran closed his eyes and focused on regulating his breathing as memories of that night replayed in his head.

"Hey," Finley said, reaching over and covering Kieran's hand with his own. Kieran opened his eyes, and they locked gazes. "You don't have to say anything else if you're not ready."

Kieran appreciated Finley's consideration, but he wanted to give him this much at least. "I convinced myself the incident was all a big misunderstanding, even when they cuffed me and hauled me into the back of a cop car. I knew they'd let me go once they talked to Ritchie. He'd have paperwork on the client who'd brought in the vehicle, and the cops would shift their attention to them. I continued to hold on to that hope, even after I told my story no less than a dozen times during the thirteen hours the officers and detectives interrogated me." Kieran's stomach pitched a little, but he swallowed and continued the story. "I demanded to know why they kept asking the same questions on an endless loop when they got the same answers each time. That's when they told me they'd called the body shop, and Ritchie had told the cops he didn't know anyone with my name." Kieran's breathing turned shaky, and he rotated his hand to link his fingers with Finley's. Green eyes widened ever so slightly, but Finley didn't look away from his face. "I didn't believe the detectives. Ritchie had kissed me and said he loved me when he'd handed me the keys to the Jag. It had to be a nightmare. That was the only explanation. I kept telling myself that I'd wake up in our bed any minute, roll over, and cuddle up against him."

Finley's fingers tightened on his, and Kieran wasn't sure what part had gotten a reaction out of him. "But you never woke up."

"Nope."

"Things just got more surreal. I found out that there'd been a similar theft spree on luxury vehicles the year before. They were stolen from garages and driveways with the keys still in them. Of course, the officers thought I was involved, and I didn't blame them at first. I just stuck with my story about moving the Jag for my boyfriend. It occurred to me that they'd lied about Ritchie to get a confession, so I confronted them." Kieran's breath froze just as he had on the sidewalk when seeing Ritchie again. Finley squeezed his hand, and he expelled the trapped air from his lungs. "The detective played the call he'd recorded with Ritchie. I heard my boyfriend's voice as he denied knowing me."

"I'm so sorry," Finley said. Unshed tears pooled in his eyes, making his irises look like polished jade.

"They tried to break me down, and that's when I realized I wasn't dreaming and asked for a lawyer. They didn't have any evidence tying me to the other cars. My public defender was an excellent lawyer, but the jury still found me guilty. I was inconsolable for quite some time. My cell mate got tired of my brooding and handed me the jail library's copy of *The Count of Monte Cristo*. That's when I turned my fury into fuel."

Finley leaned closer. "How are we going to take Ritchie down?"

"*We?* I can't involve you."

"Too late," Finley replied. "I'm invested now." He narrowed his eyes when Kieran opened his mouth to protest. "What's the plan?"

Kieran debated for a second before relenting. It wouldn't be a bad idea to get an objective opinion. His voice of reason cautioned that Finley wasn't impartial. Their fingers were still entwined after all. Kieran eased his hand free and rested it on his lap. He missed Finley's warmth immediately, but there was no future for them. "I need to get my hands on surveillance equipment. I want to get eyes on the warehouse to record and document the movement of cars and people in and out of there."

Finley leaned back against the sofa cushion, crossed his arms over his chest, and gave Kieran a smile that only promised trouble. "I can help. My grandfather was an amateur photographer, and his favorite subject was nocturnal wildlife."

"Did he take the images hanging in your office?"

"He did," Finley replied. "Pops left his photograph collection and his equipment to me when he passed. The cameras and recording devices have night-vision capabilities." His smile morphed from Cheshire cat to the Grinch. "And they can capture images from a long distance." Finley held up a hand to thwart any protest. "I'm aware this could get dicey and dangerous, but I'm stronger than I seem. I promise." Finley held his gaze and added, "I won't let you down."

Kieran knew he should refuse Finley's help, but Edmond didn't go it alone. It might've been a mistake, but he said, "When do we start, Jacopo?"

chapter

TWELVE

FINLEY RUBBED HIS HANDS TOGETHER GLEEFULLY. "I'M READY whenever you are," he said. "I just need to retrieve the equipment from my mom's garage and test it out to make sure I remember how to use it."

Kieran narrowed his eyes. "I want to keep this between us."

"Naturally." Finley added a nod for emphasis. He loved being the only other person to know Kieran's plan.

"That means not drawing any unwanted attention. If you and I just hightailed it off to Colorado Springs…"

Finley's bubble burst a little. "Everyone would notice, and their tongues would wag."

Word would get back to Harry, and his sister would worry about him. He'd seen her interact with Kieran enough to know she liked and trusted him, but that didn't mean she would want him romantically involved with her little brother. Finley had vowed to stop seeing men who were emotionally unavailable, and Kieran was the reigning king of unavailable. Harry wouldn't hesitate to remind Finley of his promise, and she would probably even tattle to their mother. Neither of them would believe Finley was just being helpful, and they would be correct. At least partially. He wanted to help Kieran get even with the guy who'd sent him to prison. Most people would call him naïve and foolish for believing Kieran's story without corroborating evidence, but they hadn't witnessed his reaction firsthand. Kieran hadn't been faking his emotions on the sidewalk or in the alley, and he wasn't bullshitting Finley in his cabin. While he sensed there was more to the story, and there always was, Finley believed Kieran and wanted to help him, even if it cut their time together short. He'd worry about the repercussions later.

"I don't want the other hands thinking we're together," Kieran said.

"Ouch," Finley said, rubbing his chest. He kept his tone light and playful to disguise his internal flinch.

Maybe Kieran saw through his ploy because a somber expression washed over his handsome face. "I don't want them to think you'd lower your standards to date a guy like me."

"There's absolutely nothing wrong with you," Finley said firmly, "but we don't need to invite extra scrutiny." Kieran looked relieved when he nodded. Then the solution hit him. Finley snapped his fingers and said, "I got it. There's a dressage show in two weeks in Colorado Springs. Tiny Dancer, one of our former foster horses, is performing that night. I received an invitation from her new owners last week."

Kieran pursed his lips and furrowed his brow. "Won't some of the other guys want to see her too?"

Finley grinned until his face hurt. "If it were any other equine show, they'd jump on it. They all think dressage is too prissy and fussy."

"What's dressage?" Kieran asked.

"It's a specific equine discipline, judging riders and horses on a series of prescribed movements and musical freestyle."

Kieran's brow shot up. "Musical freestyle? Like dancing to music on horseback?"

"Yeah, it's really awesome. The horses follow nearly imperceptible cues from their riders." Finley retrieved his phone from his back pocket and pulled up the video Owen had shot of him working with Tiny Dancer. He specialized in the gaits they were required to perform. Finley had taught the horse basic commands that her new owners

126

expanded on to train for competitions. "This was Tiny Dancer when I first started working with her." Finley pushed Play, and they watched a brief clip of him teaching her how to trot. She was awkward at first but eager to learn. He cued up a later video where she fluidly transitioned from one gait to another.

"Wow," Kieran said. "You're guiding her?"

"With my knees and hands. Very slight gestures she can feel but most people won't see."

Kieran scooted closer to Finley until they were practically pressed together. "I want to see her dance now."

Finley chuckled. "I don't dance. That skill set is beyond me. I don't have any rhythm myself, so it feels counterintuitive to teach an animal to do it."

Kieran looked up from the phone and locked dark eyes on him. "But you trot and prance around like the horses?"

Snorting, Finley said, "Well, no, but I could with proper incentive. Dancing is beyond me." He tilted his head to the side. "What about you? Have any sweet moves you could show someone with two left feet?"

Kieran's cheeks colored slightly, and Finley braced himself for another revelation, but he shook his head. What was he hiding? That he had moves or that he would share them? Finley decided not to push. He'd made some pretty big inroads and didn't want to blow it. Instead, he clicked on his Instagram account and pulled up Tiny Dancer's page. Joy swelled in Finley's heart as they watched clips from her most recent competition. The horse looked so happy as she trotted and danced before the crowd. His eyes misted over when she stood proud and tall as the audience clapped for her at the end.

"I think she's amazing," Kieran said.

"I'm a little fond of her myself." He set his phone down and looked at Kieran. "Some performances are stuffy, but most riders use modern music and show a playful side. There are a few horses in the stable who might be a good fit for dressage."

"Nellie?" Kieran teased.

Finley laughed. "Maybe if you were sitting astride her."

"I've never been on a horse before, so you'd have to teach me the basics before I could teach them to Nellie."

"Deal, but you'd probably want to start with a more docile horse."

"She's a marshmallow," Kieran countered. "But I will cede to your expertise."

If Kieran wanted the other guys to believe he was interested in dressage, he'd have to show it with his actions. So that's how they would spend nearly all their free time together leading up to the horse show.

Finley chose Loretta, a stunning Tennessee Walker with a shimmering brown coat and an indulgent personality. Like all the other animals on the ranch, she was smitten with Kieran and all too eager to help him train. They spent the next few nights going over riding basics that any beginner needed to know before progressing to intermediate skills.

"You're a natural," Finley told Kieran when they graduated to dressage basics.

The thing Finley liked most about Kieran was that he soaked up the new skills like a sponge, never hesitating to ask questions if he needed additional direction. Though he caught on quick with verbal instructions and cues, he worked best with hands-on guidance. He was a doer, which meant Finley didn't just have to tell him how to work his knees and thighs. He had to show him. Finley saddled Dolly and joined him in the indoor arena to demonstrate how to press his knees and thighs to guide her movements. Loretta's stunted movements signaled Kieran was sending mixed signals. The horse could do the maneuvers in her sleep, so Finley needed to rethink his approach.

"I think you're going to need a different approach," he told Kieran after a few more attempts.

Kieran's lips hooked into a smirk, something that came more easily since he'd arrived. Finley still hadn't seen a genuine smile, but then again, his heart might not survive it. "How handsy do you need to get?"

Finley laughed and shook his head. A flirty rejoinder was on the tip of his tongue, but he let it dissolve there instead of letting it fly. "I didn't say handsy."

Not ready to let it go, Kieran followed with, "Where do you plan to put your hands, then?"

"How about you dismount and come over here so I can show you on my body?"

Kieran's cheeks flushed, and his lips parted. "You want me to come over and watch you touch yourself?" He looked around the barn and met Finley's gaze. "Here?"

Heat engulfed his body, and Dolly pranced as if she felt the tension rising in the arena. "You're deliberately twisting my words into something dirty." God, he loved it and was dying to give it right back—physically and verbally—but he remembered the shame he'd felt after their alleyway kiss. "The alternative is for me to come over there and show you how to use your body to get what you want." Kieran's eyebrow shot up because, yeah, that didn't sound suggestive or anything. "I mean, how to guide the horse."

"Okay."

Finley just blinked. Was that a ghost of a smile that flashed on Kieran's lips? Did his obsidian eyes darken? Probably just wishful thinking. "To which option?" he asked.

Kieran raised his hand and crooked his finger. Finley nearly got his foot caught in the stirrup in his haste to dismount. He hadn't pitched to the ground face-first since he was a kid, and he didn't want to ruin his streak in front of Kieran. He took a calming breath and told Dolly to stay, then crossed to Loretta. She neighed and rubbed her muzzle against him when he greeted her. He took the time to shower her with affection before shifting his gaze to the man sitting astride her.

"Are you sure you're okay with this?" Finley asked before moving closer.

"Positive."

Finley patted Loretta's sleek neck one last time before stepping closer to Kieran. His thighs tensed when Finley placed a hand on his knee, and Loretta pranced in place. "I need you to relax and…um… spread your legs a little." Kieran nearly choked on his next breath, but he did as Finley asked.

"Perfect. This," Finley said, moving his hand to the inside of Kieran's knee, "presses here." He used his other hand to indicate where on Loretta he should push and when to use those cues before lowering his arms and giving the horse and rider some space.

Kieran repeated back to him and demonstrated. "Like this?"

"Perfect," Finley said, noticing he sounded a little breathy. "Try the other leg." Once Kieran mastered those, he moved closer again. "I need to place my hand up higher now." Kieran swallowed hard but nodded. His thigh bunched under Finley's hand, and what he wouldn't give for the privilege to slide it up even higher. Finley explained how Kieran should use his inner thighs and what those cues told Loretta.

"Okay," Kieran said. "I think I understand better." They ran through a sequence of moves, but Kieran's tension and posture countered the correct cues he gave the horse. He turned frustrated eyes to Finley. "What am I doing wrong?"

"You're doing great," Finley replied. "You're making the same mistakes all rookies make."

Kieran sighed. "Bring those hands over here and show me."

Finley couldn't resist waggling his brows and earning a snort from Kieran. He tried to keep his touch indifferent and professional as he helped Kieran adjust his posture in the saddle. He quickly discovered Kieran was trying to give cues with one side of his body but tightening his resting side to maintain balance in the saddle. After some slight adjustments through practice, Kieran and Loretta were in sync.

"Relaxing in the saddle and trusting your horse is easier said than done," Finley told him. "You're doing great."

Kieran grew more confident with each lesson, and before long, he didn't need to fake interest in the skill. He wasn't quite ready for dance routines to music, but there was no doubt in Finley's mind that he could pull that off with enough practice and commitment. He'd nearly said as much the following Saturday when they were testing the night-vision capabilities on Finley's equipment. Kieran had asked if the others would think it was weird the two of them were sneaking off toward the trees together, but Finley reminded him it was poker night.

"I can't believe that night was your first time playing poker."

Finley laughed. "I make enough bad decisions without adding

gambling to the mix. Trust me when I say I deserve the razzing the guys give me about my love life."

Kieran stopped suddenly when they reached the edge of the woods. The shade from the trees blocked the moonlight and shielded his expression. Kieran placed a gentle hand on Finley's bicep. "Did someone hurt you?"

Finley's eyes adjusted to the dark, and he couldn't look away from Kieran's glittering gaze, not even to drop his head in shame. "Not physically, but let's just say you and I both know there are other ways to cut a man."

Kieran's fingers tightened around his arm but not too hard, more like he didn't want to let him go. "I hate that for you."

"I hate it for you too." Finley's voice sounded huskier than he'd intended.

"Finley," Kieran said, his voice a rough rumble that teased every nerve ending awake. "I don't want to be just another guy who hurts you or brings sadness into your life. Maybe we—"

Finley moved closer, planning to cut him off before he could sever their burgeoning bond, though he hadn't chosen a method of distraction. A pitiful meow came from the darkness surrounding them, beating Finley to the punch. He turned his flashlight on and shone it around. *Meow.* The wail was closer, but Finley hadn't located the cat. He stepped deeper into the shadows looking for gleaming eyes.

"Here, kitty kitty," he called.

Kieran followed his lead but aimed his flashlight in the opposite direction. "We have a cat?"

Finley didn't miss that he'd said we but didn't dare point out his blunder. "We do now. It would seem someone recently dropped a cat off near the road, and it wandered down here like the sorry assholes had hoped."

"How could you possibly know how long the cat has been out here, and why assume someone dumped him?"

Finley moved deeper into the woods. "Come on, sweetheart," he said, doing his best impression of Kieran when he wooed Nellie.

"Outdoor cats don't survive out here long. There are too many predators. It's a miracle the poor thing made it this far."

"God, I hate people sometimes," Kieran growled, then lowered his voice to call out, "Here, kitty, kitty." Unsurprisingly, a calico cat slowly climbed out of a tree and headed right for Kieran. A quick look at her swollen belly explained why someone had dumped her. "I *really* hate people," Kieran corrected. Finley watched in awe as he knelt and picked the cat up, cradling her against his chest. The feline released another cry, but this one was of relief, not fear. "She weighs next to nothing."

"She looks young, not much older than a year or two, and soon to be a mama herself."

"Little Mama," Kieran said, scratching her ears. "That's what we'll call you."

"We can test out the camera equipment another night. Let's take her back to the barn and check her over. Ivan has two house cats at the old homestead. I bet he can spare some litter and food, but I think we should keep her separated from the other kitties right now."

"I'll take her," Kieran said. "She can bunk with me." He looked at Finley. "Unless that's against the rules."

"Cash won't have a problem with it," Finley said.

They worked together removing burrs and washing the cat. If someone had dumped her as recently as he thought, her existence beforehand must've been pure misery. She was malnourished and filthy to the point she didn't even resist a bath. Then again, who would when Kieran Sullivan was running gentle hands all over your body while telling you how pretty you were? Finley reminded himself to hold on to his heart. While Kieran was nothing like the assholes he'd fallen for in the past, he probably wouldn't stay once he got his revenge on Ritchie. Finley couldn't let himself forget that.

"Our vet will stop by for a routine checkup on the horses on Monday. I'll ask her to examine Little Mama and see if she needs treatment. She can probably tell us how much time she has before the babies arrive."

Once they finished, Kieran took Little Mama to his cabin, and Finley interrupted the poker game to talk to Ivan.

"What's up?" the foreman asked.

"A pregnant cat wandered into the barn a little while ago. We got her cleaned up, but I think she's malnourished. Can I borrow some food and litter from you until I can get supplies?"

Ivan held his gaze for several moments. "We?"

"Huh?"

"You said 'we got her cleaned up.'"

He knew damn well who Finley was talking about, but he wanted to make things more difficult. Everyone on the ranch liked Kieran, even Tyler and Owen. Why couldn't Ivan let up on him? "I'll just drive into town. Sorry I bothered you." Finley moved to step around Ivan, but he sidestepped to block his path. Finley tilted his head back to meet his friend's gaze.

"Of course you can have the supplies," his friend said. "If you promise to do something for me in return."

Finley quirked a brow. If Kieran had said the same thing, many innuendos would've popped into his brain. With Ivan, all he felt was dread. "What?"

"Guard your beautiful heart, Fin."

"There's no danger to me here."

Ivan pursed his lips as if mulling something over, then said, "Everything you need is in the utility room. I even have an extra litter box. There's some special food for malnourished cats at the top of the cabinet. My big boy doesn't need it anymore." Finley remembered the condition Scruffy had been in when Ivan had adopted him. He'd lovingly nurtured the cat back to health. As if he knew they were talking about him, the big, beautiful tabby swaggered into the room and rubbed up against Finley's leg.

"I appreciate it, Ivan. I'll replace what we use when—"

Ivan shook his head. "That's not necessary. Where are you going to keep the cat?"

"Little Mama is going to stay with Kieran." He smiled as he recalled the adoring look on the cat's face as she stared up at her rescuer during her bath.

"Not in danger, huh?" Ivan asked.

Finley rolled his eyes. "I was thinking about how the cat is already smitten with Kieran."

"Everyone else seems to have fallen under his spell, so why should she be any different?"

"No witchery is afoot," Finley replied. "We just gave him a chance. Why can't you do the same?"

Ivan stepped closer but not threateningly. A hand the size of a dinner plate landed softly on Finley's shoulder. "I'm just concerned about the time you spend with him. He has an agenda, Fin. I don't know what it is, but Kieran Sullivan isn't here to find redemption."

Finley knew just how wrong his friend was. Kieran had come to the ranch for redemption, but it was just a different kind. His secret wasn't hurting anyone, and Finley would rather lose a limb than betray Kieran like everyone else had. "You're wrong, Ivan. And if you can't believe me, then at least trust Cash."

The remark landed hard. There was no one Ivan liked or respected more than their boss. Finley saw his acquiescence in the big man's gaze first before the rest of him relaxed. Ivan lowered his arm, and it seemed like they stared at each other for an eternity until Owen yelled that it was Ivan's turn. The big man returned to the game without another word or a backward glance. He hated that his budding friendship with Kieran was a source of discord, but he wouldn't turn his back on his new friend to please his old one. Ivan was in the wrong, and Finley refused to back down. He retrieved the supplies and hurried to Kieran's cabin. He'd set one of the throw blankets on his bed and the cat had already curled up and was fast asleep. Finley set the litter box in a free corner and unpacked the contents.

Kieran pulled down two bowls from the cabinet. He filled one with water, then set them on the floor. "These will do until I can pick up dishes for her."

Finley pulled the tab on the cat food can, and Little Mama sprang right up. "Not too tired after all," he teased when she jumped down and pranced while he emptied half the can into the bowl. "Probably need to give her smaller meals more frequently until the vet can give us some guidance."

On Monday, Rebecca gave her a cursory exam in the barn and cautioned that Little Mama was teetering on the edge of malnourishment. She gave them advice on what to feed her and how often. The vet said the cat might have another month to go before her kittens arrived, but she might deliver them sooner. Finley scheduled a follow-up appointment at the vet's office when he picked up Little Mama's special food.

Finley and Kieran started spending more evenings in his cabin with Little Mama than training in the barn with Loretta and Dolly. It didn't take the kitty long to flourish under their care, and it took even less time for Finley to realize he was in deep trouble. They passed their evenings playing games, watching movies, and talking. On the surface, their conversations were frivolous and shallow, but Finley could learn a lot about a man based on his choice of music, movies, and preferred peanut butter brand. Their chats varied from a debate over which red licorice was superior, Red Vines versus Twizzlers, to a game Finley called Meal or Side Dish. One of them would call out a random food, and they'd debate if you could make a meal of it or if it was strictly a side dish. They'd seen eye to eye on most things but disagreed on cereal being a side dish.

"Hello, rice crispy treats," Finley said, which led to a discussion on whether dessert was a meal or a course. It was how everything flowed between them—easy and organic.

By the time the next Saturday rolled around, Finley felt like he knew Kieran better than he knew anyone else besides a blood relative, which made no sense. Most everything about Kieran's life before he'd arrived was still a mystery, but it didn't seem to matter. If that didn't raise huge red flags, nothing would, yet his internal warning system stayed quiet. The only waving flags were dream-induced erections inspired by Kieran, but Finley took care of those alone in the dark or in the shower.

On the night of the horse show, their chores and errands had taken longer than Finley had planned, leaving no time to rub one out before they left. He settled for ice-cold water to cool his ardor and hoped the chill lasted through the show and stakeout. He wrapped a towel around his waist, picked up his dirty clothes off the bathroom floor, and opened the door. Finley collided with a wall of muscle when he barreled into the hallway and staggered backward.

Ham-sized fists gently gripped his biceps to steady him. "Whoa there," Ivan said as he dropped Finley's arms. "Is there a fire?"

Aware of the towel wrapped precariously around his hips, Finley laughed nervously. "No. Just running late for the show."

"Oh." Ivan's voice was flat and disapproving. "I forgot about your date with Kieran."

Finley inhaled slowly and fought for patience. Tensions had amped up between him and Ivan ever since their last conversation about Kieran. After counting to eight, Finley slowly inhaled. "It's not a date, Ivan. I invited you to go to the horse show along with everyone else. There's still time to change your mind."

Ivan snorted and shook his head, a ghost of a smile tugging at his lips. "You invited us because you knew damn well we wouldn't go." He leaned closer and whiffed. "You only wear that body wash when you go on dates."

Finley snorted. "No, I just don't wear it when I'm working. You've teased me enough about wearing it during trips into town for lunch at the diner with you. Did you assume we were on dates?" He'd meant to make a flippant rebuttal, but the blush on Ivan's cheeks indicated Finley might've hit a little closer to home than either of them would like. "Of course you didn't," he continued, trying his best to dance his way out of an awkward situation. "Kieran is my friend—nothing more, nothing less. Now, if you'll excuse me, I'm running late."

Ivan shrugged, stepped to the side, and made a sweeping gesture with his arms. "By all means."

Finley made it to his room and shut the door before his towel fell off his hips and landed on the floor. Whew! Any sooner and things would've gotten really awkward, especially after suspecting Ivan's feelings could be more than platonic. He shook his head, unwilling to think about that or the ramifications. Finley and Kieran had an important mission to carry out, so he ran the plan through his head while getting ready. He'd debated his outfit choices before his shower and had landed on the olive-green shirt with mother-of-pearl snaps and his favorite faded jeans. He swapped out his boxer shorts for the pale blue jockstrap and refused to dwell on the reason for his last-minute decision. Finley dressed quickly, then grabbed his brown leather jacket, phone, wallet, and the keys to his personal truck before exiting his room. Finley stuffed his phone and wallet into his pockets and whistled his way toward the front door. He frequently sang, hummed, or whistled, so there shouldn't have been any raised brows or catcalls from the guys who came over for the weekly poker game, but there were.

Finley stopped at the door and looked over his shoulder. Everyone gathered around the table smiled at him except for Ivan, who wore an I-told-you-so smirk. "Not a date," Finley called out before turning the knob and wrenching the door open. For the second time in thirty minutes, he ran headlong into a man. Finley snapped his head up and met the dark gaze that heated his blood during the day and scorched his dreams at night. Kieran wore a burgundy button-up with a pair of dark jeans and boots. His shoulders looked broad and sexy beneath a sherpa-lined denim jacket he'd picked up during a return trip to the thrift store. "Hi," Finley said breathlessly.

Kieran's lips curved up but didn't quite form a smile when he raked his gaze over Finley. Obsidian eyes met his once more, approval sparkling in their depths. "In a hurry?" Kieran asked.

"As a matter of fact…" Finley smiled at him, hoping to entice a matching reaction…but not yet. It was just a matter of time, though. He was certain of it. "Are you ready?" The question was loaded, and Finley could tell by Kieran's determined expression that he understood.

"I've been ready."

Finley led Kieran to the truck he'd inherited from his grandfather. It was a late nineties model with a bench seat and an outdated stereo system, but he'd kept it in pristine condition. Finley had driven it from Tennessee when his family had made the move, and he kept the truck inside one of the equipment barns on the ranch. He and Kieran had discussed their plan backward and forward the past few days, and driving something that wouldn't lead back to the ranch was ideal. His silver work truck with a large logo would draw too much attention, but the black paint on his personal truck would be perfect to help them blend in during their clandestine adventure.

"Are you hungry? The Morrisons gave me Tiny Dancer's performance time, so we could swing through a drive-thru. Or would you prefer to grab something from concessions at the show?"

"What will they have at the arena?"

"Anything and everything," Finley replied. "Rows of food booths, stands, and trucks."

Kieran released a little groan, and Finley knew he'd hear the sound in his dreams. "I want that." Those words would make an appearance too, and he was looking forward to bedtime.

They feasted on smoked beef brisket, macaroni and cheese, baked beans, cornbread, and apple hand pies before making their way into the stands.

Kieran leaned over when they took their seats and said, "I might have to loosen a button." A button? Did that mean he wore button fly jeans? So freaking hot, but Finley didn't let his mind wander too far in the crowded arena.

The goal was to stick around long enough to watch Tiny Dancer perform, then meet the Morrisons at her trailer for a quick reunion before sneaking off for their stakeout. Tiny Dancer was smack dab in the middle of the lineup, which allowed plenty of time for anticipation to bubble, brew, and give Finley anxiety. At one point, Kieran reached over and settled his hand on his knee, bringing attention to his bouncing leg. They locked eyes for several moments and Finley found his center of calm once more and enjoyed the show. Finley and Kieran weren't confronting anyone; they were just going to take some pictures from a safe distance. They'd scoped out the area using satellite images from Google Maps and found the perfect spot to park and watch the warehouse for suspicious activity.

Finley expected Kieran to be too distracted by the stakeout to pay much attention to the performances, but he frequently leaned into Finley's space to comment on the various elements and point out the obvious directional cues. And then the announcer introduced Tiny Dancer and sixteen-year-old Addie Morrison to the crowd. Tears filled Finley's eyes as the horse trotted to the center of the arena, looking so proud.

"God, I love that horse," he said as Addie and Tiny Dancer performed the prescribed movements.

"It must be hard to let them go after you bond with them."

Finley looked over at Kieran and caught him watching him instead of the show. "Yeah, it really is, but then you get pictures or videos of the horses living their best lives, and you find joy in the role you played in their rehabilitation." Finley looked back at the arena. "It isn't often I get to see the horses in person once they leave the ranch, so I might blubber and make a fool of myself." He for sure would hug Tiny Dancer's neck.

"You won't get any judgment from me," Kieran said. "Look at the cat dad I've become."

Finley thought about the plush setup Little Mama had in Kieran's cabin. He'd bought her a fluffy bed, matching pink dishes, and a few catnip toys after ensuring they wouldn't be dangerous for an expectant mother. Kieran Sullivan was the best kind of people, even if he didn't know it yet. Finley understood that he wouldn't be the person who helped him realize his worth, but he hoped Kieran found that special someone after leaving the ranch. It would break his heart just like when the horses left him, but he hoped that one day he'd witness Kieran living his best life. He'd try really hard not to be bitter about what could've been, but he wouldn't make any promises.

Music filtered through the speaker system, and Finley laughed when he recognized "Hold Me Closer," the Elton John and Britney Spears remix of "Tiny Dancer." Finley often thought of the horse when he heard it and couldn't resist humming along and dancing a little in his seat.

Beside him, Kieran chuckle-snorted. Finley turned and caught his first genuine smile since arriving on the ranch, and it was a thing of beauty. And contagious. Finley grinned back, though he didn't know why. Then they both laughed, feeding off one another's energy.

"This was the song you were trying to sing on the day we met," Kieran said. "I couldn't place the lyrics until now."

Finley tilted his head to the side. "You're right, but I sang the hell out of that song."

"Screeched the hell out of it, did you say?"

Finley playfully pushed Kieran's shoulder before focusing on Tiny Dancer's performance again. The horse looked amazing, and Addie radiated love and joy for the horse she sat astride.

"She's a natural rider like you," Kieran said.

Finley met his gaze once more and the rest of the world faded away until the arena erupted in cheers and shouts for the duo when they finished. Finley gestured for Kieran to follow him once Addie rode Tiny Dancer out of the arena. Shelley Morrison had told him where they'd parked their trailer, so it was just a matter of walking there.

"These events are huge," Kieran said, taking in the rows of horse trailers, RVs, and pickup trucks.

"This is a small crowd compared to some of the other jumping shows and rodeos. Dressage is gaining in popularity in the US, though."

"It's beautiful," Kieran said, and his sincerity rang true in his words.

Addie squealed when she spotted Finley and launched herself at him. He swept her up in his arms and spun her around while her parents laughed.

"You two were amazing," Finley said when he set her down. He extended his hand to Ben and hugged Shelly, then introduced everyone to Kieran. "Thank you so much for letting me know you were in town. You don't know what this means to me."

Shelly tipped her head toward the arena stall where Tiny Dancer was eating a snack. "Go say hello to your girl. She'll be happy to see you."

Finley took a shaky breath as he felt a familiar sting in his nose. "Ignore the blubbering." Shelly smiled and squeezed his hand encouragingly. The horse lifted her head and knickered as Finley approached. "Hello, beautiful. Remember me?" She met him at the gate and nuzzled her head against his cheek. Finley wrapped his arms around her neck and leaned into her as hot tears fell. He loved all the horses that passed through Redemption Ranch, but some took a piece of his heart when they left him. Finley pulled back and wiped his tears.

The Morrisons joined them after a few moments and talked about her daily life. Tiny Dancer moseyed over to finish her snack while they talked about her. She contributed some noises once in a while to let them know she was listening. Finley gave her one more hug and scratched her ears before forcing himself away. The Morrisons promised to stay in touch and send him a full video of the performance. A sense of peace washed over Finley as he and Kieran made their way toward the parking lot.

"Do you know the only thing that could make this night better?" Finley asked when they reached his pickup truck. Kieran smiled at him for only the second time. The first grin was full of humor and joy, but the follow-up was sly and sexy. *Keep your mind out of the gutter.* "Someone is going down tonight," Finley vowed, only realizing how it sounded when Kieran's smile turned downright dirty. "I'm just going to shut up before I make a bigger fool of myself."

He turned to put the key in the door lock, but Kieran placed a hand on his arm to stop him. Kieran's expression was so warm and tender Finley thought for a moment he might kiss him, but Kieran pulled him into a tight hug instead. Heat unfurled low in Finley's belly as Kieran's warmth bled into him. Their embrace lasted longer than a platonic hug should, but Finley couldn't let himself hope.

"Never change a single thing about you. Promise me," Kieran demanded.

"I promise."

"Good." Kieran pulled back and placed a soft kiss on Finley's forehead before dropping his arms and walking around the hood of the truck.

Finley would've told himself to hold on to his heart, but he figured it was already a lost cause.

chapter

THIRTEEN

Ritchie's warehouse was in a commercial area that was quiet after dark, making it easier for them to avoid detection. Kieran had sketched the layout of the structure from memory. Then they used Google to pick the perfect spot to get eyes on the back of the building, where the garage doors were located. Tall fences topped with barbed wire surrounded all the storage facilities in the area. The only way in was through code-protected gates, and Ritchie's gate was at the front of his warehouse. They didn't need to see someone pull in through the gate; they wanted to see the cars pull into the warehouse.

From their vantage point behind a medical equipment supplier, Kieran scoped out Ritchie's building through binoculars while Finley adjusted the camera lens until he was happy. The only thing separating them was Finley's equipment bag on the bench seat between them. The only thing keeping him from reaching for Finley and drawing him near was the last shred of decency he clung to, but he was barely hanging on. They'd spent nearly every waking hour together over the past two weeks, and Kieran had never met anyone he admired more than Finley Ashe.

He was compassionate, intelligent, quick-witted, and competent in everything he did. Finley was the most gorgeous person he'd ever met—inside and out. No matter where Kieran landed after he left Redemption Ridge, he'd be a better man for knowing Finley, who'd filled his waking hours with sunshine and his dreams with sultry images. Kieran had nearly used all the Monkey Grease and was trying to figure out how to get more without letting on that he'd used the bottle meant for Finley. Resisting temptation had become especially hard when breathing in his woodsy, masculine scent in close quarters. It reminded him of pine trees and citrus groves and something that was uniquely Finley. It wasn't lost on Kieran that his attention had veered way off course the past few weeks, but he struggled to find remorse or the whim to steer it back.

His cohort reached over and nudged him. "You didn't hear a thing I said, did you? Already tired of my prattling?"

"Nah. I was just going over everything I remembered about the warehouse. There are two entrances besides the three garage doors at the back. You can see one entrance at the rear and the other is at the front. Ritchie never gave me the front entrance code, and I don't think he ever used it. I had numbers for the rear door and the gate."

"What are the chances the codes for the gate and back door are still the same?" Finley asked.

"Not likely, and we won't find out."

Finley chuckled and nudged him again. "I wasn't about to suggest we try. There are security cameras all around the building."

Kieran did a sweep with his binoculars and counted at least four cameras on the rectangular building. "What did I miss when I zoned out?"

"Oh," Finley said as if he'd already forgotten. "Do you think it's likely someone other than Ritchie is pulling the strings?"

Kieran worked to keep his breathing steady. "I do actually."

He wouldn't confess to suspecting Cash, the man Finley admired more than any other. Hell, even Kieran struggled to believe it after his brief time living on the ranch. He'd suspected the operation was a way to groom men for Cash's and Ritchie's illegal operations, but he'd found no proof of that. Then again, he'd spent all his free time with Finley when he should have been trying to find a way into Cash's home office.

The rancher seemed sincere and invested in how Kieran was getting by, but he wouldn't be the first or last man to hide a sinister soul behind a handsome face and kind countenance. If Kieran was right, bringing Cash down would have serious repercussions for the good people who depended on him. They'd all turn on Kieran, but he couldn't let that sway him.

"Any idea who?" Finley asked, breaking into his thoughts.

"Not really. I'm not even sure how I'll figure it out yet. I guess we start by seeing who is delivering the vehicles to the warehouse and document the vehicles moving in and out of storage."

They went back to scoping out their surroundings in quiet, but the conversation didn't lull for long.

"Macaroni and cheese," Finley said a few minutes later.

Kieran smiled but kept his gaze trained at the end of the building, where visitors would first appear as they drove around. "Side dish."

"You have no imagination," Finley replied.

Kieran snorted. If Finley knew the things he fantasized about, he would take that back. Kieran had imagined taking him in every position and in every location on the ranch. "How do you figure macaroni and cheese as a meal? Just because you can make yourself sick on it doesn't make it a main course."

"Haven't you ever heard of lobster macaroni and cheese? Chicken, bacon, ranch macaroni and cheese? Buffalo chicken macaroni and cheese? Pulled pork macaroni and cheese? If it combines meat and macaroni, it's a main course."

Kieran lowered the binoculars and looked at him, but Finley kept the camera trained on the building. "You didn't specify any of those types of macaroni and cheese, or I would have said they were a meal. I win by default."

Finley smiled, teeth flashing white in the dark truck cab. "It's not a contest."

"I've been keeping score," Kieran admitted.

Finley peeked away from the viewfinder for a moment before looking back through it. "Who's on top?"

Kieran swallowed hard. The other man could make everything sound dirty. "We're tied after the macaroni misfire."

Finley darted a glance at him. "I assure you I never misfire, but I'm willing to hear the arguments you think I lost." Before Kieran could respond, Finley held up a hand. "I think we've got movement."

Kieran looked back through the binoculars. The corner of the building was lit up brighter than it had been just a few seconds ago. The flood light on the corner had turned on. "Those are the motion-sensor security lights I told you about. Ritchie always said they seemed like overkill with the barbed-wire fence and coded gate. Since he leased the building, he wasn't able to make modifications. Now I know why he didn't like them. Those security lights shine right on his illicit activities for anyone watching. Until now, no one took a closer look at what was going on at the warehouse."

A moment later, a Mercedes SUV eased around the corner of the building and stopped outside the first garage bay. Finley's camera clicked and whirred as he took several images of the vehicle.

"I got the license plate," Finley said. "Windows are tinted, so I couldn't get a shot of the driver as he came around the side of the building."

"You'll get your chance," Kieran assured him. "Those big garage doors aren't connected to automatic openers. Ritchie had wanted to install them and even offered to pay for the upgrades himself, but no dice. I guess Ritchie could've convinced the landlord since then, but I doubt it." A moment later, the driver's side door opened. "Here we go."

"Ready," Finley said, his voice so breathless Kieran nearly lost sight of his aim. But then the driver slid out from behind the wheel. Rapid clicking filled the truck bed as Finley captured the driver standing by the car and looking around him as if he sensed someone was watching. "It's the same guy we saw him with in Last Chance Creek."

Kieran thought the same but wanted a better look. He got it when the man triggered additional security lighting as he strode toward the door. "Definitely the same man."

"And I sure as hell don't need night-vision lenses with those lights on," Finley said as he made quick adjustments to the camera. "Damn, they've lit the place up like a football field."

"Or a prison yard when an inmate makes a run for it."

Finley fumbled and dropped the lens and it rolled into Kieran's footwell. "Oops. I didn't expect you to make jail jokes." Finley placed his hand on Kieran's thigh and leaned forward to retrieve the lens, but Kieran stopped him. He couldn't afford to have Finley's head anywhere near his crotch.

Leaning forward, Kieran retrieved the lens and handed it to Finley. The air surrounding them crackled with electricity when their hands brushed against each other. "I'm learning that I still have a sense of humor. Sometimes poking fun at something gives it less control over you."

Finley snapped the lens into place and captured Ritchie's boyfriend entering the code at the rear door and letting himself inside. "Good to know. I'll use that strategy next time instead of putting myself on a no-sex diet." Kieran nearly choked on his saliva but passed it off as a throat tickle, or at least he hoped he did. Unaware of Kieran's struggle, Finley added, "I'd have better luck giving up carbs, and you've seen firsthand how I can mow my way through bread, potatoes, and sweets."

Was Finley currently on a no-sex diet? Had he recently ended one? But with who? It wasn't really any of Kieran's business, but they'd spent so much time together. How had he found an opportunity? Did he make a detour after leaving Kieran's cabin? Finley shared the house with the burly foreman and Dylan. Hooking up with one of them would be pretty damn convenient and discreet. But Dylan was as straight as a man could get and head over heels in love with Harry. Was it Ivan? Is that why the foreman still glared at him? Kieran thought about the interactions between Finley and Ivan and couldn't recall a single spark of attraction, at least not from Finley's end. Ivan was another story. Were the two of them hooking up?

Finley's soft chuckle interrupted his spinning thoughts. "Breathe, Kieran. And stop thinking so hard. I'm not involved with anyone right now unless you count my right hand and my dildo. They've both seen a ton of action."

"Oh god," Kieran said as torrid images flooded his mind, heating his blood and sending it south.

"Yeah, I've been moaning that into my pillow a lot lately." If he didn't stop talking about getting himself off, Kieran was going to come in his underwear. "Oh, heads up. Another car just arrived."

Kieran resentfully slammed the door on his fantasies, but he'd take those babies out later when he was alone. He recognized the BMW sedan right away. "That's Ritchie's car. He's probably there to give his boyfriend a ride. Sometimes I would drive one vehicle over and take another back to the shop when it was due for pickup. Other times, Ritchie would follow so we could go home afterward."

"Home? You lived together?" Finley asked.

"Not technically," Kieran replied as Ritchie parked his sedan next to the Mercedes. "We'd dated for a year, and most of my stuff was at his place. I thought living together was the next logical step, but Ritchie got squirrelly every time I brought it up, even though he got mad when I stayed at my place. He accused me of throwing a fit because I didn't get my way. Ritchie did this push-pull thing that made me feel like I was crazy. He'd hurt me, and I'd end up being the one who apologized."

"Gaslighting 101," Finley said softly. "He won't be able to bullshit his way out of trouble when we get done with him." Kieran loved the vehemence in his voice. Finley made him believe, which was something he thought was no longer possible. "So Ritchie had all your stuff while you were in jail?"

Kieran shrugged. "I didn't have much. I learned at a very early age to travel light, and those habits transitioned to adulthood. He could've easily tossed my shit in a trash bag and fully erased me from his life. My name wasn't on any documents connected to the apartment. Not the lease, not the bills, nothing. I hadn't even updated the address on my ID yet. That's how he could get away with claiming not to know me."

"Why did you have to travel light? Were one of your parents in the military?"

Kieran snorted to cover up his anxiousness. They were veering into uncomfortable territory, but Finley had made himself vulnerable for Kieran. Then again, their confessions were drastically different. Finley's disclosures were arousing, while Kieran's revelations would extinguish the desire between them as quickly as it had arrived. Then again, maybe that was for the best. "No one wanted to keep me long enough for me to accumulate much."

Finley's breath hitched, and he reached over to squeeze Kieran's hand. "This is why I prefer animals." The forcefulness in Finley's voice contradicted the gentleness in his touch. "Present company excluded." He gave Kieran one more squeeze before releasing him. "Ritchie's windows are tinted too, but they're not as dark as the Mercedes. It looks like there are two people inside."

Kieran adjusted his binoculars and peered through the rear windshield. "You're right. Maybe it's the person calling the shots."

A few minutes passed by without the boyfriend exiting the warehouse. The driver's side door on the BMW opened and Ritchie stepped out. Finley went to town with his camera. He could become a paparazzo if the horse training gig didn't pan out. Ritchie bent down and spoke to the person inside his car, and they pushed their door open too. Kieran didn't recognize the silhouette when the passenger stepped out of the car and into the shadows. *Click. Click. Click.* He could only tell it was a tall man with linebacker shoulders. When the mystery man stepped into the light, Kieran noted a square jaw, flat nose, and a dark buzz cut. *Click. Click. Click.*

"Whoa," Finley said. "Dude's nose looks like he went several rounds with a heavyweight boxer." The warehouse door opened, and the boyfriend reappeared. "Probably worried Ritchie was up to no good with Brick House," Finley said. *Click. Click.* "You recognize the bruiser?"

"Nope."

They fell quiet, Kieran watching the tableau play out through the binoculars as Finley captured every second. The boyfriend looked more annoyed than pissed. He called out something to the other two as they approached. "Too bad I can't read lips," Kieran said.

Click. Click. Click. "He said, 'It's about damn time. I thought you changed your mind.'"

Kieran looked over at Finley, who hadn't taken his eyes off the scene. "Seriously? You read lips too? Is there anything you can't do?" Finley shrugged, so Kieran looked through the binoculars in time to see the three men enter the warehouse.

"Now what?" Finley asked.

"We wait and see if anyone else shows up. If not, we document what they drive off in."

Finley lowered the camera to his lap and narrowed his eyes. "We need to figure out who the other two men are in the trio and learn everything we can about them. Hopefully we'll uncover some leverage we can exploit."

Kieran's mouth fell open in shock. "Like blackmail?"

"Whatever it takes," Finley replied. "I say we follow Brick House if he drives off in a second vehicle." Before Kieran could respond, Finley's eyes widened. "Shit! We've been made."

Kieran looked out his window and saw nothing, but then he noticed an orb of light bouncing in the truck's side mirror. "Must be a security guard." The bouncing increased and drew closer. "They probably already have your license number, so speeding away won't do us any good."

Finley stashed his camera in the green military bag with PFC Finnigan Donovan stamped on the fabric, then he hoisted it onto his lap. Since the truck was a single cab, there was no place to stash the bag. The guard would want to know what was in it and would call the cops if they didn't comply. Finley glanced in the side mirror again and said, "We don't have much time. Scoot over to the middle of the bench seat."

"What? Why?"

"Just do it," he said calmly. "We need to distract this person from wanting to learn more about what we're up to in here."

Kieran scooted over, still not sure what was going on until Finley set the duffel in his vacated footwell and straddled Kieran's thighs. "This again?" he teased. "You better really sell it."

Finley cupped the back of his neck and pressed a hard kiss against his mouth. Kieran gasped and dropped his hands to Finley's hips. He hauled him closer and parted his lips, inviting Finley to deepen the kiss, and the blond fireball in his arms didn't disappoint. Finley slid one hand into Kieran's hair, pulled his head back, and slid his tongue into Kieran's mouth.

They groaned together, and Finley thrust his hips forward, grinding his pelvis against Kieran's. Was this part of the decoy, or was Finley finally giving in to the sexual tension that had been building between them since they'd met? Both of them were hard as steel, and Kieran was losing his ability to think objectively. He slid his hands lower to cup Finley's ass, wishing they were naked so he could part those round globes and finger the pucker nestled between them. Finley grunted and frotted faster, applying the perfect amount of pressure that would have Kieran coming in his pants. He growled and moved his right hand to trace the seam in the center of Finley's jeans.

Finley lifted his head to cry out, and Kieran went to work on his neck, licking and biting a trail back to his hungry mouth. Finley sucked his tongue and fireworks exploded behind Kieran's eyelids.

He realized the moment the flashlight was aimed at them, but he didn't let up. Finley thrust harder and Kieran held him tighter. They kept at it until the guard tapped their flashlight against the window. Finley and Kieran faked their surprise and pulled apart like two teenagers caught by their parents. The guard looked to be in his late fifties, and a disgusted sneer pulled at his lips as he stared at them.

"You can't be doing that shit here," he yelled through the glass, not bothering to ask them to roll down their window. "Get out of here before I call the cops and have you arrested for lewd behavior."

Finley quickly situated himself behind the wheel, shifted the truck into drive, and sped away. Once they drove around the building and reached the exit, he snapped on his seat belt. He looked at Kieran, who still sat in the middle. "Buckle up."

Instead of moving back to his original seat, Kieran stayed there and used the lap belt.

"That was close," Finley said breathlessly when he turned onto the street and drove away. "Should I apologize?"

Kieran turned his head and smiled at Finley. "Because the guard caught us or because we didn't get to finish what we started?"

Finley's breaths came fast. He glanced over and smiled but didn't answer. At least not with words, but he turned the truck into the parking lot of Dexter's Roadside Motel not two minutes later. Most of the lights were out in the sign, but it was lit up enough for Kieran to see rooms went for sixty-nine dollars per night. Doubtful the price was a coincidence. Finley put the truck in park and closed his eyes.

"Well then," Kieran said huskily.

Finley's eyes snapped open and met his gaze. "What?" Kieran waggled his brows, and Finley looked around them. "Oh no. I wasn't...I didn't mean..."

Kieran tsked and shook his head. "That's too bad. I'd give every dollar I have for one night of kissing you." Finley sucked in a sharp breath. Kieran saw his pupils dilate even in the dimly lit parking lot. "This wouldn't be my first choice of a place to lay you down, but when in Rome or at"—Kieran reread the blinking neon sign—"Dexter's Roadside Motel."

Finley fumbled his seat belt free and pushed his door open. "Kissing sounds great, but I'm not leaving this dive until you bury your monster cock in my ass." He exited the truck, slammed the door, and jogged toward the motel office before Kieran could respond.

Alone with his thoughts, Kieran had enough time to think things through and talk himself out of going into a motel room with Finley. That isn't where his mind went, though. He was too busy thinking how this and everything to do with Finley felt right. And for the first time in his life, Kieran had to acknowledge that the emotional connection between him and Finley fueled the physical attraction, not the other way around like he'd experienced with past lovers. Of course he'd noted Finley's gorgeous attributes. Hell, he could barely tear his eyes off the man's ass until he stepped inside the building and he had no other choice.

Finley's looks weren't the reason he'd stopped thinking about life after the ranch. They weren't the reason he pulled Finley into one silly conversation after another. Kieran loved listening to him talk and discovering the quirky way his mind worked. He loved how Finley never pushed to know more about him, even though curiosity shimmered in his green gaze. The acceptance made Kieran want to divulge...everything, something that had never happened until he'd met Finley. And if he were honest with himself, Kieran had to admit to being more than halfway in love with his boss. If he conceded that, he'd have to acknowledge what he'd give up when he walked away from the ranch.

Reasons for why this was a bad idea flooded his brain, threatening to drown him, until Finley pushed open the office door and strode purposefully to the truck. Kieran shut down any part of his brain that wasn't committed to making Finley Ashe come harder than he ever had before. He unbuckled his seat belt and exited the truck, meeting Finley at the hood.

The gorgeous blond lifted his hand to show a plastic keychain dangling from his forefinger. Kieran cupped the back of his neck and pulled him forward for a hot, hungry kiss, not easing up until Finley whimpered so prettily in the back of his throat.

Kieran rested his forehead against Finley's and closed his eyes. "That sounded even sexier in person than in my fantasies." Finley's breath hitched, and Kieran reopened his eyes. "It's true. I've tried to stop wanting you and even thought I could rub you out of my system, but…" He took a fortifying breath, still in disbelief that he was spilling all his secrets. "I only want you more."

Finley wrapped both arms around Kieran's neck and smiled up at him. "That makes me feel so much better. I was feeling guilty about all the times I rode my dildo while wishing it was you." He stepped closer until they touched from head to foot. "Remember those times you asked if I was sore?"

Hell yes, he recalled the hitch in Finley's step and the soft grunts that escaped now and then. Kieran opened his mouth to speak, but no words tumbled forth, so he nodded.

"I wore my ass out thinking about you, coming so hard I nearly blacked out."

Finding his voice, Kieran said, "You're the only person to make me come for almost two years."

Finley gasped, stepped back, and grabbed his hand. "Let's go. I don't want to wait another minute."

Their eagerness faltered once they stepped inside the motel room and got an eyeful and a whiff of Dexter's accommodations. It smelled like stale beer, greasy food, and three dozen ashtrays overflowing with cigarette butts. It was hard to tell what color the walls, carpet, and bedspreads used to be under the decades of dirt and neglect. A series of flamingo paintings hung on the wall, making Kieran think the décor might've matched. The motif would work in Florida, but Colorado?

"Oh god," Finley said, his horror mirrored in his voice and expression.

"I've stayed in worse places," Kieran said. "I mean, at least there isn't a steel toilet in the center of the room."

Finley snorted and met his gaze. "Was that more jailhouse humor?"

"Trying to soften the disappointment. Are you willing to ignore the stench and the unsightly décor so I can plow your ass like you so eloquently requested, or should we find someplace else?"

Finley faced him. "And risk you changing your mind? Hell no." He walked forward and yanked the bedding off the mattress, revealing some sketchy stains. "Not ideal, but you can bend me over and—"

Kieran cut him off with a hard kiss. Lust burst inside him like a flashbang grenade and fog filled his brain, blocking out everything but the man in front of him. Their hands went into action, fingers once nimble now stumbling to release pearl snaps, belt buckles, and buttons. Their mouths separated long enough to kiss or nuzzle the newly released skin until they were down to Kieran's briefs and Finley's fucking blue jockstrap.

Kieran slid his hand over one taut ass cheek. "Planning to ride, were you?"

Finley's scorching gaze threatened to burn him up alive. "A man could hope." He reached forward and pumped Kieran's cock through his briefs. "Need this in me." Kieran's eyes drooped to half-mast when Finley slid a finger beneath the elastic band and traced the length of his shaft, producing a body-racking shiver. He pulled his hand free and licked Kieran's precum off his fingers. "Need it now." Finley bent over and retrieved his wallet from his jeans, putting that delicious bubble butt on display. He removed a condom and lube packet and tossed them on the bed.

Kieran dropped to his knees behind him and shoved his face between his ass cheeks. Finley cried out and bucked forward, grabbing onto the bed frame for support.

"Fuck," he called out when Kieran swirled his tongue over his quivering pucker and sucked it. Finley didn't just stand there and take it. He reached behind him and gripped Kieran's hair, then widened his stance to give him better access. "Christ, I hadn't let my mind go here." Kieran wiggled his tongue against Finley's opening, and Finley released the longest, loudest, and sluttiest moan he'd ever heard. "Get in their deeper. Fuck me with your tongue."

Kieran pulled back and spit on his crinkled entrance, using his saliva to work his tongue inside the tight rim, twisting and turning to make all his nerve endings sing. Gripping Finley's hips, Kieran worked his tongue in and out until Finley's lustful cries turned into needy whimpers. He ghosted his hands over Finley's thick thighs, loving the way his muscles bunched and trembled. Kieran pulled his tongue free and paid equal attention to Finley's taint and firm balls before urging him to stand up straight. "Give me that dick," he commanded.

"That's my line." Finley's voice held a sweet pout, but he complied immediately, putting his drooling dick at eye level.

Kieran rested his ass on his heels and licked a slow path from root to tip, swirling his tongue to catch the trail of precum around the engorged head, then wiggled the tip of his tongue against the slit. "Mmmm. You taste so damn good."

"Then get to sucking." Finley fisted his hair and guided Kieran's mouth down his shaft. The little minx liked to seize control, something Kieran hadn't imagined but loved.

Kieran worked his shaft up and down, changing pressure and angles to build him to the edge and back him off before he fell over it. When Finley's entire body thrummed in frustration to match his growls, Kieran rose to his feet and devoured Finley's mouth with a combination of passion and tenderness he never knew existed. Finley kissed a path down his body, but Kieran halted him with a firm hand on his nape.

"I'm too far gone, and you wanted my dick in your ass," Kieran reminded him.

Finley grabbed the condom and lube packets he'd dropped onto the mattress and handed them to him. Then he turned around and bent over, bracing his hands on the cleanest spots on the mattress. Kieran shoved his underwear down his legs, tore open the condom, and rolled it on. Just that slight friction was enough to make his balls draw tight. He squirted a tiny amount of lube on the latex and only worked his hand up and down enough to coat it thoroughly. Then he squeezed the rest onto his fingers, rubbing them together to coat them well, and slid his middle finger knuckle-deep in Finley's ass.

"Yessss," the sexy blond groaned, pushing back and fucking himself. "Give me more."

Kieran bit his right cheek hard enough to make him gasp, then gave him the two fingers he wanted. He worked them in and out until Finley's first ring of muscle relaxed a little. Kieran pulled out of him, then lined his cock up against Finley's pucker.

"Balls deep. Let's go."

Kieran placed one hand on Finley's shoulder, the other on his hip, and impaled him balls deep in a single thrust, hard enough to drive him up onto his tiptoes. Finley's cries of ecstasy were loud enough to rattle the walls.

"Again!" he shouted.

The walls rattled again, and Kieran realized the people in the next room were pounding on the wall to shut them up. Fuck them. He eased back and slammed into Finley, eliciting another exultant shout for Kieran to fuck him harder, faster, and longer.

"Never stop," Finley begged.

A blush spread up his back, and Finley's skin felt fevered wherever Kieran touched him. His pleading became incoherent when Finley reached down and started jerking himself off as Kieran plowed into him.

He leaned over Finley's back and whispered, "Come for me now." Then Kieran sank his teeth into his neck.

Finley's body stiffened, and his breath caught in his throat. His asshole clamped down tight on Kieran's cock, and the air in his lungs escaped in short bursts as he jerked in Kieran's embrace. The scent of Finley's release teased his senses, and he slammed home a few more times. Kieran's climax slammed into him, seizing the air from his lungs and muscles, then setting him adrift in a euphoric freefall as he flooded the condom. He remained bent over Finley, fighting off an urge to cry because that hadn't just been sex; it was something transformative.

Finley eased free, stood, and wrapped his arms around Kieran. They kissed and panted until the last tremors left their bodies. No one had ever felt so good in his arms, no coupling so right. Finley broke off their kiss and leaned his head against Kieran's collarbone. "There's so much more I want to do with you, but this place is so gross."

Kieran tangled his hands in Finley's hair and tugged until their gazes locked. "We're consenting adults who know the score. I have a cabin with four walls, a roof, and a door that locks. This doesn't have to be the end." A little alarm went off in his head that he was sending mixed signals. The closer they got, the harder it would be to say goodbye. He'd be another loser to hurt Finley. But his cooler head didn't prevail when he said, "You'll need to be a little quieter, though."

"Got that right," a man shouted from the other side of the wall.

Finley buried his head against Kieran's neck and laughed until his body shook. Then he pulled back and gave Kieran the most beautiful smile he'd ever seen. "Deal."

They sealed their pact with a series of kisses that alternated between sweet and hungry. Kieran reluctantly pulled back and said, "I better get Cinderella back to the ranch before midnight."

Finley snorted but reached for his clothes. They cleaned up with a wet washcloth because Kieran was convinced the disgusting shower had been a crime scene at some point.

"I take it back," he said when they stepped onto the sidewalk in front of the room. "Even jail was cleaner."

Finley laughed as he leaned into him. Kieran wrapped his arm around Finley's shoulders and pulled him flush against his body. He couldn't remember a time when he'd ever felt so happy, but that all shattered when they arrived at the truck, and he noticed the door was unlocked and someone had taken the camera equipment.

"No, no, no, no," he groaned.

They'd been too focused on fucking to secure the vehicle properly. No, that was on him. He'd been the last one in the truck, and he was the one who'd let Finley down. Bad things happened when good people like Finley got tangled up with guys like him.

chapter
FOURTEEN

FINLEY OPENED UP THE DRIVER'S SIDE DOOR, AND HIS STOMACH rolled when he realized the source of anguish in Kieran's voice. His duffel bag with his grandfather's equipment and the potential evidence against Ritchie's operation was gone. Then his heart plummeted when he recalled the other photos on the memory card. He'd captured dozens of images of Kieran astride Loretta in the arena to hone his skills with the equipment.

"Fuck!" Kieran shouted, his voice echoing off the pavement. "I'm so sorry."

Finley snapped his head up and met Kieran's desolate gaze. As sorry as he was about the missing equipment and photos, he had a bigger fire to extinguish. Kieran was clearly blaming himself, and that just wasn't fair. The progress they'd made and the promise of sexy nights in the cabin were in jeopardy if he didn't act fast. "This isn't your fault." Kieran's tormented expression didn't change, and Finley couldn't be sure Kieran had even heard him. He closed the door, rounded the front of the truck, and gripped the taller man's biceps. Finley shook him and Kieran blinked a few times, but his regret remained.

"I'm so sorry," he whispered. "I know how much that equipment meant to you, and I shouldn't have been so reckless."

"This isn't your fault, Kieran."

"I was the last one in the truck. It would've taken seconds to secure the vehicle, but I was in too much of a hurry."

To claim me. Finley could never regret what they'd shared, not even after this setback. If he didn't get Kieran to come around to see his side of things, he'd never get a chance to experience that passion again. Even worse, Finley couldn't allow Kieran to add another thing to his overburdened soul, so his brain went into damage control mode.

"Hear me when I say this," he said, both his words and grip resolute. "The thief wouldn't have hesitated to bash out a window to steal the equipment, so locking the door wouldn't have mattered. That gear belonged to me, and it was ultimately my responsibility to secure it." Truthfully, it was a miracle he hadn't left his keys in the ignition too. "I will get my stuff back." That earned a quirked brow at least. "They're going to take it to a pawnshop, and I will buy it back."

"They'll remove the memory card before pawning it."

Finley had already thought of that and had a solution at the ready. "We'll take more pictures. This changes nothing."

Kieran's dour expression said it changed everything. "Not we," he replied. "I'm not involving you in my stupid scheme anymore."

Finley wanted to argue with him, but he could tell by the firm set of Kieran's jaw that he'd just be wasting his time. He had to focus on what he could do instead of beating his head against Kieran's brick wall. Finley hadn't managed to knock it down or even scale it, but he'd managed to knock a brick or two loose. He could almost hear the splatter of the mortar and the scraping of the trowel as Kieran built the wall taller and thicker. "It's probably a waste of time, but I'm going to talk to the motel clerk to see if there are security cameras on the parking lot. Then we'll head back to the ranch."

Kieran narrowed his eyes like he was going to protest but nodded. Finley was reluctant to release his biceps, fearing he would bolt like a skittish horse, but they couldn't stand there all night. He'd just have to trust himself to reach the place where Kieran had retreated to lick his wounds.

The clerk didn't look up from his computer when Finley entered the office again, and he only responded to his question with a snort and head shake. Their first encounter hadn't been much livelier, but Finley had been too eager to get naked with Kieran to care. He left the cramped space as quickly as he'd arrived and headed toward the truck. His heart faltered when Kieran wasn't standing by the vehicle, but he breathed a little easier when he made out his shape through the windshield.

"No luck," Finley said when he climbed into the cab, "but I didn't expect much."

Kieran's countenance was even stonier and his posture more rigid than the first day they'd met. The man in his passenger seat was a stranger again, and he bit back a heavy sigh. It would be a battle of wills, but Finley believed he'd come out on top. He had to. They rode back to the ranch without uttering a word. Finley played the radio softly because complete silence would've driven him mad. But he made a last-ditch effort when he parked his truck and killed the engine.

"I figure they'll fence the equipment fast. Do you want to check out the pawn shops and grab lunch after morning chores?"

"No," Kieran said. Then he opened the door and shoved out of the truck without explaining his answer. Finley watched him disappear into the shadows with a sinking heart.

His misery deepened when Kieran didn't show up for breakfast the following morning. Finley kept his head down and focused on eating to avoid the sympathetic looks everyone tossed his way. Well, everyone except Ivan, who looked too damn smug for Finley's liking. His nerves got the best of him, and he pushed back from the table without finishing his breakfast. The rare occurrence didn't go unnoticed either.

"Whoa," Rueben said before he got very far. "I'll take those sausages and pancakes."

Finley extended his plate and let Rueben take what he wanted before rinsing his dishes and placing them in the dishwasher. His thoughts tangled and spun in his brain like a thorny tumbleweed. He wasn't sure which emotion to latch on to until he reached the barn and found

Kieran mucking out the stalls. Indignant fury won out over hurt and dismay. At least he could do something productive with that one; the others just caused him to mope around like a sad sack. Tyler and Owen had kitchen duty once they finished eating, so it would be just the two of them for a while.

"Assigned yourself the shit jobs as penance?" Finley asked. He tried to keep the anger from his voice, but Kieran stiffened before turning his head and meeting Finley's gaze. He fought back a sob and the urge to throw something when he couldn't find a trace of the man he was falling for in the stranger looking at him. "So this is how it's going to be, huh?" Kieran didn't respond or even blink. "Carry on then."

Finley retreated to his office and slammed the door hard enough to make the hinges rattle. He tangled both hands in his hair and pulled to keep from screaming, then paced the length of the small room. Fuck, he was good and pissed. It took several minutes for him to wind down enough to realize their friendship wasn't meant to be if a minor setback could cause this much damage. He closed his eyes, exhaled slowly, and adjusted his thinking. Kieran's anguish was more important than his hurt feelings and pride. If Finley gave up, he'd never see another one of Kieran's beautiful smiles, and that would suck. But if Finley failed to deliver on the promise he'd made to Kieran, that would be a tragedy. He would not let Kieran down.

Calmer, he opened his door and sat at his desk to work on the schedule for the day. He hung the clipboard on the wall for the crew to find and retrieved his rake and shovel. Kieran stiffened when Finley opened the stall beside him and started cleaning. Finley's new tactic was to pretend the past few weeks hadn't happened. They were back to square one. Finley started singing as he worked and thought he caught a faint chuckle during one particularly off-key note. Kieran's demeanor had softened a little by the time they finished cleaning all the stalls, but he didn't instigate conversation. He returned to the dining room with everyone else at lunch but didn't interact with the crew. They accepted the change just as Finley had and went about their business.

He compiled a list of pawn shops between the ranch and Denver. Finley was shocked by the sheer volume but was determined to check them all. He could've enlisted help to divide and conquer, but it would've required an explanation, and he didn't want to betray Kieran's confidence. So he hit up a few each night after dinner.

Things improved a little over the following week. Kieran rejoined the crew for meals and the two of them were polite when working together. On the occasions that they physically bumped into one another, their eyes met and held. Electricity charged the air, but Finley didn't tear down a single brick in the wall. Instead of hanging out with Kieran in the evenings, Finley spent his free time checking out the pawn shops in and around Colorado Springs, working his way closer to Denver as he went. He kept hoping that finding the camera would blast a crater in Kieran's resistance, but he kept striking out.

Finley planned a trip to Denver for the following Saturday and recruited Harry to help. He'd told her about the stolen equipment but said it happened when they stopped for a bite to eat after the horse show. "I've searched all the local pawnshops but haven't found the gear."

"What a crappy ending for a date," Harry said.

"Not you too. You're sounding like Ivan."

Harry giggled. "Because he cares about you." She paused, then added. "You could do a lot worse than Ivan. He's so handsome, hard-working, and—"

"A dear friend," Finley supplied.

"Love can develop from friendship. I've heard it's the best kind."

Finley rolled his eyes. "I don't want to talk about Ivan or Kieran."

"Of course you don't."

"I want to talk about Dylan."

Harry groaned. "Don't start this again. He's too young for me."

"Ten years isn't much of an age gap," Finley argued. "You're just not willing to take risks."

"Why should I when you take enough risks for both of us?" she countered.

"Ouch." Finley rubbed at a spot above his heart.

Harry leaned over and rested her head on his shoulder. "I'm sorry. That was mean."

"But honest."

She knew what their grandpa's camera meant to Finley and happily agreed to help if he could get her back in time for her mani-pedi appointment in Last Chance Creek. She had another girls' night out that evening and apparently pretty nails were important. They set out early because there were several pawn shops in Denver and the surrounding area. He'd felt hopeful during the ninety-minute ride to the big city but dejected on their way back to the ranch still empty-handed. Harry had let him stew in his thoughts while she read a book, which only reminded him of Kieran.

A pang of longing gripped his heart and squeezed until he wanted to howl. He missed the physical dynamic that they'd barely started to explore, but Finley craved their quirky conversations, quiet evenings, and the little pack they'd formed. But if he were objective, Finley had to consider he might've fallen into his old pattern of making something more than it was because his heart desired it.

He had two options: move on or try to work out the issue with Kieran and make the most of the time they had left. One path was logical and the other fanciful, yet there was no doubt about the route he'd choose. He didn't want to live with any regrets when Kieran left the ranch, so he wouldn't wave a white flag.

When they neared Last Chance Creek, Harry suggested they meet their mother at the diner for a bite to eat before the ladies indulged in their pedicures. Finley had eaten little for breakfast, so he was more than ready to sink his teeth into something delicious. Hope was already at the diner, and she wasn't alone. A dark-haired man sat beside her in the same booth he and Kieran had used on the night of the art festival. His mother laughed at something the stranger said, and Finley had a sinking feeling he knew the handsome man's identity.

He stopped inside the door and rounded on Harry. "You guys set me up."

Harry patted his cheek and smiled sweetly. "I'm calling it an intervention. I can't watch you break your own heart again." Finley had been on the verge of walking out of the café, but Harry's pleading gaze softened his resolve.

"Fine, but I will get even."

Harry hooked her arm through Finley's and led him toward the booth. Hope saw them first and waved. The mystery man looked in their direction, and his warm brown eyes widened when they landed on Finley. He looked to be roughly the same age and was undoubtedly handsome. Finley forced himself to relax and decided to let nature take its course. Harry gestured for him to slide in first so he'd be across from Michael, but he knew she just wanted to box him in so he couldn't bolt.

Finley slid into the booth and smiled through introductions. Michael reached across the table and Finley shook his hand. No spark or shiver of awareness followed. Suddenly unsure of what to say or where to put his hands, he reached for a menu, even though he'd memorized it long ago.

Merri arrived to take their drink order, but Hope held up her hand. "I just remembered I need to meet a client for a private yoga session." She grimaced like a seasoned actress and rose to her feet. "I forgot about our pedicure appointments. Do you think they can bump us back a little?"

Harry stood up too. "I'll go find out. Excuse us for cutting out on you."

Michael smiled up at them. "No problem," he said while Finley shook his head. Once they were alone, Michael laughed and added, "Not real subtle, are they?"

Finley laughed. "Nope. But I think they mean well."

Michael's brown eyes twinkled. "I'm definitely not sorry for an opportunity to get to know you better." His smile was beautiful, but it didn't give Finley butterflies in his stomach.

"Likewise." *I can always use another friend.*

Could it develop into something special like Harry had said? He didn't think so, and a part of him just couldn't give up on Kieran yet. Honesty and a free lunch were the only things he could offer. Michael took it well and even delighted Finley with a wonderful sense of humor. It felt good to laugh, and Michael must've fed off his energy because he kept it rolling throughout lunch. Midway through their burger and fries, someone tapped on the window beside them. Finley turned his head and saw Rueben smiling and waving at him. Then he shifted his gaze to the right and locked eyes with Kieran. Finley found it hard to breathe as they stared at each other for several moments. Kieran shifted his gaze to Michael, then back to Finley before he turned and walked away, leaving Rueben to scramble after him.

"Do you need to leave?" Michael asked when Finley continued to stare at the empty sidewalk.

Finley's knee-jerk reaction was to slap some bills on the table to cover lunch and chase after Kieran, but he squelched the notion. He'd done nothing wrong. Finley decided to finish lunch, make a new friend, and seek Kieran out after he cooled off.

"Nope," Finley said. "In fact, I'm going to order dessert. I just can't decide if it will be the apple crisp or chocolate cream pie. Would you like anything?"

"I don't eat sweets, but thank you."

Finley sighed inwardly. He wasn't sure they could even be friends now. *So long, Michael.*

chapter
FIFTEEN

KIERAN HAD NO RIGHT TO FEEL SO RATTLED AFTER SEEING Finley at lunch with another guy. The gossip around the ranch was that Finley had left shortly after dinner each night and hadn't returned for a few hours. Kieran thought he was scouring pawn shops and thrift stores to find his camera equipment, but maybe he'd been meeting that guy. Were they on a date at the diner?

In the same span of time that Finley had found a potential replacement, Kieran had lived two existences. The first half of the week, Kieran had locked himself down so tightly that he blocked out all emotions, leaving no space for sorrow, anger, regret, pining, or lust. It was like he'd been sent right back to jail. He had work, and he had Little Mama, who must've sensed his agitation or was getting closer to having her kittens. She'd been extra cuddly and had soothed him with her purring, providing comfort he wanted to refuse but couldn't. Maybe it was her affection that had cracked his façade enough midweek to let the pining and regret drip into his psyche.

Kieran spent those evenings sketching scenes from his memory. His fingers were clumsy and out of practice at first, so he warmed up with landscape renderings. Who cared if some of them were a little more abstract than he'd intended. Certainly not Little Mama, who curled up in his lap and purred until Kieran found the courage to draw the subject that called to him most. He'd closed his eyes, recalled all the special moments he'd shared with Finley, and recreated them with a charcoal pencil. When he finished each sketch, Kieran slapped a bandage on his leaking defenses, and reminded himself that Finley was better off without him.

Thinking it was one thing, but actually seeing it was another. Finley laughing with the handsome stranger punched a hole in his dam, and everything he'd suppressed flooded into his mind. Kieran felt the heat they'd shared in the motel, the happiness and sense of rightness Finley evoked. The sharp longing was a knife to the heart, but he kept moving forward. Shame for letting Finley down moved in next, followed by humiliation for hurting Finley when he'd only wanted to punish himself. As strong as those emotions were, they paled in comparison to the jealousy coursing through his blood. Finley belonged with him, not that slicked-back, toothy fucker in the diner.

"Wait up," Rueben called out.

Christ, he'd forgotten he wasn't alone. Kieran slowed so Rue could catch up. "Sorry about that."

"The scene back there isn't what you think it is," Rue said, sounding a little winded.

"Doesn't matter." Then he stopped and whirled to face Rueben. "But why do you think that?"

"Finley stares at you the way I stare at the last piece of German chocolate cake."

Kieran waved the remark away, but it burrowed into his brain like a beetle. He had just witnessed Rueben lusting after the dessert the previous night, so he had a visual reference. Did Finley look at him like he wanted to devour him? He gagged his inner cynic so he could attempt objectivity when he replayed their encounters. God yes, Finley looked at him like he was cherry crisp. A lightness he definitely had no right to feel entered the fray, picked up a sword, and prepared to battle. *Joy, you fickle bitch, what are you doing here?* Then he realized the feeling wasn't as foreign to him as it should've been. Kieran had grown too complacent and had allowed himself to get caught up in the spirit of community on the ranch. Attachments were formed, bonds were made, and he'd nearly let himself fall in lo—

"I gotta get out of here," Kieran said desperately.

"I'm ready to go back to the ranch too." Rue had misunderstood his sense of urgency and Kieran didn't correct him. Instead, he started to plan. Normally, he'd wait until the poker game started, but he had a feeling Finley would want to talk to him when he got back.

Cash was in Denver until Sunday night again, Ivan wouldn't return from Colorado Springs until after dinner, and Harry was excited about her mani-pedi and another girls' night with her friends. She'd told everyone at breakfast they had to fend for themselves, so he presumed she would be gone. Tyler and Owen were delivering Big Stanley, a gorgeous chestnut stallion, to his forever home, and Kieran rarely ran into the other guys unless it was mealtime, so he only needed to worry about Rueben. If he was distracted, Kieran would be clear to search Cash's office for answers.

As if fate had intervened, Rueben's phone rang when they were a mile or two away from the ranch. Kieran had learned enough Spanish in jail to determine Rue was talking to his grandmother. Rueben's rapid cadence made it hard for him to follow, but he definitely heard Rue's promise to call her back in ten minutes.

"There goes the rest of my afternoon," Rue said once he disconnected.

"Maybe wait a while to call her back. Kick back and watch some TV."

Rue chuckled as he turned onto the ranch's long driveway. "No way, man. You don't keep my abuela waiting. She acts like she is going to die any minute and what she has to say is too important to take to the grave. I told her I'd call her back in ten minutes, so I'd better make it eight."

Kieran planned to hang out in his cabin long enough for Rueben to become engrossed in his conversation. Then he'd return his borrowed book to Cash's library and search his office next door. Little Mama didn't greet him when he stepped inside, nor did he see her on the furniture.

"Little Mama," he called out in alarm. A weak meow greeted him from the bathroom and he found her lying in the shower. She'd already given birth to one kitten and its placenta and had managed to break the sac open on its tiny body. Her stomach contracted, and she panted softly, making him think the next kitten's arrival was imminent. Finley had a lot of experience with cats in Tennessee, and prior to the disaster at Dexter's, he had given Kieran pointers on what to look for and how to help.

"You're doing great, Little Mama," he whispered as he rubbed behind her ears. Kieran grabbed a washcloth, wetted it in the sink, and then made sure the first kitten had a clean airway. He talked soothingly to the cat while she delivered kitty number two. She immediately started licking her baby to break the sac open, and Kieran stayed out of her way until her struggle became obvious. "Let me help," he cooed, taking over caring for the newest addition.

Kieran continued the process until all five kittens had arrived safely. They looked like little alien bodies as they sought their mama. She had two black kittens, two calicos, and one solid orange. Kieran retrieved a box from the barn and made a soft nest with an extra bath towel. He helped Little Mama get cleaned up and moved her and the babies to the box. The sight of them together as a family made him tear up. Finley had told him that nature kicks in and the kittens would seek nourishment. He just made sure they didn't have far to go before latching on.

He checked the clock and saw that forty-five minutes had passed. If he wanted to search Cash's office, it was now or never. Kieran forced himself to walk at his normal pace to the ranch house, but he made a beeline for the office once he was safely inside and returned the book. Patsy didn't bark or come running, so she was either in the kennel training with the other dogs or Cash had taken her to Denver with him. He found the office door unlocked. Kieran wasn't sure if it was because Cash was too trusting or because he didn't keep incriminating evidence in his house.

Kieran closed the door behind him and headed straight for the massive wood desk. He started with the large bottom drawer on the right, where there were dozens of hanging files suspended from a rack. Kieran rifled through them, noting they were all ranch related. He stopped on the one marked Brewery and Winery. Cash had written Hooch and Honey with a different pen, so he really had been serious about using the name. Kieran pulled out the file and found a note Cash had written on top. It was a reminder to pay Kieran for naming rights and to call his lawyer to make everything legal.

Guilt stirred in his conscience. Cash intended to keep his word even when he didn't have to. Who would believe Kieran's claim? He shoved the file back into its place and kept thumbing through the stash. He barely resisted yelling "Aha!" when he found a folder with his name on it. The file wasn't the smoking gun Kieran expected it to be. Inside were the typical tax documents employers had for their employees and Cash's evaluation of Kieran from Arrowhead and why he thought he'd be a good fit for the ranch.

Kieran Sullivan reminds me so much of myself when I was in jail. He thinks it's him versus the world and has a chip on his shoulder the size of Texas. I suspect his grievances are justified, and I'd really like to help him learn there is a better future for him. He's incredible with the animals, even if he's not confident around them yet.

Kieran wanted to believe Cash meant what he'd said, but he couldn't allow the kind words to sway him. He finished rifling through the files, then searched the other drawers, but he came up empty. He'd found nothing remotely incriminating in the desk and the computer was password protected. Kieran blew out a frustrated breath and turned his attention to the credenza, where he found more useless files and office supplies. He looked around the room for anything that could hide a safe, and Kieran's eyes landed on a closet.

He crossed the room and opened the door. A row of shirts and jackets hung from a rack, and a collection of hats rested on the shelf above them. He'd accepted his search had yielded nothing until he realized the clothing could hide a safe. He shoved his hands in the middle between a corduroy jacket and a black dress shirt and pushed the clothing to create a gap in the center. The clothes didn't hide a safe, but there were rows of shelves. And on the center sat an army-green duffle bag with PFC Finnigan Donovan emblazoned across it. There was the proof that Cash was up to no good.

But how had he gotten his hands on the bag? Had he followed them? Used a tracking device to locate them while they'd been fucking in the hotel? Had Kieran's presence on the ranch been part of a bigger plan? Had he played right into their hands? His chest tightened and trapped the air in his lungs. He was back in his cell the first night, suffocating on panic. The vibrant colors around him started to dull and turn gray. Kieran braced one hand on the doorjamb and the other on his throat. His pulse fluttered beneath his thumb, a reminder that he was still alive. He could breathe. Nothing was restricting his airway but his own brain. He closed his eyes and took a shaky breath, pulling it as deep as it would go. The next breath came easier, and the one after that was better still. Each inhale expanded his lungs and loosened the panic. Each exhale cast the anxiety out like exorcised demons.

Excited barking came from inside the house, followed by toenails clicking on the hardwood floors. *Fuck.* Patsy was in the house, and she'd picked up on his scent. Even worse, Patsy wasn't alone. Heavy footsteps joined her clicking toenails, and the sounds grew closer as they drew near. There was only one way in and out of the office because the big windows behind the desk were decorative etched glass that didn't open. His only choice was to duck into the closet and hope whoever was with Patsy wouldn't think to look in Cash's office. How would Kieran explain his presence in the office to Cash or anyone else? He pushed the clothes back into place as quietly as he could and pressed his back against the shelves. His legs and shoes would be visible to anyone who opened the door, and he felt ridiculous. His heart pounded in his chest as Patsy barked loudly outside the office door until it swung open. Patsy headed straight for the closet, barking louder than ever before.

"What is it, girl?" Finley asked.

Kieran swallowed a groan. *Damn it!* Anyone but him. Patsy barked louder, and he could tell by the clicking that she was prancing or turning in circles.

"No way," Finley said. "I've seen this in movies. I'm not opening the closet door." Patsy persisted and Finley sighed. "I better live to regret this." The closet door swung open and Kieran knew by his startled gasp that Finley saw his denim-clad legs and boots sticking out from beneath the clothes. Patsy barked excitedly as if it were a game and she'd found the treasure. Her barking must've clued Finley in that the man in the closet wasn't a threat, or maybe he recognized the legs and boots because Finley jerked the hanging clothes aside and glared at him.

Kieran held his hands up in the air. "It's not what it looks like."

Finley narrowed his green eyes. "Funny, that was going to be my line about the lunch you witnessed. Now that I've found you hiding in Cash's office closet, I'm changing my comment to *what the actual fuck?*"

"I can explain."

Finley crossed his arms over his chest. "Then do it now."

chapter
SIXTEEN

"**Y**OU WON'T LIKE IT," KIERAN REPLIED.

That was a given. Finley wasn't sure if he should roll his eyes at the absurdity of the statement or sag with relief because the person hiding in Cash's closet wasn't an ax-wielding maniac. Then again, his life might not be in physical danger, but his heart was barely hanging on. "What could be worse than the silent treatment you've been giving me all week?"

Kieran flinched, and Finley thought he saw regret flashing in his dark eyes before the guilt returned. "I'll explain everything back at my cabin. You can meet the kittens."

Finley took that news harder than finding Kieran in a space where he didn't belong while acting cagey as hell. They'd spent a lot of time talking to and about Little Mama over the past few weeks. Kieran had asked dozens of questions about what to expect during her delivery, and it hurt to be cut out of the process. Finley swallowed down his disappointment and said, "When did they arrive?"

"After I got back from Last Chance Creek." Kieran stepped out of the closet and reached for Finley. He must've thought better of it because he dropped his hands. "But before we go, I need to show you something."

Kieran stepped to the side and revealed a row of shelves in the closet. Was there a safe behind it he was trying to break into? Finley squelched the snort bubbling inside him as he dismissed that theory. He was embarrassed he'd even flirted with the notion. Then Finley's gaze landed on his duffel bag. He'd lost all hope of seeing his grandpa's camera equipment again. Finley stepped forward to retrieve it, but Kieran held out a hand.

"We can't take it with us," Kieran said softly.

Finley felt like he'd landed in an episode of the *Twilight Zone*, or maybe he was still dreaming. A warm hand wrapped around his forearm, and he met Kieran's dark gaze. The sympathy caught Finley off guard, injecting more confusion into an already muddled situation. "Why can't I take back what belongs to me?"

"Because Cash will know the bag is gone, and it won't take him long to figure out who took it."

Finley looked from the bag to Kieran. "I at least want to make sure all the equipment is still there."

Kieran held his gaze for several moments, then nodded and dropped his hand. Finley stepped into the closet and unzipped the bag. Everything was there except for the memory card. Someone had removed it from the camera. The lighting in the small space was poor, so Finley felt around in the bag to see if the small card had fallen to the bottom, but it was just gone.

Finley rezipped the bag and spun to face Kieran. "What the hell is going on?"

"Let's head to my place."

Finley didn't want to wait five seconds for answers, let alone ten or fifteen minutes. He reached for his phone in his back pocket. He'd just call Cash and get an explanation. There had to be a good one.

"Please don't call Cash yet," Kieran said. He didn't reach out and physically restrain Finley, but the desperation in his gaze stopped him short.

Finley put his phone back in his pocket. "Don't think you're going to distract me with kittens or sex," he said crankily.

Kieran's mouth twitched at the corners, and Finley was suddenly desperate to see one of his smiles. He chided himself as Kieran restored order in the closet, shut the door, and showed Patsy some affection. Gaining favor with the man who'd shut him out should've been the last thing on his mind. Finley took a fortifying breath and forced himself to remember why Kieran had done it, which brought him right back to the stolen equipment.

"The only people with interest in the memory card are Ritchie or one of the other guys in the photos," Finley said softly during the walk to Kieran's cabin.

"Or the person pulling the strings. If any of those men go down, they could lead the authorities to him to get a bigger deal."

Finley tripped and stumbled. Kieran steadied him with a hand on his bicep but didn't let go when Finley righted himself. The warmth of Kieran's touch threatened to hijack his thoughts again, but Finley gave himself a mental shake. "You can't mean—"

"Shh," Kieran warned. "Wait."

Once inside the small cabin, Finley couldn't resist following the tiniest meows coming from a box by Kieran's bed. He eased over, careful not to scare Little Mama, and cooed to her as he sat crossed-legged on the floor. "Look what you did. Such a good mommy already."

Kieran sat down close enough for their knees to touch. Was it a distraction ploy, or had Kieran missed him just as much? Finley couldn't allow his thoughts to go there, so he focused on the kittens who were climbing over one another while their mama rested. He wanted to reach inside, scoop the babies up, and cuddle them, but it would distress Little Mama too much.

"They're so precious." Kieran sounded awed and smitten with the family, and Finley couldn't help being a little jealous. "She was exhausted and struggled to clean off their faces. I remembered what you told me to do, even though I was nervous as hell."

That was the most Kieran had spoken in his presence since leaving

Dexter's. Call him stupid, but it seemed natural to reach over and hold his hand, so Finley gave in to his urge. "You did good."

Kieran shocked him by rotating his wrist and sliding his fingers through Finley's. Warmth surged into him from both the connection and the naked longing in Kieran's obsidian gaze. It was as if the theft hadn't occurred, and they hadn't lost a week together. Or maybe the separation was the reason his heart was threatening to gallop out of his chest. It felt so right being back in Kieran's cabin that Finley didn't question it. The chemistry they'd shared at Dexter's was still there, maybe stronger, as if the week of tension had been mere foreplay. But this wasn't the re-union Finley had allowed himself to imagine during weaker moments.

"I owe you an explanation." Both Kieran's voice and expression were filled with dread, and the food Finley had consumed at the café turned to a brick in his stomach.

"Not in front of the children," Finley whispered, hoping to lighten the mood.

Kieran's mouth curved up slightly on the right side. Ah, progress. Finley reminded himself he shouldn't want to make inroads with Kieran until he understood better why he'd searched Cash's office for the stolen equipment. No way in hell it was an unhappy coincidence, but he also refused to believe Kieran was up to no good. Did that mean Cash was? He just couldn't go there because there was few people he respected more than Cash.

They moved over to the loveseat, both migrating toward the middle rather than choosing separate cushions. The impulse to touch Kieran again surged through Finley and he gave in. As before, Kieran rotated his wrist and laced their fingers together.

"I didn't come to Redemption Ridge for a clean start or to learn a new set of skills," Kieran said softly. "Well, maybe I did, but it wasn't the only reason. I came here because I suspected Cash Sweeney was the puppet master pulling Ritchie's strings."

Finley heard the words, but they didn't compute. "I don't under-stand how any of this happened. Will you tell me?" Kieran nodded, and Finley squeezed his hand. "From the beginning?"

Kieran exhaled slowly and said, "I didn't plan to stay in Colorado, but I fell in love with the mountains during a layover at the Greyhound station. They just called to me in a way I still can't understand. When it was time to board the bus to California, I didn't. I stayed at a home-less shelter that first night, and a volunteer gave me the number of a contractor who was always looking for help. It was hard work, but the guy was honest and always paid. His brother owned a bar and would always say a looker like me could pull in big tips." Kieran shrugged. "So I decided to give it a go."

Finley nearly wrenched his neck. "You were a bartender? The guy who doesn't do idle chitchat?"

"I talked to you a lot."

"You wanted to see me naked," Finley countered. "You weren't about to dole out relationship advice to patrons, and I don't see you flirting to get big tips." He narrowed his eyes and studied Kieran. "But you didn't need either of those things, did you? People fell for your brooding looks and aloof demeanor. There's just something about it people can't resist. I bet you raked in the money."

A soft blush bloomed on Kieran's cheeks. "I did pretty good. But you're right about the aloof bit. That's been a part of me since I went into foster care when I was ten." Finley's heart broke for the innocent boy he'd been. He started to ask, but Kieran stopped him with a gentle kiss. "I promise to tell you everything, but let's focus on the most press-ing issue right now." Finley pointed to his mouth, signaling he'd coop-erate for another kiss. Kieran complied with a smirk, lingering longer this time. "I missed you so much."

Finley sighed and briefly closed his eyes. "We'll address that later too, preferably while naked. For now, you were an unattainable bartender who the patrons couldn't resist. I suppose that's how you met Ritchie?"

"Yeah," Kieran replied. "He was determined to get my attention, to make me smile, and to get in my pants."

"I hate that I have a single thing in common with that asshole, and it turns out we shared at least three goals."

Kieran snorted and shook his head. "Do I need to get a muzzle for you, or will you let me finish the story?" Finley mimed zipping his mouth shut and throwing away the key. Kieran briefly nuzzled his neck before pressing his lips to Finley's ear. "I hope you have a spare key. I'm fond of that mouth and there are places on my body it hasn't been yet."

Finley didn't bother trying to hide the arousal thrumming through him. He could feel his focus shifting to his nether regions, which wasn't his fault. It also wasn't where his mind needed to be. He lassoed his lust and tethered it to a fence post for the time being.

"Ritchie's tactics were different," Kieran said. "His approach was consistent and deliberate. He showed up regularly and made it obvious he wanted to get to know me, not just take me home for the night. Sure, Ritchie flirted with words and actions—a wink or a glancing touch when I set his drink down on the bar, but what grabbed and held my attention were the notes he left behind on the napkins. Sometimes he complimented me, other times he poked fun at my choice of shirt or how I'd handled a situation. He occasionally quoted lines from a book, movie, or song. I threw the first napkin away with barely a glance because it wasn't an original approach. People often left their phone numbers along with the things they wanted to do to or for me."

Jealousy churned in Finley's gut as he imagined greedy eyes and hands all over his—no, not his man. An internal voice whispered *not yet*, but Finley was afraid to let that kernel of hope blossom. He clenched his jaw and pressed his lips together to keep from interrupting Kieran again.

"Eventually, I started reading the messages before throwing them away, and then I saved the notes." Kieran paused for a deep breath. "I tucked them away because no one had gone to such lengths to be with me. My resolve weakened after two months, and we went out on a date that lasted four days. There was part of me that expected Ritchie to move on afterward, so I retreated behind the wall I'd built. He'd knocked down a good chunk of it, but he hadn't demolished the barrier entirely."

"But he showed up," Finley said softly. He slapped his hand over his mouth when he realized he'd spoken his thought out loud. He parted his fingers and added. "Sorry."

"I'm the one who's sorry. I should've told you all this before I let anything physical happen between us because it gets worse."

"Worse than imagining the fuck fest you shared with Ritchie?" Finley shook his head. "I doubt it."

"You're not emotionally invested in Ritchie, but you are in Cash Sweeney."

The reminder that his mentor was tangled up in this mess felt like getting doused with water, and a shiver rolled through him. Finley centered himself and said, "I'm ready."

Kieran peppered him with a few more soft kisses. "If you believe nothing I say today, I want you to believe this next part." He waited for Finley to nod before continuing. "I have never connected to anyone as swiftly or completely as I did with you. At first, it was physical, and I nearly rubbed the skin off my dick during the first few weeks. I'd gone twenty months without sexual release, and you overwhelmed my circuit boards." Kieran smiled at Finley's wide-eyed response to that bomb. *Twenty months?* Then he recalled Kieran's remark about having no privacy in jail, and Finley understood the kind of hell that would be for someone as private as him. "But then I got to know you through our quirky conversations," Kieran continued, "and I observed the real you when you interacted with the horses and ranch crew. You accepted me without conditions or demands." Kieran swept his thumb over Finley's mouth and inhaled hard. "That time with you at Dexter's might've been brief, but it was transcendent. Being inside you was the first time I'd ever felt at home. What we shared obliterated anything I'd ever experienced with anyone else, and that's the part I need you to believe."

The sincerity in Kieran's gaze warmed Finley's heart, but it couldn't thaw the fear over what Kieran might say next. It would be too easy to transition to "I'll miss you when I leave" or "I'll carry our memories wherever I go." Finley couldn't stop the inevitable goodbye, only delay it. He wouldn't ask Kieran for more than he could give, but he would keep his promise to not let him down, so he said, "I believe you."

"Thank you." Kieran pressed a quick kiss to his lips before continuing. "Yes, Ritchie showed up at the bar during my next shift and the one after. I practically moved into his place the next weekend, and we made it official within a month. When I wasn't working at the bar, I hung around his body shop, helping wherever I could, and sometimes that meant moving vehicles to and from the warehouse. I started cutting my shifts at the bar to spend more time with Ritchie. He consumed me and monopolized my time until I turned over everything to him. He reeled me in and pushed me away depending on his mood. It took me going to jail to see how manipulative and controlling he'd been."

"You had no hint that anything criminal was going on?" Finley asked.

Kieran shook his head. "No. I had Ritchie's full attention when we were together. Napkin notes became messages on the bathroom mirror or sticky notes on the coffee pot. We took weekend trips to Black Hawk where we gambled, and ate, and—"

Finley held up a hand. "I think I get it."

"Your jealousy is really cute," Kieran said. Finley didn't bother denying it. He gestured for Kieran to keep talking. "Ritchie kept me so busy wallowing in his affection that I didn't have the time or desire to question his business practices or what he was doing when I wasn't around."

"How long did the good times last?"

Kieran leaned back against the loveseat, and Finley followed. He rested his head on Kieran's shoulder and swung his legs over Kieran's thighs. "Six months. Maybe seven. Ritchie started taking secret phone calls and putting distance between us. We stopped taking weekend trips. No matter how hard I tried, I couldn't get us back to where we'd been. The notes stopped, and Ritchie's disinterest spread everywhere, including the bedroom." Kieran worked his bottom lip between his teeth, and Finley hated for him to relive the painful memories. But Kieran clearly felt the information was necessary for Finley to understand how they'd arrived at this point. "That's when I knew something was going on," Kieran said. "I obviously suspected an affair when we went from sex four or five times a week to Ritchie being unable to keep it up with me. I'd caught him jerking off plenty of times in the shower, which made it clear it wasn't a medical issue. He'd always tell me he didn't bottom, yet I caught him riding a dildo. I think he got off on knowing how his rejection fucked with my mind."

Finley lifted his head. "I'm so sorry. I can't imagine how hurtful that was for you."

"Devastating." Kieran's voice was scratchy like he'd yanked the answer from his chest and it had fought him the entire way. "Of course,

I blamed myself and tried harder to please him. I'd achieve success occasionally, but it never lasted. I should've just packed my shit and left, but I'd had a taste of something wonderful and couldn't let go. I'd suppressed the addictive personality I'd inherited from my parents until I met Ritchie. I was hooked on him just as strongly as the drugs my parents had injected into their veins or snorted up their noses."

With his head tucked under Kieran's chin, he couldn't see the tears stinging Finley's eyes. Christ, he had so much damage to undo. He remembered the vow he'd made to Kieran and silently doubled down. Finley committed right then that he wouldn't let Kieran go without a fight. He'd ensure the battle was clean and would avoid any form of manipulation, but Finley would play for keeps. Finley couldn't allow his imagination to run wild and conjure an idea of what his victory would look like; he had to stay rooted in the present so he could learn exactly what he was up against.

Kieran held him tighter as if Finley brought him comfort and helped to ground him, or maybe he was bracing them both for what came next. "I paid closer attention to who Ritchie was talking to and where he was spending his time when we were apart. And I randomly dropped by the body shop with dinner or asked questions about the secret calls. I went through his messages, but he was too smart to leave incriminating evidence. Ritchie was quick with answers that sounded plausible, and he was always where he was supposed to be, but I knew I wasn't wrong.

"Questions turned into accusations, and we started fighting. He accused me of being paranoid, and I accused him of gaslighting me. We would make up and fall out again and again. As we approached our one-year anniversary, I kept trying to make plans to celebrate. Ritchie always had one excuse after another about why we couldn't go away for the weekend or even have a nice dinner. I took the night off at the bar without telling him and brought the romantic dinner to his shop, but the place was empty. All his employees were gone for the night, and Ritchie wasn't in his office, even though his car was in its usual spot."

Finley tilted his head and kissed the underside of Kieran's jaw. "I wish I could go back a few weeks and knee him in the balls."

A chuckle shook his chest before he continued with his story. "My heart sank because there was really only one valid reason he wasn't there. Someone had picked him up for dinner. I searched his office and found a second phone I didn't know he had buried in his desk. The battery was dead, and I figured I didn't have time to charge it and go through it. I found nothing out of place until I went through his trash can and found a note that he'd scribbled on a fast-food napkin."

Finley snorted. "Dude sure has an MO." He worried he'd over-stepped until a chuckle vibrated through the muscular chest beneath his head. It made Finley want to snuggle closer, but that was impossible unless he could burrow into Kieran's skin.

"Yeah, he does," Kieran agreed. "This time the note was to himself. It read, 'Cash Sweeney. Mackenzie's Chophouse at 7.'" Finley bolted into a sitting position but didn't let go of Kieran's hand. "The meetup was scheduled on our anniversary, which was why Ritchie wasn't in his of-fice working as he'd claimed. I drove over to the restaurant and parked where I could see the entrance. They didn't come out until eight thirty or later. Cash was dressed like a millionaire cowboy and Ritchie had put on a sport coat I didn't know he owned." Kieran inhaled shakily. "I felt so humiliated seeing them together on our anniversary, but I tried to observe them objectively. It was plain to me that Ritchie was being his most charming self. Cash was laughing at whatever he'd said and didn't pull away when Ritchie laid his hand on Cash's bicep or forearm." Kieran tilted his head to one side. "Now that some time has passed, I think Cash was tolerating Ritchie's flirtations. He didn't reciprocate or initiate anything, at least not in public. Not everyone is comfortable with PDA, so I can't say for sure they weren't fucking." His mouth curved into a sneer. "Just not that night. I sent Ritchie a text that I'd gotten off early and was heading toward him with dinner. I watched the fucker fish his phone out of his pocket and read the text. He didn't reply, but Cash drove him straight back to the body shop."

"What happened?" Finley asked.

"I beat them back to the shop and was sitting at Ritchie's desk, dan-gling the napkin from my fingers when he returned. I'd never seen him look so furious. He verbally attacked me and turned the whole thing around on me. He said it was just an innocent dinner with a potential investor and anything more was all in my imagination. Ritchie reminded me that he had big dreams and Cash was the kind of man who could help him achieve them. He did it for *our* future." Kieran shook his head. "But I'd recognized the look in Ritchie's eyes, that determination to get Cash Sweeney in his bed. I knew if it hadn't already happened, it would only be a matter of time."

"But you stayed?" Kieran dropped his gaze but not before Finley saw the shame in his dark eyes. Finley cupped his chin and raised it until their eyes met again. "Don't do that. If you stayed, you thought you had a good reason at the time."

"No one had told me they loved me until Ritchie," he said, swallowing hard. "I couldn't give up. I begged Ritchie for forgiveness." Tears spilled out of his eyes. "I hate him most for that. I'd never begged anyone for anything until he came along. Ritchie's love poisoned me and made me weak. I depended on him for everything—the food I ate, the clothes I wore, and even the car I drove belonged to him. My beater died not long after I met Ritchie. He arranged for me to sell it to a junkyard for scrap, and I told him to keep the money toward monthly expenses. I barely worked enough to pay for the apartment he insisted I keep. He was my entire world, and I couldn't imagine starting over without him. I know that makes me sound pitiful."

Finley's heart plummeted, and he dropped their joined hands so he could straddle Kieran's lap. Cupping his face, Finley said, "Baby, no." The endearment slipped out, but he wasn't sorry, and he didn't want to take it back. "You weren't weak or pitiful. Ritchie preyed on you from your very first meeting. Everything you've described so far is the work of an abusive bastard. Ritchie wanted you to catch him jerking off and fucking himself with a dildo. He wanted you to feel insecure and beaten down. It's how he kept you in place. I'll never understand people like him."

Had Ritchie cheated on Kieran with Cash? That didn't explain why Finley's camera equipment was in Cash's closet. Or did it? Finley knew where Kieran was steering him, but he didn't want to travel that path. He wanted to think Cash was just another of Ritchie's innocent victims, but it was getting harder to do. Kieran had alluded to his suspicions earlier but hadn't come right out and said it. Finley had tried to say it for him, but Kieran had shushed him, presumably so they wouldn't be overheard. Most of the crew was gone until dinnertime or later, but Kieran had been wise to be cautious. Alone in the small cabin, he no longer had an excuse to put off the inevitable. There was a minimum of three sides to every story—Kieran's, Cash's, and the truth. Finley wouldn't stop asking questions until he'd probed all the angles.

He held Kieran's gaze and said, "You think Cash is the puppet master." Finley didn't frame his remark as a question. He knew fully well what Kieran suspected. "And you deliberately sought out Cash's K9 program at the jail, hoping to learn more about him and make a good enough impression to get an invitation to work on the ranch." Again, he didn't ask.

"At first, I just wanted to see if Cash recognized my name," Kieran said. "I suspected Ritchie was involved in a rash of car thefts but knew he didn't act alone. Cash felt like a good fit for the person pulling the strings. If that were so, he would've known about my connection to Ritchie and my arrest."

"Do you think he recognized you?"

"Not that I could tell, but I didn't expect him to give much away."

"But you stuck with the program?" Finley asked.

Kieran gave him a genuine smile. "I fell in love with the dogs. Patsy in particular. Then I heard about Redemption Ridge, and it made me even more suspicious of Cash's character. I made it my mission to see what was going on here. If there was a way to tie Ritchie and Cash to the car theft ring, I wanted to find it."

"And have you reached a verdict?" Finley asked.

Kieran lifted his free hand and cupped the back of Finley's neck. "No. So far, all I've found is a hell of a lot of hard work and some wonderful people, but that doesn't mean my initial suspicions were wrong. The stolen camera equipment proves my point. The security guard was probably in on it if that's what he really was. We were dumb to think Ritchie wouldn't have scouts monitoring any transactions going down. Someone followed us to the motel and stole the camera out of the truck when we were in the room." Kieran's expression softened. "Just to be very clear, my only regret that night was letting you down. The moments we shared in that shitty room are branded on my soul. I owe you an apology for my behavior, and you'll have it. Let's just sort out the stuff with Cash first."

Finley nodded, though he'd already forgiven Kieran. "Why did Redemption Ridge make you more suspicious about Cash?" The answer was probably obvious, but he was too biased in Cash's favor to see it clearly. Kieran's cheeks flushed, and the dread Finley had seen earlier returned. "This stays between us, and I will not judge you. Tell me what you know or suspect so I can help you."

Kieran held his gaze for several moments before answering. "Redemption Ridge would make an excellent cover. Find vulnerable guys without families, give them a second chance, earn their trust, and… make them the fall guys for whatever illegal scheme or schemes Cash is running." There wasn't an ounce of conviction in Kieran's voice, and Finley wondered if he realized it.

Finley leaned his forehead against Kieran's. "I know the world has collectively let you down, and I understand how and why you leaped to that conclusion. But good people do exist, and Cash Sweeney is one of the best." Kieran stiffened, and Finley knew he needed to walk the tightrope. One false move could mean disastrous results. Kieran trusted him, and he couldn't blow it. "Don't lock yourself down again. I believe you, Kieran. I don't know how or why my camera equipment ended up in his office, but I will give Cash an opportunity to explain himself. It's the least I can do because I have seen this man work miracles." Finley reached up and carded his fingers through Kieran's inky locks. "Ivan has been here for five years. I know there's no love lost between the two of you, but he can smell a bullshitter ten miles away. He'd lay down his life for Cash. These guys aren't without families. They earn vacation time like everyone else with a job. Sometimes they go home to visit and sometimes their families come here. Cash hosts them at the ranch when they do. Those aren't the actions of a man who plans to use their sons and brothers as bait."

Kieran inhaled sharply and let his head fall back against the couch, exposing his throat and tempting Finley. "I feel really foolish."

"Huh-uh," Finley said, giving in and sucking Kieran's Adam's apple into his mouth. "Anyone in your position would've thought the same thing." Kieran gripped his hips and pulled him closer. "And Cash has some serious explaining to do." He sat upright and reached for his back pocket. "In fact, I'd like to hear his explanation right now." Kieran rested his hands on Finley's thighs as he dialed. The call went straight to voice mail, which was odd for Cash. When prompted to leave a message, Finley said, "I have two words for you: Ritchie Alvarez. And here's two more words: camera equipment. Call me back ASAP." Finley's phone rang before he could return it to his pocket. He tapped the button to accept and said, "Kieran and I—"

"Put me on speakerphone." Cash's voice was barely above a whisper.

Finley complied and said, "We're both here."

"Damn Hardy Boys," Cash growled. There wasn't an ounce of anger in his voice, just mild annoyance and something that sounded like... respect?

"And you would've gotten away with it too if not for us pesky kids," Finley replied, mimicking the Scooby Doo villains. They were only missing a dog and a few more sidekicks to complete the Mysteries, Inc. gang.

A soft chuckle came through the speaker. "Listen, guys, I will explain everything when I get home."

"Now works better for us," Kieran replied.

Cash exhaled a weighted sigh. "I wish I could, but I really can't. I promise everything will make sense, but I can't get into it over the phone. If my luck holds, I'll be back sooner than I'd planned."

"How much sooner?" Finley asked.

"I hope by morning." A man in the background murmured something low that they couldn't quite make out, but it spurred Cash into action. "I don't have the right to ask for a favor right now, but I'm going to do it anyway. Stay at the ranch tonight and stop digging into things that could get you hurt."

Finley hadn't looked away from Kieran's eyes, so he saw the moment resignation crept into his obsidian gaze. "We agree but reluctantly."

"Fair enough. Thanks," Cash said before disconnecting.

Finley stared down at his phone for a few moments before tossing it onto the couch. It was too much to expect either of them to feel better about the pending conversation with Cash. Finley had more questions than answers, and he would wait patiently to get them. It was time to pivot to another equally awkward conversation.

"About the diner…"

Kieran tensed and probably would've slammed his shields down if Finley hadn't acted fast. He cupped Kieran's face and planted a hard kiss on his lips. Finley pulled back and said, "Don't say it doesn't matter. I saw the look on your face and knew the conclusions you'd reached. I matter to you, and you matter to me."

Kieran swallowed hard and pressed a brief kiss to Finley's lips. "Some might say you matter too much."

Finley kissed him back, longer this time but still without tongue. "No such thing," he whispered when he pulled away. "My mom and sister staged an intervention when I started moping over you. And maybe I was, but I still had a productive week. I searched every pawn shop from here to Denver."

"So that's where you went. The rumor around the ranch was that you were seeing someone. Then I saw you with…"

"Michael."

"Yeah, him, and I assumed the rumors were true."

"I've given the guys plenty of fodder to gab about over the years, but not this time. As for Harry and Hope, I haven't yet decided how I'm going to get even with them, but I will. I'm thinking maybe I can somehow lure Harry and Dylan into the big walk-in freezer and lock them in. They'd have to stop being stupid and share body heat to stay alive."

Kieran chuckled. "Harry would kill you once she got out."

Finley grimaced. "Or she'd kill poor Dylan and make a skin suit out of him to stay warm. She'd have plenty of frozen foods to gnaw her way through to keep her fueled."

"Sounds like you've given this a lot of thought," Kieran said wearily.

"Nah, I just have an active imagination." He sighed. "They meant well, and I love them dearly, but I don't need them running interference for me."

"Thought you said it was an intervention."

Finley laughed. "Same difference."

"God, I've missed your smile and your laughter." Kieran brushed his thumb over Finley's cheeks. "I've missed everything about you, and I'm so sorry for shutting you out. I've had no guidance on how to handle relationships and powerful emotions. Maybe I'm too broken for even you to fix."

"Careful, Kieran. I love a challenge." Finley dropped his hands to Kieran's abdomen and loved the way his muscles bunched. A spark flared to life low in Finley's belly, and if he weren't careful, he'd have a raging inferno in seconds. There would be another time to explore their physical relationship, or so he hoped. Finley was on the verge of asking Kieran to stay with him at the ranch before he caught himself. The events of the day were catching up to Kieran, and if his week had gone anything like Finley's, then he hadn't slept worth a damn.

Kieran's mouth opened in a yawn big enough to swallow his face, telling Finley everything he needed to know. He slid off Kieran's lap, stood up, and extended his hand. "I could use a nap too. Then I'll rustle up something for us to eat."

Kieran rose willingly and tugged Finley into his arms. "Sounds perfect to me." He led Finley to his bed and pulled back the covers.

Finley saw a small bottle with his mom's logo on top of the nightstand. He picked it up, rolled it over, and saw Monkey Grease in her familiar scrawl. "Where did you get this?" Finley asked.

Heat suffused Kieran's cheeks when he saw what Finley held. He took the small bottle and tossed it into the nightstand before shutting the drawer. "It was included in the bag you gave me on my first day."

Finley looked up and gaped at him. "No way. I want a hole to open up and swallow me."

Kieran reached out and pulled him close as if that might really happen. Finley buried his head in Kieran's chest and held on for dear life. "I thought it was part of the welcome package. Salve for aching muscles and Monkey Grease for—"

Finley lifted his hand without looking up and covered Kieran's mouth. His lips trembled against Finley's fingers, and Kieran's chest vibrated as laughter built up inside him. Finley had never heard Kieran laugh before and was too eager to experience it to worry that he was the butt of the joke. He pulled his hand back, and laughter tumbled from Kieran's mouth. It was rich and thick like honey on biscuits, and Finley wanted to lick him up.

Kieran smiled at him after he regained his composure. "I didn't realize it was in there until the next morning, and I've nearly made myself blind from masturbation since."

Finley rolled his eyes. "That's a myth. We'd all be blind otherwise."

"I didn't find the note your mom wrote until I made use of the lube, which made it impossible to tell you about afterward."

Finley closed his eyes and groaned. "Oh no." After a moment, he cracked an eye open. "And you read it?" Kieran nodded, and the eye snapped closed again. Finley buried his head in Kieran's chest. "What did it say?" He shook his head. "Never mind. I can't handle the truth." By then Kieran had started to laugh again, so Finley snapped his head up. "That bad, huh?" Finley hung his head again. "I'm so embarrassed."

"Don't be," Kieran said softly. "Your mom and sister love you and only want the best for you, whether it's suitable lube or men to date." Kieran released another jaw-cracking yawn, and Finley stepped out of his embrace to strip down to his underwear. "This okay?" he asked when Kieran stood ramrod still. Had he taken things too far?

Kieran whipped his shirt off and tossed it to the floor. "Better than."

They climbed into bed, wrapped around each other, and lay there in silence for so long that Finley figured Kieran had fallen asleep. He willed his mind to settle down and shut his eyes, hoping to follow suit, then Kieran ghosted his hand up Finley's spine and settled it at his nape.

"My parents were drug addicts. Hard stuff like heroin." Finley wanted to comfort him but was afraid Kieran would stop talking if he touched him. "I can't recall a time when they were clean and we were happy. I remember their fighting, being hungry all the time, acting as a punching bag for my dad when his demons were at their worst, and my mom bringing strange men home and into their bedroom to pay for their habits. One of the johns brought my mom heroin that was laced with something else, and they overdosed together in the bedroom. I found them when I came home from school. We didn't have a phone, so I wandered from house to house until I found a neighbor at home. I called 911 and ran back to wait for them."

"How old were you?" Finley asked, unable to stay quiet.

"There you are. I was afraid you'd fallen asleep." Kieran took a deep breath. "I was ten." He pressed a kiss to the top of Finley's head and continued. "When I got back to the house, my dad was there. I told him what happened and that help was on the way. He was furious with me. Said I shouldn't have done that because they would get in trouble. He was beating the shit out of me when the cops and paramedics arrived."

Finley couldn't have kept from crying if someone had offered him ten million dollars. He just kept his head pressed to Kieran's chest, knowing he'd feel Finley's hot tears on his bare flesh.

"The state took me away, and I never saw them again. My mom survived that overdose but not the next one. My dad was killed in a bar fight not long after she passed. I don't think I have any siblings floating around in the world." He took a steadying breath. "I bounced around to different foster families because my biological family couldn't or wouldn't take me in, and I ended up in a boys' home until I graduated from high school. I fumbled and fucked around, barely resisting the horrible pattern my parents had taught me."

Finley looked up at him, and Kieran wiped his tears away. "But you didn't follow them, Kieran. You're better than they were."

"Sometimes I don't think I'm that different. I still hurt the one person in the world who cares the most about me." Kieran rubbed the back of two fingers over Finley's cheek. "You and the people on this ranch are the closest I've ever come to having a real family, and it scares me."

"We won't let you down." Considering the heavy conversation with Cash that lay ahead, it was a bold claim.

Kieran held his gaze for a long time before his eyelashes fluttered and his eyelids closed. His breath evened out moments later, making Finley sleepier. He tucked up under his arm once more and whispered, "Please stay," before giving in to sleep.

chapter
SEVENTEEN

K IERAN WOKE UP HUNGRY AND HORNY THE NEXT MORNING. He also woke up alone. Had he dreamed about holding Finley in his arms all night? What about the rest of it? Seeing Finley in town having lunch with a handsome man, finding the stolen camera equipment in Cash's office, and reconnecting with Finley afterward. Was it real? Kieran heard hushed whispers and tiny meows coming from the bathroom. He looked around the living space but didn't see Finley or the box with Little Mama and her babies. Kieran smiled when he realized Finley had moved the family into the bathroom so he could fuss over the babies without waking him.

It would've worked if his stomach and dick didn't ache so bad. They'd apparently slept through the night without waking up to eat or fuck. Kieran knew he should be upset about one more than the other, but damned if he could decide right then. One kitten let out a lusty cry, pulling Kieran's thoughts back to the congregation in the bathroom, and he wanted to see what was going on. He eased the covers back and padded toward the small room, stopping in the doorway because there wasn't enough room for him too. His heart lurched then leaped at the sight. Finley sat cross-legged on the bathroom floor, cradling each of the kittens against his bare chest. He'd borrowed a pair of Kieran's lounge pants and rolled the waistband a few times since they were too long. Finley's skin was flushed, his hair tussled from sleep. One kitten tried to latch onto his nipple, and he gently pulled the baby back.

"That will not give you what you want, sweetheart," Finley whispered.

Kieran had never seen something so precious in his life. The same kitten repeated its lusty cry, and Finley returned the babies to the box where Little Mama lay watching their interaction.

"Let greedy Gus go first," Finley said as he moved the vocal kitten closest to mama. "He's the smallest and needs more milk."

"Gus, huh?" Kieran said.

Finley jolted and twisted at the waist to see him. "How in the world do you move so silently?"

Kieran shrugged. "Sometimes it's necessary to survive." He regretted the words when all the joy faded from Finley's expression and the color leached from his face. *Fuck.* He didn't want to be the sad sack, mood-sucking vampire any longer. "Simply surviving isn't enough. My new goal is to thrive, and step one is getting you naked and under me." Kieran crooked his finger as he eased back toward his bed as the sweetest pink blush tinged Finley's pale cheeks.

The lounge pants were still too big and fell to the floor when he stood up. "That's convenient," Finley said. "Do you have a parlor trick to do the same for my underwear?"

Kieran hooked his thumbs in his own waistband and shoved his briefs down his legs. His cock sprang forward, hard and eager.

Finley moaned, then said, "Yeah, that'll do it." He removed his boxers and left them in the bathroom before trailing after Kieran. "I cannot wait to choke that down." But his cell phone rang on the nightstand just as he reached for Kieran's dick. "No, no, no. It's too early for my phone to ring." They both realized it meant the call was urgent. Finley flipped the phone over and revealed Cash's name on the screen. He accepted the call on speaker and growled, "This better be good," instead of his usually cheerful, "What's up, boss?"

Cash chuckled. "You're the one who demanded answers. I drove home at three in the morning so I could give them to you. How about we get this over with before breakfast? Anticipation will just give us all indigestion, and I have it on excellent authority that Harry is making Belgian waffles."

"With fresh fruit and real whipped cream?" Finley asked. He seemed to forget all about Kieran's dick. Finley started separating his clothes from Kieran's on the floor before he got an answer.

"Is there any other way?" Cash asked.

Finley snatched his clothes and headed toward the bathroom. "See you in ten or less."

Kieran shook his head but couldn't keep the smile off his face. He leaned against the bed and pulled his jeans up to his thighs while Finley searched the cabinet drawers until he came up with an extra toothbrush. He set it on the counter then turned to get dressed, spotting Kieran as he did. His mouth fell open on a small gasp.

"So this is how you're going to leave me?" Kieran asked, stroking a hand over his thick cock. "Aching, hard, and lonely?"

Finley swallowed audibly and blinked. "Aren't you going to put on underwear before we go?"

Kieran stopped stroking and pulled his jeans up the rest of the way. He stuffed his erection inside, then slowly did up the buttons. "No."

Finley narrowed his eyes. "Am I being punished?"

Kieran slid his arms into a long-sleeved tee and pulled it over his head. "No." He stalked forward, pinning Finley between his body and the bathroom vanity. "Just want you to remember what's waiting for you after we finish our conversation with Cash and eat breakfast." He reached around Finley and grabbed his toothbrush from the holder, then squirted a generous glob of toothpaste on both their brushes. "Because nothing Cash says will come between us."

Finley dropped his clothes to the floor, slid both arms around Kieran's waist, and pressed a kiss to his chest. Hope and happiness turned his irises into jade pools again. "Promise."

Kieran cupped Finley's face. "We may not agree on what Cash says or the actions that should follow, but whatever happened was set in motion before we met. I've let bitterness and suspicion affect my instincts and cause me to question my judgment. I was wrong about Ritchie, yes, but that doesn't mean I'm wrong about everyone. And since I'm being honest, I stopped giving people the opportunity to prove their worth to me. That's walking through life, not living it." *Surviving, not thriving.* "I want a second chance to do things right. Cash, regardless of his motivation, gave me that opportunity, and I won't squander it."

Finley rose to his tiptoes and pressed a quick kiss to Kieran's lips. "I have so many questions and a tiny favor to ask once we can break away."

"I'll answer them all, and I'll grant your favor," Kieran said.

"You don't even—"

He stopped Finley with a kiss. "Doesn't matter."

Finley sighed and shook his head. "You can't give me that kind of power."

Kieran trailed a finger across his jawline and over his lips. "That's exactly what I'm going to do. You make me want to believe, and someday I will."

Finley took a shaky breath and smiled. "Believe in what?" he pressed.

Kieran's heart raced as he decided how honest to be. "Myself for starters. I want to see the version of me that you see. But that's not all," he said, using an infomercial voice to inject humor into the conversation to ease the tightness gathering in his chest. Would expressing his thoughts and feelings ever come easy? Easier at least? He sure hoped like hell it would because Finley deserved the best version of him. Kieran deserved the best version of himself. "You make me want to believe that faith, hope, and joy really exist and that they're not just pretty words embroidered on bathroom towels. You make me want to believe the universe not only has room for someone like me but wants me too." As Kieran spoke, the knot in his chest loosened in places his humor hadn't reached. "You make me want to believe that anything is possible, and it's the most wonderful gift I've ever received." Finley's eyes shimmered with gathering moisture, and Kieran acted quickly before those tears became his undoing. "And if you call within the next thirty minutes—"

Finley cut him off with a hard, quick kiss. Then he shook his head and sighed. "Still have so many questions, but that gorgeous declaration will more than do for now."

After another kiss, Finley dressed and they brushed their teeth. Kieran replenished Little Mama's food and water, then they headed to the big ranch house to meet with Cash.

Harry looked up from the kitchen island and volleyed her gaze between them. She offered a tenuous smile and said, "Cash is waiting for you both in his office." Her gaze landed on Finley and held. "Perhaps you can keep me company afterward and help me prepare breakfast."

Kieran's heart sped up as he recalled Harry's attempt to fix Finley up with Michael.

"I don't need my big sister to—"

Harry held up a hand. "I owe you both an apology."

Kieran smiled while Finley bristled. "I would love to learn how you make the Belgian waffles he hasn't stopped talking about since Cash called. Served golden brown. Crispy on the outside but light and airy on the inside. Pretty sure I know how everyone on the ranch tops theirs too." Finley nudged him with his elbow and Kieran smiled at him. "It's cute."

"Ugh," Finley growled. He headed toward Cash's office without waiting to see if Kieran would follow.

"Be back soon." Kieran darted after him. He slid his arm around Finley's waist and whispered, "Don't be mad."

Finley looked up at him with a smirk. "Not mad, but keep it up, and I know what kind of topping you won't be doing."

Kieran leaned closer and whispered, "More than happy to receive."

"Let's get this meeting out of the way. I might even consider skipping breakfast—" His words died when multiple voices filtered from Cash's office. "What the hell?"

Finley picked up the pace and stopped so suddenly in the doorway that Kieran crashed into him. They both stumbled into the room, drawing the attention of the three men inside, who were drinking coffee and chatting. Cash's guests had their backs to the door, but the guy on the right had a bulky physique that triggered warning alarms.

Cash looked up and snorted. "Good of you to make it, gentlemen."

His guests stood up and turned to face the visitors. Sure enough, the man on the right was the same big guy who'd been with Ritchie on the night of the stakeout. Broad shoulders and a military buzz cut weren't exactly unique, but the square jaw and flat nose definitely set him apart. In the light of day, Kieran could see his hair wasn't black as he'd first thought. Most of the bristles were dark gray with some white and lighter gray peppered throughout. His shrewd, icy blue eyes stood out in sharp contrast to his tan complexion, and he didn't look happy to be there.

Finley gestured toward the stranger and said, "What the hell, Cash?"

"Come in and shut the door, please," Cash said calmly.

Finley crossed his arms over his chest and screwed his features into a mutinous expression. Kieran closed the door and faced the gathering, but neither he nor Finley budged from their spots.

Cash gestured toward a pleasant seating area next to a crackling fire. "Finley, you know me well enough to know I would never hurt you."

"But have you done anything to hurt Kieran? If so, our history won't save you." Big words, but the determination on his face said he meant it. Christ, could Kieran fall any harder or faster for him? The panic he expected to feel didn't materialize, showing just how far he'd moved away from no attachments and no bonding.

The burly dude held up a hand to take control of the situation, his eyes snapping with irritation. "Let's all save our breath and energy." His abrupt tone matched his no-nonsense demeanor. The man reached into his jacket and removed a small wallet from an interior pocket. Flipping it open, he revealed a badge. The agency initials were large enough for Kieran and Finley to read from across the room, but the man took a minute to introduce himself anyway. "Adam Rowland. I'm a special agent with the FBI." He gestured to the other guy, who was shorter and had sandy brown hair and easy-going blue eyes. "This is Special Agent in Charge, Nicholas Scott." Agent Scott presented his badge also and nodded a greeting.

Both men wore dark jackets over crisp dress shirts, denim jeans, and boots. Kieran figured they both had service weapons under their jackets, but his distress had turned into curiosity now that he knew they were feds.

"Can we all sit down and have a conversation now, please?" Agent Scott asked. His tone was softer and a bit more polished than his grumpy subordinate.

Finley looked at him, and Kieran nodded.

"Coffee?" Cash asked, gesturing to a carafe and full coffee service on top of the bar.

"No thanks," Finley said.

Kieran wanted something to do with his hands besides fidget. He didn't fear the federal agents, but their presence made him uneasy and triggered memories of endless interrogations. Finley joined him at the bar and leaned into him.

"What the hell is going on?" he whispered.

"I think we're about to find out, but I suspect we witnessed an undercover operation at the warehouse."

Finley's eyes grew wide, and he darted a glance toward the group gathered near the fire. "Oh, wow. I bet you're right."

Kieran dropped a kiss on his lips. "Let's find out."

"First things first," Cash said, lifting Finley's duffel bag from behind his desk. He crossed the room and handed it to Finley. "Everything is there. The FBI retained the memory card because it contained case-sensitive photos." Proving their suspicions had been correct. Finley started to protest, but Cash removed a flash drive from his pocket. "They transferred all the other photos onto this for you."

Finley snatched Cash's peace offering out of his hand and tucked it away. "I'll reserve expressions of gratitude until we conclude this conversation and I confirm my private photos are all there."

"Fair enough," Cash replied and gestured toward the sitting area.

Kieran settled his hand at Finley's back and leaned into his space. "Just how private are we talking?" Finley snorted and nudged his elbow into Kieran's side.

They settled on a leather love seat while the other three claimed the matching club chairs. The warmth from the crackling fire and the coffee soothed Kieran's frazzled nerves, allowing him to look calm and collected when energy coursed through him like a power plant substation.

"Are we in trouble?" Finley asked softly.

"You should be," Agent Rowland growled, "but your employer is best friends with my boss." He tipped his head toward Agent Scott as if Kieran and Finley struggled to follow along.

Cash had connections in the FBI? An idea formed, but Kieran was too rattled to put the pieces together yet.

"Do you mind if I take it from here?" Cash asked. Rowland didn't look too pleased, but he nodded. "About three and a half years ago, a lot of luxury cars were stolen in the Colorado Springs and Denver areas. The departments ran tight investigations but ended up reaching out to the FBI when their investigations failed to turn up solid suspects. The thieves were fast, organized, and could make the vehicles disappear without a trace. The popular theory was that a vehicle transportation company was behind moving the vehicles unseen, but they'd need someone to provide connections and tell them where to find the cars. They started checking out dealerships, auto body shops, and other types of businesses that provided services for luxury and rare cars."

The brain fog cleared, allowing Kieran to fit the first puzzle piece into place. "Ritchie and his detailing service."

"Yes," Cash replied. "Nick called in a favor and recruited me to go undercover for him as a prospective buyer for rare vehicles. There was a list of suspects for me to reach out to, and Ritchie Alvarez was one of them. I called him a few times and even swung by his shop once, but Ritchie was adamant he couldn't help me. He claimed he only serviced the vehicles. He didn't get involved in selling them, and he wouldn't budge on sharing his clients' information either. And based on the size of his operation, it wasn't likely he had the connections to pull off a large-scale theft ring, so we dismissed him."

"Mind if I interject something?" Agent Scott asked. Cash gestured for him to go ahead. "Before the FBI got involved, the Denver and Colorado Springs police even formed a joint task force, but they couldn't make anything stick. Every time they thought they had a tangible lead, it turned out to be another dead end. When millions of dollars in luxury and rare vehicles go missing in six months, it's going to get the FBIs attention. I expected the two police departments to get pissed when I showed up and requested their files on the thefts, but I almost heard a collective sigh of relief. The investigations had consumed too much of their manpower and time, and the chiefs were getting hounded by everyone from reporters to politicians. I basically started from square one, poring over every document the departments had compiled."

"Then a funny thing happened," Rowland interjected. "The thefts stopped suddenly after six months."

"My bosses wouldn't leave me on the case once it went cold, so I set the investigation aside and worked on it in my spare time over the next year," Scott told them. "Which meant I glanced at the information once every four or five months. I started with the joint task force files because all that information should've been the most recent and contained all the documents in one place. I just had a nagging suspicion I couldn't ignore and started combing the files from the separate investigations prior to the task force and comparing it to what I knew. Everything seemed to line up perfectly except for one suspect."

"Ritchie," Kieran said.

"Yes," Scott replied. "I noticed a discrepancy between DPD's and CSPD's notes on Ritchie Alvarez's operation. Denver noted a secondary location for Alvarez, but that detail was missing in CSPD's files. There were several other notations in one file, but not the other. On the surface, they seemed innocuous, but put together, there was a bigger problem."

Finley leaned forward, a riveted expression on his face. "Ritchie had someone inside CSPD covering for him. They told him to lie low once the feds swept in."

"That was my theory, though my boss didn't like it," Scott replied.

Cash raised his hand. "That's where I came in again."

"Another favor?" Kieran asked.

Cash cast a baleful expression at his friend. "He said I hadn't completed the original favor since no arrests had happened." Scott chuckled, and Cash rolled his eyes. "Anyway, I reprised my role of the interested collector. This time, Ritchie seemed eager to assist me. I thought the change of tone was interesting."

"Dude was bored. Alvarez had gotten a taste of the wild side and had a hard time settling back into his old life. It happens all the time." Rowland's tone said he'd seen it all before.

Kieran flinched because he and Ritchie would've started dating around the time the thefts stopped. Was that why Ritchie had pursued him so relentlessly? It would've explained why he'd run so hot in the beginning and cold toward the end.

Scott cleared his throat, and Rowland swung his gaze in Kieran's direction. "I didn't mean to insult you. No one would've replaced the thrill Alvarez got from boosting cars. Not even the gambling addiction he developed."

Kieran nodded. "No offense taken." In fact, the truth was liberating in a way. He told them about Ritchie's demeanor changes, the secretive calls, and the date with Cash scrawled on a napkin in the trash.

"It wasn't a date," Cash replied. "I want to be very clear about that, and I'm truly sorry you thought otherwise."

"I saw you together," Kieran admitted. "Then, I couldn't be objective, but with perspective, I realize you didn't react when Ritchie flirted with you."

Cash smiled. "You sent the text message that made him end our night abruptly."

Kieran smiled. "It was our anniversary, and I wanted him to know I'd caught him." He paused before continuing because he hated how weak he'd been. "Ritchie had convinced me nothing was going on and that I was just paranoid. We made up, celebrated our anniversary for real the following evening, and the cops arrested me for stealing the Jaguar a few days after."

"I still don't understand why none of you listened to Kieran when he explained why he was in the car," Finley said angrily. "He was the connection to Ritchie you needed."

Agent Rowland dropped his gaze to the ground, and Agent Scott ran a hand over the lower half of his face. "That's on me," he said. "Operation Silver Fox was rogue and completely off the books. I risked losing my job if it got back to my superiors. The car Kieran was driving was a luxury vehicle, but the theft wasn't the same MO as the previous cars. And though Ritchie seemed ready to play, he was more interested in helping Cash out of his clothes than helping him locate a vintage Aston Martin." Scott winced. "Sorry."

Kieran waved him off. "CSPD handled the investigation, so if one of them was covering for Ritchie, they steered the case in a different direction."

"Yes and no," Scott replied. "The initial investigator did interview Ritchie, his employees, and your coworkers. Ritchie said he didn't know you, his employees said they'd never heard of you, and your coworkers at the bar said they knew nothing about your personal life. The original detectives from the first rash of stolen cars took over your case, and they're the ones who convinced the prosecutor you were guilty."

"His employees were all blood relatives, so they never would've gone against Ritchie," Kieran said softly. "We never officially moved in together, so there was nothing tying me to his address. I've never been one to hang on to a lot of possessions, so it would've been easy to erase my existence." But he'd already figured out that much. "How'd we get to this point, though?"

"I'm guessing more stolen cars," Finley said.

"Yep, but not until right after Kieran's release from jail," Rowland said.

"That son of a bitch was trying to set you up again," Finley snarled.

Kieran's stomach churned with acid. He hadn't known until this point if his arrest had been dumb luck or an actual setup. Rowland's candor hammered home what had really happened. Eventually, the truth would set him free, but right then, it anchored him in resentment. Then Finley slipped his hand into Kieran's and infused him with his warmth and goodness.

"I'm not a fan of Alvarez, but I have to interject at this point and say that the timing of the latest car theft is a coincidence. Ritchie's gambling addiction has put him into serious debt with very dangerous people who've banned him from the casinos in Black Hawk." That explained why he was in Last Chance Creek. "He's boosting cars to pay off his debt."

"What about Kieran's arrest? Was that a coincidence too?"

"We think so," Scott replied. "I looked through dispatch records and Crime Stopper tips and there's no indication that Ritchie sent you out in a stolen car then phoned the police."

"Fair enough," Finley said. "Sorry for the detour."

"No problem," Rowland said. "Scott had received a promotion by this point and he went for gold. He tapped me to do the undercover work since Silver Fox over there had only ended up with dates." Cash flipped him off, causing the big man to guffaw. "It took me months to wear Ritchie down enough for him to trust me, and you two nearly blew my case with your amateur-hour stakeout."

Finley cringed, but Kieran narrowed his eyes. "Why are you being so forthcoming with information? Aren't you guys normally stingy with the details?"

"Very," Rowland agreed.

"And now Cash owes me another favor," Scott said, grinning from ear to ear before he composed himself. "There's a lot we can't tell you right now because there will be several trials and—"

"Trials?" Kieran and Finley said together.

Scott and Rowland looked at Cash. "You didn't tell them?" Scott asked.

Cash threw up his hands. "You told me I couldn't, and when would I have found time?"

"He makes a valid point," Scott told Rowland. "Do you want to do the honors, or should I?"

Rowland held up his hand to deflect. "This is your baby."

Scott produced his cell phone from his jacket pocket and tapped on the screen. A moment later, he turned it around so Kieran and Finley could see the headline on a newspaper article.

"Leader of multimillion dollar auto theft ring arrested after evading capture for four years," Finley read.

"In the article, they reveal that Ritchie's new boyfriend is the younger brother of Detective Snyder, who we believe misdirected and deflected the original investigation and Kieran's case. That might take longer to prove, but he's currently on suspension until further notice."

Kieran found it impossible to breathe as he stared at the caption below the headline. It showed Ritchie and his boyfriend being led away in handcuffs. "It's over?" Kieran whispered. He sat up straighter and looked at Finley. "It's really over?"

Finley's eyes swam with tears, and damn, Kieran wanted to dive into the jade depths. "It's over."

"Not yet," Cash said firmly, pulling everyone's attention to him. "It won't be over until Kieran's conviction gets overturned."

"We'll need to obtain a confession from Ritchie that he orchestrated the theft or find a credible witness," Rowland said. "That's a big hill to climb, but if Ritchie possesses a single ounce of self-preservation, he'll come clean and turn State's witness. They won't honor an agreement to place him in WITSEC if he doesn't confess to everything, though. I think you stand a good chance of getting your name cleared, but don't hold your breath. The wheels of justice don't always turn fast."

"It doesn't matter," Kieran said.

"The hell it doesn't," Cash replied.

"We'll do our best to help you," Scott said, "but you should really hire an attorney with experience in getting postrelease convictions overturned. It's not as easy as Cash thinks."

"Consider it done," Cash said.

Kieran's face heated with embarrassment because Cash had ignored the elephant in the room. "I don't have the means to hire a lawyer right now. I'm not sure how long it will take to save that kind of money."

Cash leaned forward and pinned him with his icy blue gaze. "You have me, and I have a fuckton of money. It will happen, Kieran. Not only that, but you have an excellent chance of winning a civil suit against the police department. By the time we're through, you'll have enough money to build whatever life you choose wherever you want to do it."

"How much is a fuckton?" Rowland whispered to Scott.

"More than you or I could imagine," Scott replied.

Kieran ignored them to focus on Cash. "But why? I'm nothing to you."

"Can Kieran and I have a private moment?" Cash asked without breaking eye contact.

Finley leaned over and kissed Kieran's cheek. "See you soon."

He and the two agents got up and left Cash and Kieran alone.

"Did you know who I was all along?" Kieran asked.

"No," Cash replied. "I didn't make the connection until I'd already decided you'd be a good fit for the ranch. That's when I did my due diligence and saw you'd been arrested for stealing a car. I don't know what made me do it, but I asked Agent Scott to do a deeper dive on you than my typical PI would perform. I just had this weird feeling I couldn't shake. He could've knocked me over with a feather when he reached back out after reading your file. I told Nick—Agent Scott—that you didn't do it and hounded him until he promised to look deeper." Cash smiled and said, "He kept his word, but couldn't manufacture proof out of thin air. I wish I could've done something sooner and gotten you released from prison. It would be my honor to help you clear your name."

Kieran tilted his head. "Because you feel guilty or because I remind you of someone?"

Cash chuckled. "Dug through my files, huh?" When Kieran just shrugged, Cash said, "You are familiar to me because I was you. I also had no family and nowhere to go after my release from jail. I applied for jobs all over the city, but no one wanted to hire me. The hardware store owner mentioned a rancher who was looking for help and pointed to an ad taped to a bulletin board near the front door. I hitched a ride out here, and Durrell and Lavonda took a chance on me. They changed my life forever by giving me a job, a family, and a purpose."

"And you want to do the same for me?"

"Absolutely I do," Cash replied. "I hear the skepticism in your voice, and I understand it better than you think, Kieran. All I ask is for a chance to help you tap into your real potential."

"What's in it for you?" Who would take care of the man who took care of everyone else?

Cash held his gaze for a long time. "I get a soul-deep satisfaction that money can't buy when I help people. You don't have to give me an answer right now. You must feel overwhelmed by everything you've just heard. Think it over, okay?"

Kieran nodded and rose to his feet.

"And Kieran," Cash said before he took the first step. "Men like Finley Ashe are rare and precious. Many of us could live multiple lifetimes and never find one. Don't waste your gift. If you decide you can't stay here, don't leave him behind. You'll regret it for the rest of your life."

"Thank you for everything, Cash," Kieran said before exiting his office. There was so much more he could say, but Cash wasn't the person who needed to hear it.

Kieran found Finley in the kitchen with his sister. Harry was trying to engage him in conversation, but Finley's focus was on the laptop in front of him. He must've commandeered his sister's computer to make sure his photos were there.

"Oh," Harry said breathlessly. "That's a gorgeous picture of Kieran and Loretta. I see you didn't just inherit Grandpa's skill with horses."

Finley must've sensed his presence because he snapped his head up. He didn't look like the same man who'd cuddled against him the previous evening or flirted with Kieran that morning. And he understood. Finley thought this was goodbye for them.

"Harry, could we get a rain check on our conversation?" Kieran asked. "I really need to talk to your brother."

"It won't take long," she replied hastily. Harry placed a hand over her heart as her bottom lip quivered. "I'm truly sorry for my role in Finley's intervention yesterday. I was just so worried about him." She smiled over at her brother before meeting Kieran's gaze again. "I guess some habits are difficult to let go, but I'll try harder to stay in my lane."

"No harm done," Kieran assured her.

Finley removed the flash drive and dropped it into his pocket before pulling Harry into a hug. "That Michael guy didn't stand a chance. He didn't even like dessert."

Harry released him and shuddered hard. Her gaze darted between Finley and Kieran, and she smiled sweetly. "Looks like we don't need to worry about Mom trying to set you up again."

Finley chewed on his bottom lip, and Kieran swore he could hear his heart pounding from across the room. He shot a wink in his sister's direction and rounded the island. Finley hit his usual stride and pulled ahead of him, but Kieran reached out and grabbed his hand. He didn't let go until they reached the porch, and that was just so he could hoist Finley off the ground and toss him over his shoulder.

Finley squeaked and slapped at Kieran's ass. "What are you doing?"

"You're not getting rid of me that easily," Kieran growled. "So get it out of your gorgeous head."

"Cash is right. You're probably going to receive a nice settlement. You'll get a fresh start and a clean slate anywhere you want to go."

"I'm not like the others, Fin."

Finley relaxed in his hold, making it easier to carry him. They passed the rest of the crew, who were heading to the house for breakfast. The guys tipped their hats and greeted them with cheerful "good mornings" like Kieran carrying Finley off to his cabin was an everyday occurrence.

"That will give them something juicy to talk about," Kieran said proudly. "And I better not hear about them placing a single bet on us."

Once alone in the cabin, Kieran tossed Finley onto the bed and pulled off his boots. He bent over Finley's body and pressed a kiss to his lips. "Ask me to stay again now that you know I'm awake."

Finley blushed, but joy danced in his eyes. "It was a statement, not a question."

"Fine," Kieran said. "I want to hear it again."

Finley cupped his face and pulled him closer so Kieran's lips hovered above his. "Stay," he whispered.

chapter

EIGHTEEN

F INLEY HAD PUT HIS WHOLE HEART INTO THAT ONE WORD AND waited with breathless anticipation for Kieran's response. It came in a slow stretch of a smile, the rustling sound of Kieran toeing off his socks, and the dip of the mattress beneath his knee. The answer was a long stretch of hard muscle on top of him and a thumb tenderly brushing over Finley's cheekbone. Parting his thighs to make room for Kieran felt as natural as breathing, and he wanted to make space for him in all aspects of his life.

Kieran pressed a sweet kiss to Finley's forehead, the tip of his nose, and his eyelids. "Say it again," Kieran said shakily.

The significance of the moment wasn't lost on Finley nor was it overshadowed by the events of the past few days. No one had ever wanted Kieran to stay before, and that single word could be his salvation or his undoing. Finley recommitted to the promise he'd made in the diner. He wouldn't falter or fumble; he'd double down. No one would want him the way Finley did. It was probably too soon for such a strong declaration, so he decided on a safer approach.

Sliding his fingers into Kieran's silky hair, Finley pressed a kiss to his lips. "Stay with me. We can take things as slow as you need."

A wicked smile spread across Kieran's face as he trailed his free hand down Finley's side. "I can take it real slow." Finley's breath hitched at the carnal promises shimmering in Kieran's dark gaze, but his lustful thoughts dissipated when Kieran's fingers danced over a sensitive spot under his ribs. And since Kieran was watching him so closely, he didn't miss the reaction. His southbound hand reversed course and sought the ticklish spot once more. Kieran swirled his thumb over the area and grinned like a devil when Finley squirmed and released a sound that was part giggle and part groan. "Interesting," Kieran announced seconds before he tugged Finley's shirt free from his waistband and shoved the material up under his armpits.

Finley's muscles tensed and bunched when warm fingers brushed against his bare skin. "Is this really the best use of our time?" There was no denying his arousal since his erection was on full display beneath his tight denim.

Kieran scooted down the length of Finley's body until his lips hovered over the ticklish spot his fingers had uncovered. Kieran gazed upon Finley's bare skin like it held the secrets of the universe. He'd felt no one's attention so keenly and couldn't resist squirming, which created friction everywhere their bodies touched. Finley thought Kieran was impervious to his plight until their gazes collided and he saw the impish delight dancing in his tormentor's eyes. Kieran licked his bottom lip before lowering his head and nuzzling his nose against Finley's sensitive skin. He choked back a second giggle, but his muscles tensed and goose bumps broke out all over his body.

Kieran's chuckle was a decadent, dark-chocolate brownie with extra hot fudge sauce. "I can't think of a better use of our time." He kissed the ticklish spot, then circled it with his wicked tongue. Finley bit his lip and squirmed, and Kieran used more of his weight to hold him down. Gazes locked once more, Kieran said, "I want to learn everything about you." He pressed one last kiss to Finley's ribcage before scooting higher to drop a peck near his sternum. Kieran had to feel Finley's heart hammering against his ribcage. "I want to learn every dream you've stashed here." He moved up again and nuzzled his lips against Finley's temple. "And the secrets you've locked in here." Their lips met and held for a few heartbeats before Kieran pulled back. "I'm going to be the man who cherishes everything you are. I won't make the same mistake as those other guys. They didn't deserve you, but I will."

Tears stung the back of Finley's eyes. "You already do, but I know that's a conclusion you'll have to reach on your own. Doesn't mean I can't start your journey off with an affirmation, and I'll happily repeat it as often as you need. We deserve each other. We deserve happiness."

Kieran's mouth quirked up at the corner. "You learn that kind of thinking from your mom's studio?"

Finley groaned. "Rule number one: never mention my mom or sister when we're getting naked or on the verge of getting naked. Boner killer."

Kieran chuckled. "Maybe she could bottle that up and sell it to people who get erections at the worst times." Kieran thrust his hips forward, grinding his hard-on against Finley's. "For the record, this isn't one of them."

He captured Finley's mouth in a hot, hungry kiss because the time for talking had passed. Or had it? Was Finley's offer to take things slow a reaction to their whirlwind relationship or a last-ditch effort at self-preservation? Weren't both things important? Kieran sucked on Finley's tongue, and he forgot his own name. Kieran broke their kiss to nuzzle Finley's neck, sucking the sensitive skin beneath his ear. Finley shivered hard, and Kieran repeated the action, adding tongue and teeth this time. He pressed his lips to Finley's ear and said, "This is going to be so much fun."

Kieran Sullivan gave entirely new meaning to *taking it slow* as he stripped Finley bare. There wasn't a spot on his body Kieran hadn't caressed or kissed or a ticklish spot left undiscovered by the time he rolled to Finley's side and submitted to the same torture. Kieran was better at hiding it, or he wasn't ticklish, but Finley discovered plenty of erogenous zones he exploited until Kieran waved his discarded white sock as a flag.

"But I haven't licked the best part yet," Finley said, eyeing Kieran's erection. Precum glistened on the head of his cock, making Finley's mouth water. "I've fantasized about wrapping my lips around this since you dropped your shorts the first day we met."

Kieran threaded his fingers into Finley's hair and guided his mouth toward his dick. "Show me."

Taking a page from Kieran's book, Finley bypassed the expected. He didn't lick or suck the broad head or take it down his throat. Finley nuzzled his nose in Kieran's thatch of dark pubic hair, discovered another erogenous zone on the inside of his thighs, and sucked Kieran's balls until he yanked Finley's hair and begged for release. Placing his tongue at the base of Kieran's cock, Finley licked a path toward the head, never tearing his gaze away from Kieran's obsidian eyes.

"Don't tease, baby. Suck me. *Slowly.*"

Finley swirled his tongue around the slick crown and wiggled the tip inside the leaking slit. Kieran growled and fisted the bed sheets. If he wanted slow, Finley would give it to him. He located that sweet spot on the underside of his cockhead and swirled his tongue against it until Kieran squirmed. With a dark chuckle of his own, Finley wrapped his lips around Kieran's dick and eased down his shaft. When it got to be too much, he breathed deeply through his nose and sucked his dick down farther until—

Kieran thrashed his head. "I'm going to come."

Finley eased off and restarted his oral seduction all over again. Kieran settled his breathing when Finley nuzzled his fur and kissed his thighs but was back to panting by the first swipe of tongue against his taut sac.

"Any slower and I'm going to die," Kieran begged after the fourth round of oral edging.

Finley had never gotten so turned on just by giving someone else pleasure. The barest friction against his cock would set him off, and he refused to come until after Kieran did.

Finley retrieved a condom from his wallet, then realized the only lube they had on hand was the Monkey Grease his *mother* had made. The urge to close the drawer and bury his face in the mattress was strong.

A firm hand fisted his cock and pumped. "Don't overthink the lube's origin right now. Let's test it out on my ass."

Finley tossed the condom onto the bed and squeezed the lube onto his fingers. "It's a little thin for anal sex."

Kieran parted his thighs, exposing his pucker, and said, "Good. Come here."

Positioning himself between Kieran's legs, Finley rubbed the oil against his entrance. It was slick and silky, allowing Finley's first finger to glide right in. Kieran groaned and pulled his legs toward his chest. "More."

Finley knew it had been almost two years since he'd bottomed, so he ignored Kieran's demand, taking his time to tease and tantalize with one digit and waiting until Kieran's hips moved on their own before adding a second. Finley crooked his fingers and rubbed them against Kieran's prostate, earning a strangled gasp. Kieran's cock jerked like a phantom lover was caressing it, signaling he was close. Easing his fingers free, Finley ripped the condom wrapper open and suited up. He slicked more lube along his erection before lining his cockhead up with Kieran's entrance and pushing in to the hilt.

His channel was so tight and hot that Finley had to stop or risk coming already. Kieran held his gaze, an impish gleam shining in his eyes as he reached down and stroked his dick.

"Right there with you," he said. "We'll go slow next time."

Next time. Finley loved the sound of that and quit fighting the inevitable. He gripped Kieran's strong thighs and fucked him until dots danced before his eyes. Kieran pumped his hand faster, crying out when he came all over his chest and abdomen. The vise around Finley's cock tightened, milking his orgasm from him with enough force to render him mute. His breath snagged in his chest, and not even a squeak escaped his lips. He fell forward, nearly forgetting to put his hands down to brace his fall. Kieran chuckled and pulled him down the rest of the way. Finley took his first breath when Kieran wrapped his arms around him and held Finley against his chest. He didn't care that Kieran's spunk would likely seal them together like glue. He eased up enough to pull his oversensitive dick from Kieran's ass, then returned to rest his full weight against Kieran's solid chest. Lips pressed against his temple and his hair.

"How soon?" Finley asked, his voice gruff and unrecognizable.

Kieran's chest rumbled under him. "I've regressed to a horny teen-ager since arriving at the ranch, so I should be good to go before your sweat dries."

Finley chuckled and pushed up to support his weight on one fore-arm. He reached for the lube and lifted it into the air. "I can see you've been busy."

"What can I say? I went nearly two years without so much as jerk-ing off, then landed on a ranch where my walking wet dream also lived."

Maybe he should've thought the wet dream comment was crude, but Finley wanted to preen instead. It kept him from thinking about the other thing Kieran had said was in the bag until the handsome devil grinned like a loon. Groaning, Finley dropped his head on Kieran's chest. "Okay, tell me what the note said."

"Nothing bad," Kieran replied. "I buried it in the drawer. I couldn't bring myself to throw it away."

Finley jerked into a sitting position and rifled through the night-stand's contents until he found the scrap of paper under Kieran's sketchpad.

My son,

Different cures for different aches.

Love,

Mom

Finley set the note down. "Could've been worse."

"Words I always want to hear from a naked man after sex," Kieran said.

"You think that's funny?"

Kieran laughed and nodded. Finley dove in with curled fingers, searching for ticklish spots, but Kieran was stronger and faster. He pinned Finley to the bed and proved he had an outstanding memory too, homing in on each of the spots he'd uncovered before sex. Finley would've expressed outrage that he had enough brain cells left after their shared orgasm, but he was breathless from laughing so hard.

Finley banged his fist against the mattress and shouted, "Uncle!" Kieran collapsed beside him on the bed, and they lay there, grinning at each other for a long time. Finley reached over and brushed the backs of his knuckles over Kieran's cheek. "I mentioned taking things slow because you've been through a lot, and I'm sure I don't even know the half of it. My track record with men is horrid, and I carry baggage of my own. We could have something amazing, beautiful, and rare, but I worry about codependency issues. I fear I might want too much too fast, and—"

Kieran quieted him with a kiss. "I'll tell you if I feel overwhelmed and need some solitude, and you can tell me when you need me to open up more. I trust you like I've never trusted anyone else, and it has nothing to do with codependency. It feels like I put out a call to the universe, and you answered."

"Pack," Finley whispered. Kieran cocked his head to the side in confusion. "You reminded me of a lone coyote when we met. Something about you spoke to me, and I could hear your howl echoing in my soul."

Kieran tightened his hold around Finley. "And you answered."

"And I always will." No matter what their future held, Finley would always answer Kieran's call. He pressed a kiss to one perfect pec, then pushed up into a sitting position. "Can I ask for that favor now?"

Kieran smiled, cupped the back of his neck, and pulled him back down for a kiss. "I'm lying here in a boneless heap, covered in my spunk because you rocked my world. You can have anything."

"I'm curious about your sketchbook," Finley said. "You had it with you in the laundry room, and I've wondered about the kinds of things you draw."

Kieran inhaled long and slow as he considered, and Finley knew it was a big request. He exhaled just as slowly before saying, "Nothing until the past few weeks. Some of the sketches are pretty rough."

"I don't want to critique your work. I just want you to share it with me when you're ready."

"Go ahead," Kieran said, nodding toward the nightstand.

Finley retrieved the sketchbook from the drawer and sat up. "Are you sure?"

Kieran rolled onto his side, bent his arm, and rested his head on his palm. "I am. I think you're going to get an idea of where my head has been since the moment I arrived on the ranch."

The first few sketches were landscapes and animals. Finley could tell Kieran's first strokes weren't quite confident, but the technique sharpened with each turned page. The subject changed from trees, mountains, dogs, and horses to Finley. Images of him performing various tasks filled the page. Finley's favorite was a sketch Kieran had made of him hugging Tiny Dancer. He'd drawn it so beautifully that it looked like a black-and-white photo. The tears shimmering in his eyes in the sketch were so lifelike. And because life imitated art, Finley's eyes filled again.

"You're killing me," Kieran said. "You've been staring at that drawing for several minutes."

Finley jerked his head up. "Have I?"

Kieran bit his bottom lip and nodded. "Do you like it?"

Swallowing hard, Finley said, "I love it. You're so talented."

Kieran snagged Finley's hand and brought it to his lips. "The subject obviously moves me."

Finley struggled to tear his gaze away from the sketch. He'd never looked better than through Kieran's eyes. "Have you ever wanted to pursue a career in art?"

"It's always seemed like a pipe dream," Kieran replied. "I'd hoped to take some courses to hone my skills, but I've never been able to pull it off."

"Until now. You're surrounded by people who want to see your dreams become a reality."

Kieran captured his mouth with a long, lazy kiss that left him reeling. "I want to see your art too."

Finley snorted. "Even my stick figures are unrecognizable."

"Nice try," Kieran replied. "I want to see the photos that made Harry gasp."

Finley released a long exhale and set the sketchbook down. If Kieran could put himself out there, then he could too. He leaned over the edge of the bed and retrieved his phone from his pocket. "I used Harry's laptop to save them to my digital storage." He tapped on the app and accessed the folder before handing over the device.

Kieran lay beside him and held the phone where they could both see it. He said nothing as he scrolled through the photos twice. He set the device on the bed and rolled onto his side. Finley turned his head and bravely met his gaze. "I've never liked pictures of myself. They were a visual reminder of how I never fit in." He set his hand on Finley's racing heart. "I always looked so out of place…until now."

"You *do* belong. Pack."

"Pack," Kieran whispered.

A loud knock at the door interrupted their beautiful moment. "Special delivery from the kitchen," Harry hollered from the small porch. "Don't get used to this and give me a two-minute head start before you open the door. I don't want to bleach my eyes."

Finley pulled on his jeans and only zipped them before heading to the door. "Thank you," he shouted at his sister's rapidly retreating form. She waved her hand without turning around, and Finley laughed. He hoisted a heavy paper grocery sack into the air and got a whiff of waffles and bacon. "This is without a doubt the best day of my life." He set the bags on the coffee table and went into the kitchenette for utensils. Kieran slid off the bed and located the lounge pants Finley had borrowed that morning, then hooked his arm around Finley's waist when he tried to return to the food.

"Should I be insulted you didn't express that sentiment until after the food arrived?" Kieran asked, his breath tickling Finley's ear.

"The food is just the whipped cream on the waffle," Finley replied, turning in Kieran's embrace.

"Whipped cream?"

Finley grinned and waggled his brows. "Mmmhmm. And I'm pretty sure there's enough food to sustain us for the day." Sunday was a minimal chore day, and there were more than enough crew members to share the tasks.

"It's settled," Kieran said. "We'll hide away in here all day." With a playful wink, he added, "Save some whipped cream for later."

They ate and dozed, had sex again and dozed some more, then ate and dozed again. Finley awoke to an urgent erection pressed against his backside. It was something he'd love to get used to but reminded himself to take things nice and easy. The room was dark except for light from the full moon invading the tiny crack between the curtains. As much as he wanted to roll over and kiss Kieran or simply part his legs in invitation, an even better idea was taking form.

"Can I show you my Colorado?" he whispered in the dark.

Kieran nestled closer. "This is my Colorado."

Finley's heart threatened to melt, but his determination persisted. "I promise you won't regret it."

Kieran huffed out a short sigh. "Fine, but not on horseback. I'm not confident enough in the saddle to attempt riding in the dark."

Finley laughed. "Grandpa's truck will be our steed."

He left Kieran at his cabin long enough to make a thermos of hot chocolate and grab his sleeping bag and more lube. He'd have to suck it up and get a bigger supply from his mother but not yet. She'd ask too many questions and push for meeting Kieran. The time for that would come but on his terms, not Hope's, which was an unfamiliar concept to her. He hustled back to Kieran's cabin and smacked into a wall of muscle as soon as he rounded the corner of the original homestead. He immediately recognized Ivan's scent and braced himself for another lecture.

Instead of releasing Finley, Ivan wrapped his arms around him in a hug. "I was wrong to be so critical of your man. I'll try harder."

Finley rested his forehead against Ivan's muscular chest as tears tickled the back of his eyes. What was with the waterworks lately? "Thanks, Ivan. That means the world to me."

"I'm still going to give him shit."

Finley stepped back and looked up at the big man, whose white teeth gleamed in the dark. "But that's your love language."

Ivan's laughter followed him all the way to the small cabin.

Kieran grinned when he saw the sleeping bag and quirked his brow at the thermos. "You don't need to ply me with alcohol to have your way with me under the moon."

"Trust me," Finley said, "you'll get drunk off the night view and forget I exist. This is hot chocolate to keep me warm when it happens."

Kieran snorted his disbelief as they exited his humble abode.

The radio came on loud when Finley started up the truck. "Oops," he said and turned it down. He was glad he hadn't turned the radio off when he recognized P!nk and Chris Stapleton singing "Love Me Anyway."

"These two make an unlikely duo," Kieran said.

Finley met his gaze. "Sometimes those are the best kind."

Kieran's smile was nearly blinding. "Show me your Colorado."

Finley slowly drove the bumpy, winding path down to a meadow. The moon looked huge in the sky and hung low enough to make a cowboy think he could lasso it. The burbling stream glittered in the moonlight as if the mountains had deposited a million diamonds in its depths. But the real showstopper was the stars twinkling in the sky.

"Oh, wow," Kieran said breathlessly. "I think this is what they call a religious experience."

Finley turned his head and narrowed his eyes. "You better not be thinking about joining that damn cult."

Kieran looked at him with eyes as big as the moon, and Finley burst into laughter. "How could you even joke about that?"

"The same way you joke about jail," Finley replied. "I'm taking away its power over me." He unbuckled his seat belt and leaned toward Kieran. "And if you want a religious experience, I'll give you one." He didn't wait for a reply. Finley got out of the truck and walked around to the back, where Kieran met him with an eagerness that made his heart leap with joy. After lowering the tailgate, Finley unzipped the sleeping bag until it lay flat, then the two of them spread it in the truck bed before climbing up and lying on their backs. "This will be even nicer this summer when its—"

Kieran cut him off with a kiss. It started out chaste but got dirty in a hurry. Kieran pulled back abruptly and looked up at the sky. He reached over and laced his fingers between Finley's. "I don't know who I am or what I want to do with my life. There's so much I still need to figure out." He turned his head and met Finley's gaze. "I don't know what I can give you except for my tomorrow and the tomorrow after that."

So this was what love really felt like.

"I'll take all your tomorrows," Finley whispered.

chapter
NINETEEN

"Everything okay?" Finley asked. "You've been awfully quiet."

Kieran squeezed his hand and smiled over at him. "Not going to lie. I'm more than a little nervous about meeting your mom."

As much as he'd protested otherwise, it turned out that Kieran had wanted to take certain things slow, such as meeting the parents. Finley had been dodging and deflecting Hope's attempts to orchestrate an introduction for over a month after Harry let the cat out of the bag. *So much for her staying in her lane.* The gesture was for Kieran's benefit, and he worried it would create friction between Finley and his mom, which was the last thing he wanted, and not only because she kept them well lubed with a constant supply of Monkey Grease. *Bless her heart.* But what if she decided Kieran wasn't good enough? She'd wanted Finley to date that Michael guy, who exuded confidence and success. That dude wouldn't freak out about meeting anyone's family. Kieran had nothing to offer Finley besides a drawing from his sketchbook. *And my tomorrows.* What mother in her right mind would want that kind of uncertainty for her son?

"Maybe we should've called first? This feels like an ambush," Kieran said.

Finley hip-checked him on the sidewalk. "Knock it off. Hope is going to adore you. Stop making a big deal out of this. We're just making a low-stakes swing by her shop to say hello."

"And get more lube."

Heat flooded Kieran's cheeks, and Finley laughed. "And that too." Finley stopped a few feet away and tugged on Kieran's hand to halt his progress. "Don't let her see you blush," he cautioned in the same tone others used to say *don't feed the wild animals.*

Kieran snorted and shook his head. "Or what?"

Finley's eyes widened in alarm. "Oh no, I think you just challenged the universe to give you a Hope Newton performance."

As usual, Finley knew the perfect thing to say to ease Kieran's nerves. Their lives had become so beautifully entwined over the past four weeks. Finley's photographs decorated Kieran's cabin, and Kieran's sketches joined Finley's art collection in his office. Well, at least the drawings and photos that were made for public consumption. The racier images and drawings were kept for private viewings only. They worked and played together like a well-oiled machine, and even spent most of their nights in the small cabin. Kieran did have moments of overwhelm that Finley intuitively detected. On those nights, he'd kiss Kieran tenderly and head back to his bedroom at the old homestead without need for excuses or explanations. The first time it happened, Finley had been a little tentative the next morning, so Kieran had backed him into his office, shut the door, and demonstrated just how happy he was to see him. After that, Finley didn't worry that the time away meant they were growing apart. Each day brought them closer together, and meeting the rest of Finley's family felt like a natural next step.

Something cold and wet smacked against Kieran's back. He stiffened and spun around and saw an ice cream cone on the sidewalk.

"Men shall not lay with other men," said a man with white hair and a white beard. Hostility and something akin to madness shimmered in his pale eyes. "I will cast out all the sinners."

Kieran was too stunned to speak, but Finley didn't suffer from the same affliction. He stepped around Kieran and planted himself between Kieran and the threat.

"Your grammar is the sin. It's *lie*, not *lay*. The word *shall* is a future tense auxiliary verb." Finley took a few steps toward the man, who had the wisdom to ease back. "I assure you I shall lie with this man whenever and however I want to."

The old man trembled as he pointed a finger at Finley. "You're the witch's son."

Before Finley could answer, the door to his mother's shop burst open and a young man with dark blond hair darted onto the sidewalk. He was dressed just like the man who'd accosted them and didn't look like he was faring any better. He froze like a deer in headlights just as a woman burst through the door with a Super Soaker. He recognized Hope from Finley's photos and watched in awe as she leveled her weapon of choice at her harasser.

"I warned you assholes," she said before she pulled the trigger, hitting the man at center mass with a blast of water. His arms pinwheeled and he flailed about as people on the sidewalk darted to the left and right to avoid the woman's wrath. Her victim staggered to one knee before scrambling to his feet and fleeing for safety. Hope cackled like a madwoman the entire time, her gray-and-white hair flowing behind her, and Kieran was pretty sure he fell in love with her a little just like he'd fallen for her son.

"Witch!" the white-haired man called out.

"Oh shit," Finley said. "Now you've done it."

Hope spun around and marched forward, Super Soaker locked and loaded. "It's bitch, not witch. Get it right." She unleashed a torrent of water at their white-haired accoster until he staggered off into the crowd that had gathered to witness the spectacle.

Finley looked over his shoulder at Kieran. "And the universe answered."

The crowd cheered for Hope, and she grabbed the skirt of her flowing yellow dress and gave a little curtsy. Then she gave her full attention to her son. It was that moment when she realized Kieran was with him. Her eyes went wide and excitement danced in green eyes several shades darker than Finley's. It was also at that time Hope realized her finger was still on the trigger because she pressed it in her excitement and blasted Kieran in the chest.

The cold stunned Kieran for a second, and he froze in shock. Finley, the valiant knight, jumped in front of him once more, taking the brunt of the blast.

"Let off the trigger, you madwoman," Finley yelled while trying to use his arms as a shield to block the water.

Hope eased off and lowered the weapon, and the three of them howled with laughter.

"What the hell is going on out here?" A lanky man stepped out of the shop and searched the sidewalk until his gaze landed on the trio. "Hope, what have you done?"

"Gary, your wife is unhinged," Finley said as he pulled his soaked shirt away from his chest.

"You're just figuring that out, kid?" he asked. Gary's sandy brown hair was going gray at the temples. His black-framed glasses sat slightly askew on his nose, and he assessed Kieran with kind eyes. "As far as meet-the-parents encounters go, this must be one for the records." He extended his hand. "I'm Gary Newton. Husband to this wonderful woman, and stepfather to this incredible young man. You must be the Kieran we've been dying to meet."

Kieran didn't know if their first meeting broke any records, but it sure did shatter the ice. "Good to meet you, sir," Kieran replied, shaking the man's hand.

Hope hip-checked her husband out of the way and was on Kieran faster than Nellie on a denim-clad ass. Unconcerned about his wet shirt, she flung her arms around him and hugged him tight before stepping back and smiling up at him. "I'm so happy to meet you, and I'm sorry I blasted you with the gun."

"That Salvation Anew leader had just baptized me with an ice cream cone, so no worries."

Hope growled protectively as she looped her arm through Kieran's and led him toward the store. "I have a shirt you can have."

"Mom, he'd rather go naked on the streets than wear a shirt with one of your slogans on it."

"How bad could it be?" Kieran asked over his shoulder. He understood Gary's and Finley's laughter when he surveyed the options in his size a few minutes later. He could claim that a yoga session a day could keep the bad sex away, boast that good health includes sexual health, or advertise that her Monkey Grease puts the self in self-care.

"I'll just wear my wet shirt," Finley announced.

Kieran snorted and tossed him the sexual health shirt while he chose the Monkey Grease for himself. Finley's eyes twinkled with mirth as he reached for Kieran's hand and tugged him into the changing rooms attached to the yoga studio. He reached for the hem of Kieran's wet shirt instead of his own, so Kieran reached for his. But they stood there staring into each other's eyes instead of undressing.

"The young guy my mom first hosed down is my ex."

Kieran didn't get a very good look at him, and it was impossible to see much with the beards anyway. "He's an idiot. Bet she really enjoyed blasting him."

"Damn right I did," Hope called out from the other side. "You boys want us to step out for a little bit?"

"No," Finley said. "We're not fooling around. I just wanted to make sure you haven't scared Kieran off."

Kieran pointed to where Finley's hand had shifted on his body. Instead of moving away from Kieran's crotch, Finley gave it a good squeeze.

"Are you scared off, Kieran?" Hope asked. It was cute that she actually sounded concerned.

Finley squeezed his junk a little harder like he might be trying to influence Kieran's answer. Like he had anything to worry about. "Not in the least."

"Would you boys like to get a bite to eat?" Gary said. "We were just talking about closing up for a quick bite at the diner."

"Can we get a rain check?" Finley asked. "We've got a big poker game back at the ranch soon, and I'm in charge of ordering food."

They'd started playing every Saturday, which had allowed Kieran and Ivan to get to know one another better. The ginger giant turned out to be a teddy bear when he let his guard down. They also discovered Finley's winning streak wasn't limited to his first time, and the two of them still treated the showdown like foreplay. Finley looked for ways to outdo the menu each week, and he had planned a big barbecue feast that made Kieran's mouth water.

"How about we do family dinner at our house tomorrow night?" Hope asked. After a pause, she added, "Don't worry. I won't try to cook. I'll order something from a local restaurant."

"Thank goodness," Gary replied.

Finley, whose hand still gripped his lengthening dick, arched a brow in question. Kieran nodded and tried not to lean further into Finley's touch.

"We'll be there. Text me the time."

"Great," Hope said. "We're going to head out now. Just use your key to lock up after yourselves. Take your time. I'm going to leave a goodie bag for you on the counter so you can try my latest product."

Finley groaned and dropped his hand, and Kieran breathed a little easier. He too let go of Finley's shirt and waited to follow his lead. "Mom, we're not going to bang in your dressing room."

"You're such a prude," Hope told him. "It was lovely meeting you, Kieran. I can't wait to get to know you better."

The situation was completely surreal, but somehow charming as hell. "I'm looking forward to it too." And he realized he meant it.

Gary and Hope started chatting about what they wanted to eat. Their voices got softer as they got farther away. The bells jingled over the front door when they exited, leaving the two of them alone.

"I really would love to drop to my knees and suck you off," Finley said. "Or bend over and grab onto that bench and let you plow me."

"Okay."

Finley laughed and pulled his wet shirt off. "But not when my mother suspects we're doing it."

Kieran waggled his brows and tugged his off too. "She's going to suspect it one way or another, so we might as well do it."

Finley grabbed his dry shirt and pulled it on. "Still grosses me out."

Kieran laughed and put his dry tee on also. Smoothing it down, he said, "How does it look?"

Finley grabbed his crotch once more. "You'll never need to stroke it alone again. Let's grab our goody bag and get back to the ranch. Maybe we'll have a little time to fool around before the food arrives."

They picked up their wet shirts and made their way into the store where a purple bag waited for them on the counter. Finley peaked inside the bag and laughed. He removed a tube with a label that read Butt Stuff.

"I'm looking forward to test driving this," Finley said.

"Pretty sure I adore your mom."

They made it back to the ranch with enough time to give Butt Stuff two trial runs.

"Think I shall *lie* here the rest of the night," Kieran said breathlessly. "You go on to poker without me." They laughed at the reference to the cult leader's bad grammar and Finley's witty reply.

"Short ribs," Finley whispered. "BLT macaroni salad. Jalapeño and brown sugar cowboy beans."

"Okay, okay."

The food arrived before they made it to the homestead, but amazingly the guys hadn't tucked into it yet. They treated Finley like a rockstar, though their worship would turn to jests when the cards came out.

Ivan pointed to Kieran's shirt. He hadn't realized he'd put the tee from Hope's studio back on, but that was all Finley's fault. He had noodles for legs and mush for brains. "Nice shirt. I have the yoga one." When Kieran quirked a brow, Ivan just shrugged. "I have depth."

Kieran patted him on the broad shoulder. "I don't doubt it, big guy."

"Don't start without us," Cash said as he and Harry hustled in.

Harry hoisted two pies in the air. "I brought dessert."

The guys cheered at her announcement. Ivan added another leaf to the dining room table and procured a few more chairs from someplace in the house. They filled their plates and sat around the table, stuffing their faces on delicious barbecue and pie before Finley kicked their asses at cards. Cash was brilliant with business and people but horrible at poker. He ran out of chips first but stuck around to engage in the constant banter. Cash looked around the room with a fond expression on his face and smiled when their gazes met. He'd hired Kieran a legal team as promised and mentored him on several things. Kieran had felt a pressing need to make decisions about his future but was clueless about what his big picture should be. Cash had promised him that he'd figure it out when the time was right.

Kieran repeated that to himself every time the uncertainty made him anxious. He performed his jobs with pride, worshipped Finley with everything he had, and hoped lady justice would drop the hammer on Ritchie and his cohorts. He knew the latter would take a lot of time, but he expected to figure out his future quicker. Then again, Kieran had so many avenues in front of him, and maybe that was the problem. He went from living a life of limitations to having limitless opportunities. He'd gone from having no family to having a great, big found family. It was overwhelming to say the least. But giving Finley his tomorrows was his constant, and though he could visualize that big picture, he knew it would include asking Finley for his forever.

In August, pieces of his future snapped into place like a jigsaw puzzle. The picture wasn't complete, but enough of the image formed for him to recognize it and the accompanying sense of rightness. He was working with the vet, Rebecca, to help irrigate and bandage a fairly deep wound on Buttercup's hind quarter. Finley had left Kieran to assist the doc while he searched out the source of her injury. Buttercup started to get nervous when Rebecca flushed the lesion, and he soothed the horse with gentle hands and a calm voice.

Rebecca stood up and came to stand beside him when she finished, offering Buttercup apple slices for being a good girl. The horse gave the doc serious side-eye while chomping on her treat. "Has anyone ever told you that you have an amazing temperament with animals?" she asked Kieran.

He averted his gaze and busied himself cleaning up the exam room in the barn. Receiving compliments was still hard for Kieran, even when they came from the most genuine people. Finley found his affliction charming, but he hated the way he shut down and retreated behind his wall during times of overwhelm. Finley hadn't knocked his defenses down; he'd carved out a door instead. Kieran could retreat behind it any time he needed to, but he never locked the door. It was the kind of compromise they made as they worked through their issues together.

Kieran cleared his throat and forced himself to meet Rebecca's kind gaze. "I might've heard it a few times."

The vet smiled. "And did that certain someone also mention a future for you in veterinary medicine?"

"I'm not smart enough to be a vet." The admission heated Kieran's cheeks and made him want to look away again, but he remained locked on Rebecca's earnest gaze.

"I don't agree with your assessment," the vet replied. "But there are other careers in the field that won't involve sacrificing a minimum of eight years in college. My vet techs have associate's or bachelor's degrees. And you wouldn't be limited to just vet clinics either. You could utilize your skills right here or perhaps work for animal rescues. I know several wildlife vets who need technicians. You should look into all the options to see what fits you best."

"I appreciate the suggestion."

Kieran didn't say anything to Finley about the conversation right away. He waited until they saddled up the horses for their nightly ride. "Who's the best girl?" Kieran asked Nellie. They'd been working on her tolerating a rider for a while. They started by letting her get used to the weight of the blanket first before adding the saddle. When Finley deemed her ready to attempt the rider, he made Kieran wear protection practically from head to toe, including a jockstrap and cup. Finley called out tips from a safe distance while Kieran mounted the horse. Nellie whinnied and tossed her head but not because she was ready to buck him. It was her version of an eye roll at Finley's theatrics.

Before they took a chance in the wild, Finley had them ride around the arena for a week. Kieran used that time to teach her a few of the moves he'd learned with Loretta. Nellie picked up quicker than either of them anticipated. Kieran didn't have a desire to perform dressage competitively, but it was a blast teaching Nellie the techniques, and he was looking forward to learning more himself. One day, they'd put something together to music. He thought Nellie would prefer a tune from Disturbed or Eminem over Britney Spears.

"Her first ride out in the wild," Finley announced as they exited the barn. "Are you sure you're ready for this? Loretta could use some exercise."

Kieran leaned forward and mock whispered, "See how he talks about you gals when you're not around?" He straightened in the saddle and paid close attention to Nellie's body language. She gave off no clues that she was agitated or was about to bolt. Both her body and gait were relaxed. They'd decided to keep her to a leisurely canter to start, but Kieran was eager to see what she could do during a full-on gallop. Once he was assured of her cooperation, he filled Finley in on the conversation he'd had with Rebecca.

"So you give the idea merit when Rebecca suggests it but not me," Finley replied. The wry smile showed he wasn't in the least bit upset.

"You're more than a little biased when it comes to me," Kieran pointed out.

"True, but I would never suggest someone work with animals if they didn't have the right temperament and tools. And you definitely have what it takes. But neither Rebecca's opinion nor mine counts. What do you think?"

"Working with animals feels right. I'm just not sure what the next step will be."

"We find out what opportunities are available and how to access them," Finley replied.

We. Kieran loved how everything shifted to *we* with them. He'd never been half of a whole before meeting Finley. "You make everything seem possible."

"Well, Hope Newton's kids know there's no such thing as impossible. Only I'm possible."

Kieran smirked and shook his head. "Can't believe she doesn't have that on a T-shirt."

"She did years ago. She swaps out her merch every year or two."

"Wise woman," Kieran said.

"Well, I'd have to agree since she adores you." Finley called her a cougar at least once during Sunday family dinners, usually when she hugged Kieran or kissed his cheek.

"I adore her too."

Kieran more than adored Hope's son, but the words felt too big to speak out loud. He used every opportunity to *show* Finley his affection, such as the long kiss they shared when the horses stopped for a drink at the stream. He ran his fingers through Finley's hair, loving the play of light and colors where the sun had turned some strands copper and others spun gold. Kieran wanted to kiss the freckles on his nose and feel the warmth radiating off his tan skin. God, this man meant the world to him. It was scary and exhilarating, and he longed to express all the things Finley made him feel.

"I know," Finley said, reading the emotions he couldn't yet verbalize. "Me too."

They shared many more kisses until it was time to return to the ranch.

"I think you can loosen the reins with Nellie on the way back if you're comfortable with it."

Kieran nodded eagerly. "She's ready."

Excitement sparked in his soul when he shifted his body weight forward and signaled with his legs for Nellie to gallop when they were nearing the ranch. The breeze whipped through his hair and the landscape around them became a blur as she ran with the wind. Her fears no longer imprisoned or hobbled her. She was regaining the parts of herself abuse had stolen. Tears stung his eyes because this sweet girl was healing, and so was he. They both owed it to the gorgeous man on the horse behind them, shouting out his relentless encouragement.

They were free.

epilogue

"It's over," Kieran said. He'd lost track of the number of times he'd said it since leaving Denver.

"Really over," Finley repeated. He reached over and squeezed Kieran's hands before turning into the ranch. Cash had given them the day off, but they were eager to share the good news with him.

Still in disbelief, Kieran said, "And almost a year to the day that I arrived at Redemption Ridge." And, wow, had things changed. Whenever Kieran caught his reflection, he didn't recognize himself as the same person who'd stepped onto the ranch. Hope, faith, and joy had erased the cynicism from his expression and softened his harsh edges. This Kieran had a future, a family, and Finley.

"Makes your exoneration that much sweeter. Happy anniversary."

That's right. He also had a fucking clean record. Kieran looked over at Finley and quirked a brow. "Anniversary, huh?"

Finley smiled broadly. "Yep. I handed you my heart the moment I saw you, so our anniversary is tomorrow in my eyes."

That was the closest they'd gotten to a verbal "I love you," though their mutual actions loudly announced their devotion.

"I like that," Kieran said. "Let's go out and celebrate."

"Why wait?"

Kieran looked out the windshield and saw that someone had erected a large tent between the barns. A banner hung across one side and read: Congratulations, Kieran! Dylan flipped something on the grill and talked to Harry while everyone else mingled with Hope and Gary.

"What's this?" Kieran asked. The banner gave it away, but he couldn't believe Finley had pulled off a surprise after the botched birthday party attempt in December.

"Surprise!" Finley cried.

Kieran laughed. "I know what it is, but planning a party was pretty presumptuous."

"Nah. Hope consulted her crystals."

Kieran quirked a brow because he knew Finley didn't really believe in that stuff. "The tent, tables, and chairs were already here on the ranch. I texted Harry from the courtroom as soon as we got the judge's ruling, and she put everything in motion."

"The banner?" Kieran asked.

"I ordered it a few months ago when your lawyer told you about the hearing. I didn't need crystals to know I was going to need it someday. If the judge was a blind fool who couldn't see the truth, then I would use it when you graduated from college."

Finley's faith in him never ceased to amaze Kieran, and he leaned over and kissed him when he put the truck in park. "Thank you for going with me today."

"There's nowhere else I'd rather be," Finley replied.

Clapping and cheering erupted from the people gathered to help Kieran celebrate. They all came over to greet him when he stepped out of the truck. He received hugs, backslaps, and bumped fists. Everyone on the ranch had turned out to congratulate him with only two noticeable exceptions—Cash and Ivan. None of this would've happened without Cash's financial and emotional support. Kieran would be able to repay the debt when his settlement was finalized in a few months.

"You guys missed the excitement," Rue said. He leaned closer and lowered his voice. "A sedan with government plates pulled in about thirty minutes ago. Two guys got out and went inside the house with Cash. The tall guy with sandy brown hair dressed and moved like an agent." Sounded like Agent Scott. "I couldn't get a read on the dark-haired guy with him. He was slightly shorter, leaner, and moved like he didn't have a care in the world." That definitely wasn't Agent Rowland. "About ten minutes later, Cash texted Ivan and asked him to come to his office. None of them have come back out yet."

"Quit hogging Kieran," Hope called out.

He slapped Rue on the shoulder and went to mingle with everyone, but his thoughts never wandered far from the meeting that was taking place in Cash's office. When Dylan needed the barbecue sauce he and Harry had made, Kieran volunteered to go get it so he could nose around a bit. He wanted the opportunity to thank Agent Scott for whatever role he'd played in Ritchie's cooperation. His ex had struck an agreement to turn State's evidence and enter WITSEC like the agents thought he might. As part of the deal, Ritchie had confessed to his participation in the past and present auto theft rings, which exonerated Kieran. Without that, he would've remained a convicted felon. Ritchie had asked to speak to him, but Kieran had declined. His cooperation was to save his own ass and wasn't for Kieran's benefit. There was nothing left to say between them, and Ritchie had settled their score. Ritchie wanted the feds to think he was the mastermind, but everyone knew better. Ritchie had ensured he stayed alive and nothing more.

Kieran was at peace for the first time in…ever. He wanted to thank those who had made it possible, and he was damn nosy about the meeting taking place in the house. His curiosity grew when he stepped inside and heard Ivan shouting. Kieran couldn't make out his exact words, but it was definitely his voice. He eased down the hallway but stopped short when he rounded the corner and found a stranger in the kitchen. It was the dark-haired man Rue had described. The stranger had sun-kissed skin, a neatly trimmed dark beard, and sky-blue eyes. He somehow leaned against the counter just as indolently as the stride Rue reported. Kieran had walked in just as the guy had taken a bite of an apple he'd filched from Harry's fruit bowl. His pale blue eyes assessed Kieran as he chewed. Though this guy was weary, he'd bet money he never served time. So why was he here?

"This is bullshit, Cash," Ivan yelled from down the hall. "Why does paying up a favor become my problem?"

Kieran cocked his head to hear Cash's response, but his voice was too low. The stranger across the room chuckled, recapturing Kieran's attention. "Who are you?" he asked.

The stranger's mouth curved into a wry smile. "I'm the favor."

"And now you owe me," Ivan thundered. "Big time."

Heavy footfalls rapidly approached, and Kieran scooted over to the refrigerator and whipped the doors open just as Ivan stomped into the room. "You," he bellowed. Kieran peered around the door to see which one of them Ivan had addressed. Big Red stared daggers at the newcomer and pointed his forefinger at the man. "Come now."

The new guy purred and waggled his brows as he straightened to his full height. "Yes, Daddy."

Ivan's face turned an unhealthy shade of red. Kieran feared the big man was having a stroke when his face turned purple, but the foreman pivoted on his heels and stomped from the room.

Kieran turned back to the stranger with what he suspected was an awed expression because the guy shrugged casually. He tossed the rest of his apple into the trash and crossed to Kieran. Extending his hand, he said, "I'm Rory."

Kieran shook it and introduced himself. "Don't worry about Ivan. His bark is worse than his bite."

Rory's lazy smile turned purely wicked. "Let's hope not. See you around, Kieran."

He couldn't wait to tell Finley what he'd witnessed. He was tempted to request a transfer to Ivan's crew just so he could experience the fireworks on the daily. Someone cleared their throat, and Kieran poked his head around the door to find Agent Scott standing in the kitchen.

"I hear congratulations are in order."

Kieran shut the refrigerator and crossed the room with his hand out. Agent Scott shook it firmly before dropping his arm. "Thank you, sir. I'd hoped for an opportunity to express my gratitude."

Scott glanced in the direction Rory and Ivan had gone. A wry grin spread across the agent's face. "Trust me when I say it was all my pleasure." He snorted and added, "My younger brother is a lot to handle. I just hope he doesn't cost Cash a foreman." He didn't look that worried about it, but Kieran didn't point that out.

The front door opened, and Finley called out his name. "Did you get lost?"

"Be right there," Kieran said.

Cash and Patsy entered the kitchen, and he wanted more intel. "I don't think we're even," Cash said. "Seems your favor is going to create an enormous headache for me."

Scott laughed and slapped Cash on the back. "Better you than me."

"I don't know how I got mixed up in your family squabble," Cash said with a head shake. "I have something I'd like to discuss if you've got a minute."

Scott narrowed his eyes at Cash's somber tone. "I'm listening."

"I think we have a potential cult digging its claws into the community," Cash told him.

The federal agent narrowed his eyes and gestured to Cash's office. "You've got my attention."

Mine too, damn it. Especially when Kieran caught Agent Scott checking out Cash's ass.

Kieran knew he wouldn't get anything else when the men disappeared down the hall, so he retrieved the barbecue sauce from the refrigerator and headed back to his celebration. Finley was waiting for him on the porch.

"Please tell me you know what the hell is going on," he said.

"Just enough to make me dangerous."

Finley covered his heart with both hands. "Rumor has it I have a thing for bad boys."

Kieran chuckled and pulled him closer for a kiss. He repeated everything he'd heard and seen on their way back to the group.

"This day couldn't get any sweeter," Finley said, a serene smile tugging at his lips.

Kieran stopped and tugged on his hand so he would too. Finley halted and turned to face him. "Thank you."

"For what?" Finley asked.

Where did he begin? He palmed the back of Finley's neck and leaned forward until their foreheads touched. "Keeping your word and being the one who didn't let me down. For always knowing when to give me a gentle nudge or retreat. The encouragement you give me whether it's for enrolling in online vet tech classes or instructing me on how to fuck you."

Finley arched his brow. "You calling me bossy?"

"I'm calling you perfect." Kieran pressed a quick kiss to Finley's lush mouth. "And I wasn't done," he admonished. Finley mimed zipping his lips. "Thank you for being the best friend and co-cat dad a man could ask for." Though they'd wanted to hoard Little Mama and her kittens to themselves, Kieran's cabin wasn't big enough. The idea of giving the babies to strangers broke his heart, but luckily the crew members fell in love with them. The little darlings found homes with Rueben, Tyler, Owen, Ivan, and Cash. "And thank you most of all for loving me."

Finley's lips trembled. "Now look who's being presumptuous."

"And for teaching me how to love someone in return." Kieran took a shaky breath. "I do love you, Fin. More than words could ever express."

Finley's eyes widened and his lips curved into a beautiful smile. "Oh, I was wrong. Now it's officially the sweetest day. I love you too."

They shared a long kiss as everyone under the tent cheered them on.

Kieran pressed his lips to Finley's ear. "I believe." Something he never thought he'd experience until Finley had taught Kieran that guys like him were worthy of love.

The End!

Want to be the first to know about my book releases and have access to extra content? You can sign up for my newsletter here: http://eepurl.com/dlhPYj

My favorite place to hang out and chat with my readers is my Facebook group. Would you like to be a member of Aimee's Dye Hards? We'd love to have you! Go here: www.facebook.com/groups/AimeesDyeHards

other books by
AIMEE NICOLE WALKER

Curl Up and Dye Mysteries

Dyeing to be Loved
Something to Dye For
Dyed and Gone to Heaven
I Do, or Dye Trying
A Dye Hard Holiday
Ride or Dye
Curl Up and Dye Box Set

Road to Blissville Series

Unscripted Love
Someone to Call My Own
Nobody's Prince Charming
This Time Around
Smoke in the Mirror
Inside Out
Prescription for Love

Welcome to Blissville Collection (Both M/M Blissville series)

Volume One
Volume Two

The Lady is Mine Series

The Lady is a Thief
The Lady Stole My Heart

Queen City Rogue Series

Broken Halos
Wicked Games
Beautiful Trauma

Zero Hour Series

Ground Zero
Devil's Hour
Zero Divergence
Zero Hour Box Set

Sawyer and Royce: Matrimony and Mayhem

The Magnolia Murders
Marriage is Murder
Killer Honeymoon

Sinister in Savannah Series

Ride the Lightning
Mr. Perfect
Pretty Poison
Sinister in Savannah Box Set

Savannah Universe Standalone Books

Invisible Strings
Bad at Love
About Last Night
Just Say When

Standalone Novels

Second Wind
Fated Hearts Series
Chasing Mr. Wright
Rhythm of Us
Surrender Your Heart
Perfect Fit

Coauthored with Nicholas Bella

Undisputed
Circle of Darkness (Genesis Circle, Book 1)
Circle of Trust (Genesis Circle, Book 2)

acknowledgments

Many, many thanks to Susie Selva for her incredibly thorough edits and to Lori Parks for her keen eye during proofreading. These ladies are consummate professionals and are an absolute joy to work with. And much love to Jay Aheer and Wander Aguiar for this gorgeous cover and to Stacey Ryan Blake for her stunning interior designs. All of you make my books sparkle and shine so beautifully—inside and out. I thank my lucky stars that I get to work with such wonderfully talented people.

Sending much love to Melinda James Rueter and Racheal Yunk for bravely reading my rough drafts and providing priceless feedback. And I don't know where I'd be without CC Bell, my amazing personal assistant, who brings organization and so much joy into my life. Love you, ladies!

xoxo

Aimee

about
AIMEE NICOLE WALKER

Ever since she was a little girl, Aimee Nicole Walker entertained herself with stories that popped into her head. Now she gets paid to tell those stories to other people. She wears many titles—wife, mom, and animal lover are just a few of them. Her absolute favorite title is champion of the happily ever after. Love inspires everything she does, music keeps her sane, and coffee is the magic elixir that fuels her day.

She'd love to hear from you.

Want to connect? All her links are in one nifty location. Go here: linktr.ee/AimeeNicoleWalker

Made in the USA
Monee, IL
04 December 2023

48118663R00143